X Marks the Scot

VICTORIA ROBERTS

sourcebooks
casablanca

Copyright © 2013 by Victoria Roberts
Cover and internal design © 2013 by Sourcebooks, Inc.
Cover design by Jamie Warren
Cover photograph by Stephen Youll

Published by Sourcebooks Casablanca, an imprint of Sourcebooks,
Inc.
P.O. Box 4410, Naperville, Illinois 60567-4410
(630) 961-3900
Fax: (630) 961-2168
www.sourcebooks.com

Printed and bound in the United States of America
VP 10 9 8 7 6 5 4 3 2 1

To my beautiful daughter and my strapping son, may you always reach for the stars and fulfill your dreams.

All dreams can come true if we
have the courage to pursue them.
—Walt Disney

One

Royal Court, England, 1604

"GET UP, YE WHORESON."

Praying he was still in an ale-induced state and only dreaming, Declan MacGregor of Glenorchy slowly opened his eyes as he felt the prick of cold steel against his throat. A man with graying hair at his temples stood a hairbreadth away from the bed, dagger in hand.

A muscle ticked in the man's jaw. "Get up," he said through clenched teeth.

The blonde in the bed next to Declan—what was her name?—gasped and tugged up the blanket to cover her exposed breasts. Her eyes widened in fear.

"Ye defiled my daughter," the stranger growled.

Declan raised his hands in mock surrender. "I assure ye that I didnae." He stole a sideways glance at the woman and silently pleaded for his latest conquest to come to his aid.

"Papa?" The fair-skinned beauty sat up on the bed. "What are ye doing here?"

Glancing at his daughter, the man spoke in clipped tones. "This whoreson had ye and will wed ye."

"Now just a bloody minute. I…"

Whipping his head back around, the enraged father glared at Declan, repositioning the dagger—much *lower*. Feeling the contact of the blade, Declan took a sharp intake of breath while the woman sprang from the bed as though it was afire. Hastily, she grabbed her clothing and started to don her attire.

He silently chuckled, realizing the irony of the moment. What would Ciaran think? Declan had chosen to remain at court to escape his older brother's scrutiny, now only to be thrown deeper into hot water. In fact, it was scalding.

The fair-colored lass rolled her eyes at her father. "Really, Papa, ye must cease your attempts at match-making. I donna wish to wed him."

She pulled on her father's dagger-held hand, thankfully removing the blade from the most favorite part of Declan's anatomy. He breathed a sigh of relief when he reached down and felt that his most prized possession was still intact.

What the hell had he gotten himself into? The gods knew he had needs, but if he wasn't more selective of the women he bedded, the fairer sex would surely be the death of him.

He needed to escape.

Declan threw back the blankets, stood, and quickly tossed his trews into the air with his foot. While father and daughter were huddled in deep conversation, he donned his trews, pulled on his tunic, grabbed his boots, and simply walked out—unnoticed and unscathed.

When would he learn that ale always led him into trouble? The last he wanted to think of was Ciaran's constant ramblings about how he was destroying his life, but perhaps there was a string of truth to his brother's admonishments. Not wanting to contemplate that revelation, Declan proceeded out the door for a breath of fresh air.

"MacGregor!" Sir Robert Catesby called, waving him over.

In the fortnight Declan had attended court, he had met Sir Robert Catesby and Thomas Percy several times. Upon his approach, both Englishmen smiled in greeting.

Declan nodded. "Catesby. Percy."

"We head to shoot targets," said Catesby, holding up his bow. "Would you like to join us?"

The corners of Declan's lips lifted into a teasing smile. "The first time I bested ye wasnae enough? Ye are actually coming back for more?"

Catesby slapped him on the shoulder. "Perhaps it was purely luck the first time around, eh?"

"Come with us. I challenge you to a match, and we'll see if you can equal my skill with a bow," said Percy with a sly grin.

Declan refrained from commenting that Percy barely had any skill with a bow. At least the man did not challenge him to swordplay, for Declan knew he would be sorely lacking in that. Praise the saints for small favors.

His brothers had often tried to engage Declan to practice swordplay with the men, but he knew he could never match their prowess. So why even attempt it?

Ciaran and Aiden were quite skilled, whereas he was only a third son. Besides, he was interested in more manly pursuits, such as raising things of a personal nature for the lasses. The bow, on the other hand, was another matter entirely. Declan had mastered archery as soon as he was old enough to shoot. He never really practiced it—the bow was something that came naturally to him, a gift from the gods.

A bit of sport was exactly what he needed after this morning's spectacle. Engaging in some healthy competition might do him some good, cleanse his spirit, so to speak.

He nodded in agreement. "If ye are up for the challenge, it would be my pleasure to have ye *attempt* to best me again."

"That's the spirit," said Percy.

The men made their way to the targets. The sun was shining and the winds were relatively calm, a great day for shooting. When they arrived at the area, a handful of men were gathered and the boards were already in place. When Declan turned, he felt like he had been punched in the gut.

Lady Liadain Campbell stood in the distance and brushed an errant curl away from her face. Her hair was the black of a starless night and hung down her back. Her high, exotic cheekbones displayed both delicacy and strength. Her lips were full and rounded over even teeth. The flush on her pale cheeks was like sunset on snow. She looked ethereal in the sunlight. Enchanting—well, that's what he had thought the first time he held his dagger to her throat.

Percy cleared his throat. "What say you,

MacGregor? Let's have some practice shots before we compete."

Declan laughed, reaching for the bow that Percy held. "'Tis fine with me, Percy. Ye need all the practice ye can get." Declan adjusted the arrow and took aim. He studied the board and shot, the whizzing arrow flying out of his fingers. His eyes never left the mark.

Dead center.

"Well done, MacGregor! Come now, Percy. Do not let me down, young chap," said Catesby, handing Percy his bow.

Percy adjusted the arrow. He raised the bow and took aim. His eyes narrowed and the lines on his forehead contracted. At the last moment, his elbow moved and he shot—to the left. Very far to the left.

Catesby shook his head. "Well, clearly not your best shot, man."

Declan stepped forward. "Percy, ye study too much on the board. Think ye are one with the mark and just shoot. Donna hesitate. Try again." Handing Percy another arrow, Declan stepped to the side. Percy raised his arm and Declan readjusted his stance. The arrow soared through the air and landed only a few inches away from the center, but closer than Percy's prior attempt. "Ye breathed. Ye would have done much better had ye nae breathed until the arrow was released."

Percy's eyes widened in amazement and he chuckled. "Thank you, MacGregor. Truly. What a difference that even made. I will try not to breathe next time."

Declan gave Percy a knowing look. "Do ye still wish to challenge me?"

"I never back down from a challenge." Something unspoken clearly passed between Percy and Catesby before they masked their expressions.

Catesby was reaching out to hand Declan the arrows when Declan spotted the swish of a skirt out of the corner of his eye.

The daft woman leisurely walked along the edge of the forest. He stifled a sigh, trying not to let his displeasure show. Quickly making his apologies to Catesby and Percy, Declan followed the lass with purposeful strides. Where did she think she was going without an escort? He had lost count of how many times he'd lectured her about that.

Lady Liadain Campbell—healer, half sister to the late Archibald Campbell, seventh Earl of Argyll—was nothing but a thistle in his arse. He strived to be patient with her—after all, Ciaran had recently slain her brother, the bloody Campbell, the right hand of the king.

When the Campbell had disobeyed King James's orders and abducted members of the MacGregor family, Ciaran had been left with no other alternative. The Campbell chose his fate the moment he touched the MacGregor clan. Declan supported his brother completely in that regard. His nephew's screams of terror still plagued his thoughts. Since Ciaran still nursed a shoulder injury, he'd ordered Declan to attend court on his behalf to explain the circumstances. To Declan's relief, Liadain Campbell had not only affirmed her brother's treachery, but the king exonerated Ciaran.

Now she was a ward of the court, which meant there was no suitable male presence to watch over her.

And with a clan debt to be paid, he could not abandon her to all the courtly vultures. He at least owed her that much. Although he had no problem watching over her from a distance, a very far distance, times like these drove him mad.

Someone had to keep a watchful eye on the wily minx.

He increased his pace. The faster he could get to her, the better. He lost sight of her somewhere in the dense forest. Where did she wander off to now? He finally spotted her, chopping branches with her dagger.

Declan thundered toward her, his temper barely controlled. "What the hell do ye think ye are doing?" he bellowed. "Didnae I tell ye nae to—"

The obstinate woman lifted her chin, meeting his icy gaze straight on. "*Ye* arenae my husband, MacGregor. Ye have nay right to tell me what I can or cannae do!" she spat. She tossed her hair across her shoulders in a gesture of defiance.

He stepped toward her and reached out to clutch her arm.

She held something close to her chest and tugged away from him. "Careful, ye fool. I donna want them broken."

He looked at her puzzled. "What is that? Sticks?" he asked, pointing to her bundle.

The lass responded sharply, "They arenae just any sticks, ye daft man. This is willow bark for healing."

Declan smirked in response. "Willow bark? And they donna have enough for ye at court?"

She brushed past him and increased her gait. "I donna expect ye to understand."

He grudgingly trailed behind her. "I donna *want* to understand. Ye need to cease wandering off by yourself. Do ye hear me?" He quickened his pace to catch up with her.

"Of course I can hear ye. Ye are bellowing at me," she called over her shoulder.

He grabbed her shoulders and spun her around. His eyes narrowed and he studied her with curiosity. Was she completely daft? Did she have no idea of the dangers that could befall a woman without an escort? He remembered a time not long ago when he had sprung out of the brush and startled her. He could have killed her. Did she not learn a lesson?

Apparently not.

She stiffened at his silent challenge, and her emerald eyes were sharp and assessing.

Declan chuckled at her demeanor. "Tell me, healer. What if a man found ye out here alone?" he asked, giving her body a raking gaze. "What would ye do since ye have nay escort?"

Every generous curve of her body bespoke defiance. "I came this far without your assistance and I donna need it now." Turning on her heel, she started walking back without him—again.

Who was he to argue with a stubborn Campbell? She could bloody well walk back on her own.

Still, his conscience hammered away at him. "Wait, healer." His voice softened, losing its steely edge. He ran up beside her and extended his arms. He did not think she would accept his offer and she obviously weighed her response.

Looking down at her bundle, she sighed. "I donna

want the willow bark broken. It needs to be chopped. I donna like it snapped."

Damned twigs.

"Here. I will carry it for ye and promise to be careful."

Reluctantly, she released the bark into his care and they continued to walk silently. Declan was grateful for the quiet because if he heard her sharp tongue again, he might just take her back into the trees and show her what could befall a woman who was caught out here alone.

Two

LIADAIN HAD NOT INTENDED TO WANDER SO FAR FROM
court unaccompanied—well, she had, but *he* did
not have to know that. He did not understand. The
courtly games alone were enough to drive a sane
person mad. She had happened to stumble upon the
willow bark, and once she found it, she could not
turn away. This would make a great addition to her
collection of healing herbs.

Declan MacGregor had been watching over her
since they had arrived at court, but what she could
not discern was why. At every meal, every dance,
every turn, he was there, peering at her intently. The
man obviously did not think her capable of caring for
herself. And she did not need any man to protect her.
After all, she had gone behind her brother's back—*half
brother*—and brought the MacGregor women to safety.
What woman would attempt such a feat? Yet, her newfound champion continued to survey her every move.

Foolish man.

Liadain stole a quick glance at him and shook
her head. MacGregor might be foolish, but he was

definitely a man. It was hard not to notice such pure masculinity.

Clad in a red-and-green-patterned kilt with a flowing gray tunic, he wore his golden-chestnut hair plaited into two braids that hung past his broad shoulders. His powerful body moved with an easy grace. He had a strong chiseled jaw and piercing blue eyes. Her attention was drawn again to his powerful set of shoulders and she stifled a sigh. He was truly a beautiful man. And that was exactly the problem.

He knew it.

MacGregor carried himself with an arrogant grace, as if the very air itself was charged with energy, his energy. When he ambled into a room, he could command attention without speaking a single word. His mere presence was captivating.

Liadain cleared her throat. "How much longer do ye think I will be a ward of the court?"

"Anxious to take your leave, healer? 'Tisnae as if ye have somewhere else to go."

"I thank ye for reminding me of that fact," she replied sharply. She stopped, extending her arms. "I am able to manage from here. Thank ye for carrying the willow bark."

Hesitating too long for her tastes, he eventually handed her the bundle. "I trust ye to have an escort or at least your maid the next time we meet." He gave her a pointed look, waiting for her to respond.

"Rest assured, MacGregor, if I need an escort, ye will be the first to know." She turned on her heel and left him standing there.

She remembered the day she had met him. How

could she forget? He had held a dagger to her throat and would have spilled her blood where she stood. What was she supposed to have done—inform him that the Campbell was her brother? MacGregor had some bollocks. He had not exactly been forthright with the truth, having led her to believe he was his brother, Aiden. Ever since, the man had insisted on calling her "healer" and refused to address her by her given name.

Men.

Liadain proceeded to her chamber to escape his disturbing presence. She placed the willow bark on the table and removed her cloak, tossing it onto the bed. She pulled her dagger from beneath her dress and started to chop the bark into manageable pieces, not realizing she had gathered as much as she had. When memories of MacGregor popped into her mind like a pecking bird that refused to cease, she sighed. Why did she let him get under her skin?

She was not completely daft. She never left her chamber without her dagger and would be able to defend herself if the need arose. What did the man take her for? She did not ask him to be her champion and could take care of herself. What she needed was to safeguard herself from him. She wished he would just stay away.

❧

Liadain reluctantly sat and embroidered in the ladies' solar, praying for patience as they spoke of the latest fashions and discussed who was sharing a bed with whom. These women had no inkling of life outside the walls of the court. If she had a single ounce of power, she would willingly denounce the title of "lady" that had been bestowed upon her and adhere to her true calling, healing.

But because of her brother, she was stuck at court with other women of quality, forced to behave as a lady, pretending she had no brain whatsoever. It was completely maddening. Gone were the days of roaming freely and applying her healing talents to the sick. She was no more than the latest pawn in the game of men.

She rubbed her brow and sighed. More than likely, the king would marry her off to some English lord, and her beloved Highlands would be lost to her forever— only a distant memory to offer her comfort and warm her heart on the coldest of nights. She stared into the distance and did not realize her maid was speaking to her until she felt a steady tapping upon her arm.

"Are ye well? Ye appear flushed, my lady," Mary asked with concern.

Liadain smiled and handed the maid her embroidery. "I find the conversation 'tisnae verra stimulating. In fact, I think it makes me darn near daft," she whispered. "I need some air."

Mary dropped the stitching upon the chair and jumped up from her seat. "Then I will accompany ye, my lady."

For the time being, Mary was assigned as her lady's maid. The petite, eager young girl tried to accommodate her in every way, but the girl's actions were becoming smothering. Accustomed to being on her own, Liadain was not content with having no time for herself. She could barely breathe with the girl constantly underfoot.

Escorting Mary out into the hall, Liadain spoke softly. "I donna need ye to accompany me." Seeing the rush of disappointment upon the young girl's face, she quickly added, "Mayhap ye could press my gown for this eve," she said, hoping the task would keep the girl occupied.

Mary's eyes lit up. "It would be my pleasure, my lady."

Liadain watched Mary dash off, her tawny curls bouncing. Turning, Liadain made her way hastily out the door. If she could escape the exasperating crowd for only a moment and steal some time for herself, the reward would be well worth the risk. She found such an area opposite the fountains that led along the outer border of the gardens.

Lifting her face to the sun, she let the warmth bathe her skin. Everything seemed brighter and she suddenly found the corners of her mouth turning upward. She lifted her hand and pulled the ribbon from her wealth of dark hair, releasing the heavy tresses that tumbled over her shoulders. She could immediately sense the tension starting to dissipate.

Ambling along the outer path to the gardens, Liadain inhaled deeply, the smell of roses overwhelming her senses. She truly loved the open air.

≈

Declan sought the solace of the gardens. He needed a reprieve. He never thought he would admit as much, but women were actually starting to make his head ache.

"MacGregor!" shouted Percy.

Speaking of women…

He turned around as Percy punched him gingerly on the shoulder. "You are not going to back out on me again, are you? I still hold you to the challenge."

Declan's mouth curved into a smile. "Nay. If ye are free on the morrow…"

Percy clapped once. "Splendid. Catesby and I travel into the village this eve with Fawkes for a much needed eve of ale and women. Would you like to come?"

A chance to escape these walls for an eve? His mind drifted briefly to the healer, but how much trouble could one lass possibly get into in just one eve? It was a tempting offer and he did not take long to decide. "Aye. I would."

"Glad to hear it. We will meet you at the stables."

Percy turned away and Declan continued his walk to the gardens. He often found tranquillity at Glenorchy as he sat on a wooden bench in the flowery sanctuary. He ambled along the outskirts of the garden and found an unoccupied bench conveniently hidden behind a tree. He sat down and sighed. Closing his eyes, he willed away any thoughts that came to mind.

"There ye are. I have been searching for ye all day."

For the second time today, he reluctantly opened his eyes. His latest bed partner stood before him with her hands placed on her hips. He stretched out his legs, crossed his ankles, and folded his arms over his chest. "Och, ye found me." His morning conquest looked like a wolf ready to devour a lamb.

Moving toward him with a wanton purpose, the woman raised her fingers and brushed his jaw.

"Aye," she said with brazen sensuality and sat down beside him.

"What did ye want?" he asked, already afraid he knew the answer.

"Ye," she said in a childlike voice, slapping him in a playful manner. "We can meet again this eve in your chamber. Papa willnae bother us again. I assure ye."

There were a couple of things undeniably wrong with the words she said. First, he never brought a lass into his chamber. He had no qualms about bedding women wherever, but not there, his refuge.

Second, he never coupled with lasses who were wed, which praise the saints was not the case here. Being chased or hunted down by enraged husbands because he'd sated their lonely wives' desires was not on his list of accomplishments. He was not that daft. Besides, he liked his head just where it was.

Third, he never bedded a woman whose livid father threatened to cut off his manhood—well, at least not a second time, which brought him back to the task at hand. "I have something to which I must attend this eve. I donna think it wise that we meet again," he said dryly.

The woman pursed her lips and pouted.

He was sorely in need of a reprieve from the lasses. What had ever happened to a pleasant evening of satisfying each other's lust and just saying fare-thee-well in the morn? Her whining voice pulled him from his thoughts.

"Donna let Papa frighten ye off. He is all bark and no bite," she said, waving her hand dismissively.

"Lass, he doesnae frighten me and I thank ye, truly,

but 'tisnae wise for us to be together again." Declan rose. "Pray excuse me." His brisk steps could not carry him away fast enough. He had ignored the voice of his brother inside his head that nagged him to straighten his path. Perhaps if he listened even half the time, he would not find himself in these predicaments. In any event, he would just need to be more cautious.

After lecturing the healer and barely escaping from his latest disaster, Declan sought the solitude of his chamber, probably the safest place. Sprawling out on the bed, he sighed, rubbing his hands over his face. If he was to convene with the men this eve, he needed to rest. His body could not survive another brutal night of ale and women without it.

❧

Liadain donned her gown for the evening meal and pinned up her unruly tresses. Another eve filled with insincere laughter and dancing—just what she needed. She hoped she would be able to keep MacGregor, the scoundrel, at bay.

She'd been thankful he hadn't seen her in the garden because she had no desire for another reprimand for being on her own. As a safer alternative, she'd surreptitiously watched from behind a tree as he left the garden, retreating from his latest tryst. What a rogue. Did he have no respect? She shook off the memory. The man was not her concern. She had more important matters to attend to.

Reluctantly, Liadain stood tall and straightened her spine. How many more days would she be made to suffer? As she walked through the hall, a couple of men cast her leering glances. Looking past them, she entered the great hall.

"Healer," murmured MacGregor from behind her.

Startled, she turned to face him and her heart hammered in her ears. "MacGregor," she said simply, raising her brow.

"May I have a word with ye?" he asked, gently taking her arm and pulling her away from the crowd.

The mere touch of his hand sent a warming shiver through her. "Aye. What do ye want to scold me for now?"

Ignoring her words, he glanced around to make certain no one overheard their conversation. For a moment, he merely studied her intently. "I will be taking my leave—"

She tried to swallow the lump in her throat. "Thank ye for staying as long as ye did. I am joyful that your brother is cleared of any wrongdoing and that your clan is now safe."

A devilish look came into his eyes and he raised his hand. A finger tenderly traced the line of her cheekbone and jaw. He lowered his head and his voice, deep and sensual, sent a ripple of awareness through her. "And to think...I thought ye didnae care for me."

Liadain grabbed his hand, intent on stopping his light caresses. Instead, she found herself extremely aware of his masculinity. She did not have the strength to pull away, and frankly, she had no desire to move. His touch sent a bolt of sensual awareness through her that only increased under his heated gaze. There was a tingling in the pit of her stomach and her heart jolted. What the hell was wrong with her? With a steely resolve, she dropped his hand, reminding herself of what he was.

MacGregor was momentarily speechless and then his eyes grew openly amused. "If ye would have let me finish my words, I was to say that I merely take my leave to the village and wanted to make sure ye were all right. I will return in the morn."

She was helpless to halt her embarrassment and she flushed miserably, casting her eyes downward. She was aware of his scrutiny, her discomfiture quickly turning into anger. She nodded, not trusting herself to speak.

He moved closer until he left her no room at all. Lifting her chin with his finger, he smiled tenderly. "If ye donna want me to take my leave, ye only have to speak the words," he said quietly.

She stood frozen and needed a moment to gather her wits as his azure eyes studied her. "I am fine. I will see ye in the morn." Was that a flash of disappointment she saw in his eyes before he took a step away?

"Be safe, healer," he ordered, pointing his finger at her.

Nodding again, Liadain watched his broad back walk out of the hall. For some reason, she sensed an odd twinge of disappointment herself.

❧

"So I hear MacGregor is truly the best shot you have ever seen," said Guy Fawkes, addressing Percy and Catesby as they sat around the table.

Declan waved the man off and took another drink of ale from his tankard.

"I daresay that is true," said Catesby, holding up

his cup in mock salute. "I've never seen anything like him. He is quite the shot."

Declan shook his head, leaning back casually in the chair. "Ye swell my head and will curse me into bad luck by speaking such words."

Catesby smacked him on the shoulder. "I don't think that would happen. Your skill is far too superior. Do you need more ale? I am buying."

Fawkes banged his tankard on the table. "Hell, Catesby, if you're buying, I'm drinking. Bring another round!" he shouted, waving his hand in the air.

Percy filled Declan's tankard and nodded briefly to Catesby. Glancing around the table, Catesby lowered his voice. "Tell me, MacGregor, what are your thoughts toward the king?"

Declan almost choked on his ale and placed his tankard back down on the table. Wiping his mouth with the back of his hand, he cast Catesby a questioning glance. "The king?" he asked, his voice unintentionally going up a notch.

Fawkes leaned forward and his words were loaded with derision. "In April, the Commons refused his request to be titled King of Great Britain. King James still has ambitions to make Scotland and England one country under one law. I'm curious, MacGregor. What are your thoughts on the matter?"

Taking another drink of ale, Declan shrugged. He'd known Percy, Catesby, and Fawkes only for the brief time he'd been at court. They'd engaged him in some form of sport one way or another, but he was not well enough acquainted with these men to speak so openly.

"I donna judge a man by his title. Ne'er have.

His Majesty just signed a peace treaty with Spain and stopped the war. Besides, he is holding a great banquet in celebration," said Declan, holding up his tankard. This could quickly turn into a dangerous conversation. He needed to promptly change the subject. "There will surely be flowing ale and plenty of lasses."

Fawkes studied him closely. "Then tell us, MacGregor, do you side with the realm and practice the Protestant religion or do you hold fast to your roots?"

Declan leaned back in the chair. All of the men were on the edge of their seats waiting for his response when a warning voice whispered in his head. Who in the hell would care what he thought? He was no one. These were certainly not matters to be discussed freely in a tavern with so many open ears. Men had been killed for less.

He held a blank expression. "Ye know? There are two things I donna think men should speak upon when they are in their cups—politics and religion." He threw back his head and roared with laughter. Just as he thought, the men followed suit.

At that moment, Declan became astutely aware that this was not a chance gathering. These men were plotting…and they wanted something from him.

Three

Liadain stood in a corner, attempting to be a wallflower. As soon as she could manage, she would make a fleeing attempt back to her chamber. The heat was unbearable. Even with her hair pinned up, sweat dripped down her back. Reaching behind her, she gently pulled the moistened gown away from her skin.

She glanced around the room, hoping to see if any other women were just as miserable. Perhaps she could find someone to share in this brutal torture. To her dismay, the women danced and laughed as if they had not a care in the world.

They were dressed in their finery, their escorts looking much the same. She yearned for the rugged Highlands, and although it pained her to admit as much, perhaps even one Highlander in particular.

Although MacGregor sparred with her constantly, Liadain had become accustomed to his stalking behavior. At any given moment, she would be able to lift her eyes and spot him through the crowd. It was if he always knew where she was and was looking after her from afar—always from afar. Without him tonight, she felt oddly bereft.

The sounds of laughter hammered at her nerves. Now was the perfect opportunity to make her escape. Walking along the outer edge of the ballroom, she discreetly made her way into the hall.

A short man approached her with a sly grin. "Escaping already, my lady?"

Liadain returned a nervous laugh. "I am trying."

Standing to his full height, which was not much, the man extended his hand, his breath reeking of ale. "I do not believe we have been formally introduced." Grabbing her hand, he bent over and planted a wet kiss on the top of it, giving her a view of his balding top. "I am Lord Dunnehl." Lifting his head, he narrowed his dark eyes as he studied her. "And you are a very beautiful woman, if you do not mind me being so forward."

She pulled her hand away. "Thank ye. Pray excuse me." As she attempted to move around him, he stepped to the side and blocked her path.

The English lord chuckled with a dry and cynical sound. "Now, now," he said in a singing voice. "I did not mean to frighten you. Besides, you have not yet shared your name."

Liadain smiled and knew the smile did not quite reach her eyes. Something about this man made her uneasy. Whether it was his shifty stance or the lecherous looks he threw her way, she could not say, but everything about him told her to tread carefully.

Lord Dunnehl stretched out his arms to stay her. "You are a relation to the Earl of Argyll, are you not?"

Looking around for another means of escape, she shifted from foot to foot. "Aye, he was my half brother."

"Please accept my sincere condolences. And why is it that Archie never said that he had such a lovely sister?" He gave her body a bold and raking gaze.

"My brother and I werenae verra close. I am sure he ne'er mentioned me. If ye will excuse me, I will be retiring," she said hastily.

He cast a menacing look. "Alone?"

That was all she could take. Her lips pursed in annoyance as she tried willfully to control her tongue. Standing to her full height, she towered over the petite man. "Aye. Good eve, sir." Liadain brushed past him and strode away as fast as her skirts would allow. Once inside the security of her chamber, she bolted the door. At least MacGregor always kept the scoundrels at bay.

❧

Declan shared a small room in the village with the men. The floor was hard and unwelcoming. It was not as warm and soft as sharing a comfortable bed with a desirable, willing lass. When he thought of the healer, he wondered if His Majesty would marry her off to a Highland laird or perhaps even choose an English lord. Then again, what difference would that make and why should he even care? She was a bloody Campbell, an enemy of the MacGregors, and he was only a third son.

He was nothing.

Rolling over, Declan reminded himself that she was only another wily female—no different from his sister-by-marriage, Aisling.

The healer complained that he watched over her constantly and insisted she could take care of herself. Yet, when he saw her in a crowd, her emerald eyes would find him and she would grace him with a smile. She was completely unaware of the captivating picture she made when she did so. Her behavior this eve had caught him by surprise. She believed he was deserting her. He was not a total arse—well, at least not in this instance. He would remain until the king…He turned back over. Why was this woman consistently consuming his thoughts?

He must have dozed off because the next he knew, the sun's rays shined brightly through the window in the early hours of the morn. Declan rubbed his eyes until his vision cleared. Catesby slept in the bed, and Percy and Fawkes moaned from the floor.

"Too much ale," Percy groaned, reaching for the chamber pot.

Slowly, Declan pulled himself up. "I go below stairs to break my fast. Do ye come along?"

"MacGregor, how can you eat after last eve?" asked Fawkes in astonishment.

Declan chuckled. "I am used to my brother's ale and 'tis much stronger than what we drank last eve."

"Your stomach must be made of iron, my dear boy," grunted Catesby, sitting up on the bed and running his hands through his hair.

"I will meet ye below stairs when ye all can move."

Declan broke his fast companionless, chuckling to himself. Apparently, he was the only one who could handle his drink—well, he did have years of discipline. But it was the conversation from last eve, not the ale, that continued to gnaw at his gut. Why all of the questions and why ask his opinion on such matters? His instincts were definitely on alert; he would have to keep his eyes and ears open.

Sluggishly, Catesby, Percy, and Fawkes made their way down the steps a short while later. Bloodshot eyes and pale faces nodded in greeting as they mumbled something incoherent about the stables and staggered outside.

Declan tossed the last piece of biscuit into his mouth, then walked briskly to the stables. The fresh air gave him new life. He inhaled deeply, the cool breeze clearing his senses. He found the men ready to ride—more or less. Fawkes was mounted. Percy grunted, pulling himself awkwardly upon his mount, and Catesby looked as though he was going to faint.

Englishmen...

Declan swung up effortlessly onto his mount and was ready to ride. "Do we head back to court then?"

Dropping the reins, Percy clasped both hands over his ears. "Shh...MacGregor. I go to my chamber and seek my bed...for days."

Declan laughed. "Mayhap ye should just pour the ale with the other wenches and leave the drinking to the men."

"It pains me too greatly to argue. I think I will just remain silent," said Percy with a grunt.

As they rode back to court, the only sound beyond the horses' hooves was that of an occasional groan or two from the Englishmen. Returning to court, the men secured their mounts and Percy, Catesby, and Fawkes retired to their chambers. Declan was surprised that they walked on their own accord. He would see to the healer and confirm that nothing untoward had occurred while he was away. Although, he was not sure she would be completely honest with him if it had.

Stubborn female…

Perhaps she would like to go for a walk with him. Declan knew the confines of court were restricting her. And of course he felt somewhat guilty for having some enjoyment while she was stuck at court.

❧

Liadain opened her bedchamber door and MacGregor stood there, devilishly handsome. His windblown hair brushed his face and his crystal-blue eyes sparkled. She had to remember to breathe.

He nodded in greeting. "Healer."

She folded her arms over her chest. "MacGregor."

"I take it ye didnae cause too much trouble last eve since ye are standing here before me."

She smirked in response. "I figured ye caused enough unruliness in the village for the both of us."

He paused, running a hand through his hair. "Do ye wish to go for a walk?" She must have had a startled look upon her face because he quickly added, "I know ye have been confined and thought ye might enjoy some air."

"I would love to join ye. Do I need a cloak?"

"Nay, 'tis plenty warm enough." He stepped aside and she walked out into the hall.

She cast him a thankful smile as they walked to the gardens. As they ambled along the stone path, flowers filled the air with scented sweetness. Several hedges formed a trail along the way that led to the fountains, but they chose to stay on course.

"So how do ye fare?" MacGregor asked, placing his hand at the small of her back and then hastily removing it.

Nervously, she looked away from him, casting her eyes to the ground. "I am well. How was yester eve? I see ye live."

He chuckled in response. "I am alive. Howbeit Percy, Catesby, and Fawkes nae so much. As soon as we returned this morn, they all sought their beds. I am still nae sure how Percy made it back without falling from his mount."

"If ye wish it, I could make them something to ease their pain."

He shook his head. "Nay, let them suffer. 'Tis their own fault their English blood cannae handle ale."

Walking past a man and a woman, they nodded in greeting. The man placed his arm protectively around the woman's back and Liadain smiled at the loving gesture. "I know I have asked this of ye, but how much longer do ye think it will take King James to…"

He stopped abruptly. Turning her to face him, MacGregor placed both of his hands on the top of her shoulders. He towered over her and smiled down at her with compassion. "I donna know and I am sure 'tis on your mind. If ye wish it, I could request an audience with His Majesty."

"'Tisnae necessary. I donna know what he has planned for me and I donna rush to find out."

He hesitated, measuring her for a moment. "I know ye arenae fond of court, lass. If there was anything I—"

"Nay, I donna like it overmuch. My apologies that ye must suffer as well," she said, raising her hand to touch his cheek in a gentle gesture. She offered him a comforting smile, favoring him when he was like this and not being—well, an arse. There had been a handful of times when he dropped the pretenses and she had seen another man that existed within. She hoped that man would appear more often.

"Donna worry about me," he said, his eyes darkening like a summer storm.

She licked her lips and suddenly imagined being crushed within his embrace. The idea sent her spirits soaring. Whether she wanted to admit it or not, the pull was stronger each time she saw him. He made her feel like a young, breathless lass. Deliberately, she tried to shut out any awareness of him. With a firm resolve, she reminded herself that he had many other conquests, and frankly, she did not want to be added to his list of exploits.

"Ye donna think we should be together again. Yet, ye have clearly replaced me with another," said a woman's voice from behind MacGregor.

Liadain jumped back away from him. MacGregor turned and faced the woman, but Liadain could not see her face. It was not for lack of trying. The view was blocked by his massive form.

"Now isnae the time," he said dryly.

Stepping around him, the woman surveyed Liadain slowly from head to toe. The woman gave an overly dramatic curtsy. "Pray excuse me, my lady. I didnae realize he dallied…" As if she had second thoughts, the woman pulled MacGregor to the side, not even making an effort to lower her voice. "Papa took his leave this morn and I want to meet ye after the celebration."

This was clearly a private conversation—one Liadain did not particularly want to be a part of. "MacGregor, I will take my leave—"

Spinning toward her, he held Liadain in place with a wide-eyed look of desperation.

She could not stay the giggle that escaped her lips. Though it served the wretch right, she still felt sorry for him. He was clearly backed into a corner, searching for a means of escape. For a brief moment, she thought to flee, but she was a healer. She couldn't stand to see anyone suffer.

Liadain boldly placed her hand on his rock-hard forearm and fixed the blond with a withering gaze. Nodding to the woman, she said in a firm tone, "I donna share, my lady."

Liadain could feel MacGregor's stare boring into her. As their eyes met, she felt a shock jolt through her and she was amazed at the thrill he gave her. He wrapped his arm around her shoulders, his thumb making light, circular caresses.

"She doesnae share me."

The woman stammered in confusion. "My apologies, my lady," she said, bobbing a brief curtsy before she ran off.

Liadain could not help herself as she burst out laughing.

❧

Declan was rendered speechless. He could not say what surprised him more—the fact that the persistent woman would not yield or the fact that the healer actually came to his rescue.

"Why would ye do that?"

Her gentle laugh rippled through the air. "Your eyes said that ye were in desperate need…of escape."

"There is that," he said, shaking his head in astonishment as he watched the blond woman sulk away. Turning his attention back to his champion, he smiled. "I truly thank ye, and my apologies that ye heard… er, her words."

She waved him off. "A word of advice, if I may?"

Declan twisted his mouth in annoyance. "I donna think I have a choice," he said dryly.

"If ye continue to behave as a rogue, MacGregor, ye will always find yourself in these situations. Howbeit ye arenae my husband so I donna have a care," she quickly added. "But when ye settle down with a wife, she may. Just something for ye to think upon," she said with an air of indifference as she continued to walk.

For some reason, her words disturbed him. Granted, if he ever wed, his wife might have such concerns over his dalliances, but what bothered him more was the fact that the healer was not troubled. He was taken aback because she was unaffected by his wicked behavior. Perhaps he was mistaken and what he'd thought were stolen glances were only that—nothing more.

He shook off their conversation and they continued to walk as if the incident never happened. What was the matter with him? Prior to the woman's untimely interruption, the thought actually crossed his mind to kiss…the *healer*.

Hell, the lass looked so lusciously alluring. She always did. Her actions showed that she could be as playful as a young lass or as composed as an intelligent woman, a strength that did not lessen her femininity.

Casting a sideways glance, he saw that tiny curling tendrils escaped the heavy silken mass of her raven tresses. Her beauty was exquisite. She carried herself confidently, unaware of the approving glances that men threw at her. Declan studied her thoughtfully for a moment. She was truly a woman to be treasured.

"'Tis such a lovely day. *Mòran taing* for walking with me." *Thank you very much.*

He winked when he caught her eye. "'Tis my pleasure, lass."

Her smile broadened in approval. "So tell me, MacGregor. Do ye miss the Highlands as much as I do?"

He chuckled. "I hope 'tisnae that obvious, but aye."

"I bet ye miss your family."

He did not fail to notice the silent sadness upon her face. "What? The endless lectures from my brothers, Aisling and Rosalia's prodding, and my nephew's screams? Nay, I donna. I do miss Ealasaid's biscuits, though."

There was a heavy silence.

"And what of ye, lass? The Earl of Argyll was many things, but he was still your kin. How do ye fare?" Declan asked, his tone filled with compassion.

A soft gasp escaped her and she gave him a sidelong glance of nonbelief. "MacGregor, 'tis the first time I ever heard ye call my brother something other than 'the bloody Campbell.' My apologies, I just need but a moment to recover."

They exchanged a look of subtle amusement. "Ye donna realize how truly painful that was for me," he jested, holding his hand over his heart.

She elbowed him in the arm. "Cease, ye rogue."

"Ye didnae answer my question, lass."

Her features held a solemn gaze as she spoke. "Archie chose his own path, and fate decided it wasnae the correct one. Howbeit 'tis those of your clan—Aisling, Teàrlach, and Rosalia—that are in my prayers. My brother's conduct was inexcusable, and I donna know how your family doesnae hold me accountable," she said, looking down at the ground.

Declan stopped and moved to stand in front of her. He lifted her chin with his finger and saw that her eyes bordered with tears. "Look at me, healer." She glanced up at him, but he did not give her an opportunity to speak. "Ye are naught like the bloody Campbell. If nae for your actions, lass, my nephew would be dead. Ye brought Aisling back to Aiden. Ye are a courageous woman, Lia—"

A sudden uproar in the garden caught their attention. Robert Cecil, Viscount Cranborne, walked through the garden, cheered by everyone he encountered. It had been due to the man's skilled diplomacy that King James was able to sign the peace treaty that brought the war with Spain to an end. In celebration, a grand banquet was being held in Cranborne's honor.

The healer gasped and the heavy lashes that shadowed her cheeks flew up.

Declan reached out and supported her. "What is amiss? The color has drained from your face, lass."

Her eyes widened, but she didn't say a word. "'Tis Viscount Cranborne," he said as though it was the obvious answer.

Her voice rose in surprise. "Aye, I know."

Four

DRAWING A DEEP BREATH, LIADAIN FORBADE HERSELF
to tremble. Her heart refused to believe what her mind
told her.

It was him.

Robert Cecil, now Viscount Cranborne, ambled
through the garden right before her very eyes. If she
had not witnessed it herself, she would have never
believed it. Robert's dark hair, just graying at the
temples, was still full. His face was bronzed by wind
and sun, his handsome visage still familiar. How long
had it been? Three years perhaps—three years and not
a single word from him.

She remembered the first time she had met him.
She'd entered the Campbell great hall for the midday
meal and there he was, boldly confident, undeniably
attractive. She recalled Archie clearing his throat
to break their trance. Once her brother introduced
them, the two of them had conversed throughout the
entire meal. In fact, they did not even realize Archie
had already taken his leave. For well over a fortnight,
Robert wooed her, made promises. And then he

simply took his leave and did not return for her. Her musings were interrupted by a male voice.

MacGregor.

He gazed upon her with concern. "Are ye well, healer? It looks as though ye have seen a ghost."

She nodded in confirmation. "I am well. Shall we resume our walk? 'Tis such a beautiful day and would be a shame to waste it."

He looked at her hesitantly and then reluctantly nodded. "If ye are sure."

Liadain took his arm because she was too shaken to walk on her own accord. She needed time to absorb that Robert was presently here—alive. She had often inquired about him to Archie, but her brother had brushed off her words. Her thoughts continued to race wildly.

Robert, Viscount Cranborne, was now at court. What were the odds? She would be bound to encounter him again. What would she say? What would he say, for that matter?

MacGregor chuckled. "Lass, 'tis obvious something troubles ye."

His voice brought her back to reality. "My apologies. 'Tis naught, truly. I thank ye for escorting me. I really needed the fresh air."

He raised his brow and gave her a questioning glance. "I think I know ye well enough to know when something is amiss. Do ye want to speak upon it? I am a good listener, or so I have been told."

Unsettled, Liadain shook her head. "Nay, I donna, but thank ye," she said, giving him a forced smile. She stole a quick glance at him and hoped he was not aware of her discomfiture. One thing was for certain. MacGregor was not an idiot.

&

That was interesting. How did the healer know Viscount Cranborne? Perhaps through the bloody Campbell. That would certainly explain the association, but there was indisputably something more to the story than the lass was willing to reveal. If her actions were any indication, she was distraught upon seeing Cranborne in the garden. No matter, Declan was convinced the truth would eventually come to light. It always did.

She bit her lip yet again, something he recognized as being her habit when she was ill at ease. In an attempt to ease her distress, he decided to change the topic. "Lass, there are many arriving at court this day for the celebration. I donna want ye unattended. I will be your escort this eve."

She glanced up at him and raised her brow. "Are ye asking me or are ye telling me?"

He mocked the tone of her voice. "Are ye going to battle with me or just accept the inevitable?" Now his bonny healer was more like herself.

Her eyes danced with amusement. "I would be honored if ye would escort me, MacGregor."

"Ye see, healer? 'Tisnae that difficult. It would be so much easier if ye would just do as ye are told from the start," he said, exasperated.

"But then I wouldnae have the pleasure of hearing ye bellow at me," she jested, the glint of humor finally returning.

"And I hope ye donna expect me to dance with ye this eve. I donna dance." He enjoyed seeing the light come back into her eyes.

"Then fortunate for me that I wasnae thinking of having ye as my partner."

Their gentle sparring was short lived when, out of the corner of his eye, Declan spotted a man walking toward them with long, purposeful strides.

Damn. Cranborne.

Immediately stiffening at his side, the healer slowed her steps. Cranborne moved toward them and the silence grew tight with tension.

Cranborne studied them both and then stepped forward and gave an elaborate bow. "My lady."

Declan had to give his wily lass credit. She lifted her chin, meeting the man's gaze straight on. "Viscount Cranborne, a pleasure to see ye again. Pray allow me to introduce ye—"

"Declan MacGregor," said Declan, giving him a slight bow of his head.

"A pleasure." Turning to the healer, Cranborne spoke softly. "I was wondering if I might have a private word with you."

She cast an unreadable expression. Declan would have been more than happy to return the favor she had just previously bestowed on him, but the choice was clearly hers. Raising his brow, he cocked his head slightly, giving the lass the opportunity to voice her opinion.

She nodded in consent, but he was not foolish enough to leave her to face her demons alone. As she turned with Cranborne, Declan halted her with a firmly placed hand on her arm. "I will be over here if ye need me." Casting a warning glance at Cranborne, he quickly added, "For anything."

The healer adjusted her smile. "I know where to find ye."

❧

Liadain forced herself to settle down. What could Robert possibly say to her that would obliterate three years of heartache? Three years of wondering what could have been?

"I knew that was you in the garden. I would recognize you anywhere." Robert reached out to touch her and then pulled his hand back almost as a second thought. "You look well, Liadain."

"Viscount Cranborne," she said, trying to keep the censure out of her tone. She folded her arms in front of her in a protective gesture. She was irked by Robert's cool manner. If he asked her about the weather, she might have to throttle him.

"I owe you an explanation," he said softly.

She chuckled. "An explanation? After three years? I think ye are long past due, Viscount Cranborne."

Recovering, Robert spoke lightly, "You have every reason to be cross with me."

"Cross with ye? Mayhap after the first year that I received nay word from ye. Mayhap even after the second, but definitely nae after the third," said Liadain, her voice raising an octave. Where the hell had he been? What of the promises of their life together? She only knew one thing for certain.

Robert was a liar.

The man had the nerve to cast a worried look at MacGregor. "Please lower your voice."

Her jaw dropped. "Why? Ye didnae even care enough about me to say fare-thee-well. That would have been more bearable than nae leaving a single word. A single word, viscount."

Robert had pledged his loyalty to her. And then he had vanished like a thief in the night with no regard for her or her welfare. The man was clearly nothing more than an English cur who'd never given a damn about her. How could she have been so foolish? She continued to glare at him with burning, reproachful eyes.

"I have no excuse for my behavior. I had every intention to return for you and then I departed for Spain. It changed me." His voice was resigned.

Liadain reached out and squeezed his arm. Her voice was inflamed and belligerent. "I see your arm isnae broken. Ye verra well could have written."

Sheepishly, Robert glanced away from her. "I didn't know what to say. I figured after that long… you would have wed and moved on with your life."

She gave him a hostile glare. "I wasnae pining after ye, Robert. I didnae wed because I am a healer. I care for others and donna have time for the likes of a man. Nae to mention the wee detail that ye completely ruined me, but mayhap ye have forgotten that fact." She was so furious she could hardly speak.

The beastly man actually had the nerve to look offended. "Liadain, I did not mean to imply…What are you doing here at court? Where is Archie?" He had such a look of concern upon his face that she almost felt sorry for him. *Almost.*

She briefly closed her eyes when she realized Robert did not know. She needed more time to erase the pain. It was too fresh. Her misery was so acute that it was a physical pain. "Archie is dead," she replied in a low, tormented voice.

He had a genuine expression of shock upon his face. "What? When? *How*?"

Liadain glanced over at MacGregor. At least the rogue pretended to look occupied. Hesitating, she tried to prepare the words in her mind before they left her lips. "There is nay easy way…I will just speak the truth."

There was a heavy silence.

When she tried to speak, her voice wavered. Clearing her throat, she attempted once more. "Archie was determined to seize the lands of Ciaran MacGregor of Glenorchy. When my brother realized it was futile, he set fire to the stable in the village and killed a MacGregor man. Archie plotted to have Laird MacGregor declare war on the Campbells in retaliation and therefore break His Majesty's orders for peace in the Highlands. MacGregor would have hanged as a traitor."

She shifted from foot to foot. "But instead of storming the gates as Archie had planned, the MacGregor sent my brother a missive about the stable fire. Of course Archie denied any involvement. Howbeit Archie wouldnae accept defeat. He held the laird's kin and an innocent bairn, treating them horribly," she said, choking on her words and closing her eyes at the memory.

His eyes softened with compassion. "You don't

have to explain further. I understand what you are trying to say."

"I couldnae stand by and watch while he tortured innocents for the sake of his greed." She lowered her head, ashamed of her brother's actions. "Archie ordered the death of the bairn and I couldnae bear it. I helped the women escape, leaving verra little choice for Laird MacGregor. He ended Archie's life for his treachery. I traveled here with Laird MacGregor's brother, Declan, to give an account of Archie's…"

She left the words unspoken, not needing to relive the pain. "Since there is nay one to take Archie's place, the MacGregors hold my brother's lands, which are now relinquished to the realm. And I am now a ward of the court until His Majesty decides my fate."

Robert looked amazed. "I don't know what surprises me more. Archie's deceit or your bravery. I am sure it was difficult for you to speak to Archie's character or lack thereof." Reaching out, he gently touched her arm. "Listen, Liadain, I have the king's ear. Tell me what you want or where you want to go. I can at least offer you that for my ill-mannered behavior."

"I donna want anything from ye," she bit out. "Ye couldnae even give me the truth."

He sighed and held an expression upon his face that seemed regretful. "When we met, you were but a young girl, Liadain. I know I made promises to you, but then I was sent to Spain and I fell—"

"Robert! Robert!" yelled a woman upon her approach. She wore a moss-colored gown and her hair was the shade of honey. The woman appeared petite and flowerlike until she turned and displayed a rounded belly very much with child. Holding her hands under her stomach, the woman moved unsteadily toward them, the wind whipping color into her pale cheeks. "There you are, Robert."

Liadain would not have even noticed MacGregor's approach if not for the strong hand placed supportively at her back. She leaned against the palm of his hand as the woman spoke.

"Robert, I need to go back to our chamber. I feel ill. The babe pushes too much and I need to lie down." Placing her hands at her back, the woman stretched, looking totally uncomfortable. A rush of pink stained the woman's cheeks and she cast a sheepish smile. "Pray excuse my husband's comportment, my lady. I am Viscountess Cranborne."

Liadain gaped at Robert and he held some unreadable mask of emotion upon his face. At the same time, MacGregor's hand at her back suddenly became almost unbearable in its tenderness. The shock of discovery hit Liadain in full force. She stood there, blank, amazed, and shaken. This was Robert's *wife*.

All of those promises that flashed before her eyes were now blown away like petals that fell from a beautiful flower, a gentle reminder of what could no longer be. Her pride had been seriously bruised, and now her face flushed with humiliation and anger—mainly at herself for being such a fool.

An unwelcome tension loomed between them like a heavy mist.

Struggling to maintain collectedness, Robert coughed. "My apologies, dearest." He cast Liadain a gaze of complete and utter terror, similar to the same flustered expression that MacGregor had upon his face earlier.

MacGregor spoke and his voice was tender, almost a murmur. "Healer." His tone brought her swiftly back to reality and she leaned back against his massive frame. If his arms did not support her, she would have fallen.

Liadain smiled tenderly at Robert's wife, her foolishness turning quickly into annoyance. "Viscount Cranborne was ne'er one for manners. I am Lady Liadain Campbell. The Earl of Argyll was my brother. The viscount and I were acquainted from his visits with my brother. Please, I would be honored if ye would call me Liadain."

Robert's wife smiled graciously and then suddenly turned her head. "Pray excuse me," she murmured, placing her hand over her mouth. Taking a few steps away from them, the woman tossed her contents all over the ground.

The gagging sounds brought Liadain's instincts into awareness, and she immediately ran to Robert's wife, placing a nurturing hand at her back. "'Tis all right. Ye have the sickness all day, my lady?"

The poor woman nodded in response, still huddled over. She moaned loudly as another bout of sickness came upon her. When she finished, she could barely pull herself to stand. She gulped hard, tears slipping down her cheeks. "My apologies."

Robert pushed back his wife's hair from her cheeks

and his eyes were gentle, understanding. He wiped the woman's tears with his thumb. "Let me take you inside, my love. You have been up and about all day."

Liadain's hand rubbed the woman's back. "There is nay need for apologies, my lady. I am a healer. Let me help ye. I can brew something that will assist ye with the sickness."

Robert's wife smiled. "Please, call me Elizabeth."

Five

DECLAN PREPARED FOR THE EVENING'S FESTIVITIES IN honor of Viscount Cranborne, donning the courtly fashions he had borrowed from his brother. Having met the viscount, he could not say what surprised him more: that Cranborne had ruined the healer or the obvious affection the man held for his wife.

Reluctantly, Declan had to admit that the healer had handled herself with dignity and respect. He was not sure he could have done the same. When he had placed his hand at the lass's back, she had trembled, but he was relieved to see her compassion for others beat out the urge to cause bodily harm.

Feeling like an arse, he had tried not to overhear the conversation with Cranborne, but raised voices left him with few options. Cranborne had promised her a future, taken her innocence, and never returned. And that was why Declan had enough sense never to dally with virgins or women who were wed. They led to nothing but trouble. Cranborne had certainly made a mess of things.

As of late, the healer had been through a great deal.

Losing a brother, being a ward of the court, finding out that the man she was to spend the rest of her days with was now a viscount wed to another…It was enough to drive a sane person mad. The poor lass. This eve, he would make sure that the woman enjoyed herself. Perhaps he could stay his tongue long enough not to spar with her, or maybe he could even swallow his pride and choose another partner for her with whom to dance—not an easy feat, by any means. She clearly needed some joy in her life and he would see to it. It was but a small price to pay for her aiding his kin.

As Declan made his way through the halls of the castle, he sorely missed the informality at Glenorchy. The solace of his own chamber, the bantering with his brothers—well, that part was not exactly peaceful. At least he could just be himself. Granted, his family drove him mad with their constant lecturing, but they were his own and they depended on each other. At court, he had no doubt someone might drive a dagger straight through his heart as soon as he turned around. He trusted no one. His mind wandered back to the peculiar conversation in the tavern. Fortunately for him, he had no interest in political machinations.

When he entered the great hall, someone poked him in the ribs. "'Tis about time, MacGregor. Ye leave me to the wolves," jested the healer. She wore a gold-colored gown that clung to her curves in all the right places. Her throat looked warm and shapely above a low-cut bodice. Her hair was pinned up, but one curl brushed against her slim, ivory neck.

Closing what was left of the gap between them,

Declan looked down at her and gave her a roguish grin. "Looking like that, lass, I bet the packs are fighting over ye. Ye look beautiful."

She smiled at the compliment. "So do ye."

He raised a brow. "I donna think ye are to say those words to a man, lass. Ye are to consider me handsome or the like. Nae beautiful."

She waved him off. "I know exactly what I said, MacGregor. Ye are handsome and ye know it. In fact, ye are more bonny than most women." She giggled. "It should be a sin for a man to be so bonny."

As she leaned in close, her lavender scent teased his senses. "Think ye, aye? I only know one thing for certain. I am nae as beautiful as ye look this eve, healer." Her flush deepened to crimson. Declan took her hand and brushed a kiss on the top of it, looking into her emerald eyes. She was stunning.

"There you are, Liadain. I was searching for you." Viscountess Cranborne approached with a wide smile. "I wanted to thank you. The herbs that you brewed made me feel remarkably better."

Releasing the healer's hand promptly, Declan smiled in greeting. "Viscountess Cranborne. A pleasure to see ye again. Ye look well."

"Thanks to Liadain. I must apologize for my earlier—"

"Please, there is nay need for apologies. Ye are a woman with child. I am joyful I was able to assist ye. Ye look much improved."

Instinctively, the viscountess raised her hand to her face. "I do feel somewhat better. I would never forgive myself if I missed Robert's celebration. His Majesty certainly spared no expense," she said, glancing around the hall. Looking back to Liadain, Robert's wife leaned closer. "So tell me. You said that you knew Robert when he visited with the Earl of Argyll. That was when? Four or five years ago?"

"Three," the healer said.

"What was he like then? You must tell me. Robert doesn't like to speak about his past. Sometimes I think he doesn't want me to hear that he took to the drink or the women."

Declan moved in an instinctive gesture of comfort, placing his hand again at the small of the healer's back. Her body screamed with unreleased tension.

His fingers gently rubbed her.

She squared her shoulders. "There isnae much to say to that. I was young and he would visit Archie upon occasion."

Suddenly, cheers erupted through the hall as the king in his long, flowing robes entered with Cranborne. His Majesty smiled in greeting as they walked to the dais, his hand on Cranborne's shoulder. The king's actions certainly erased any doubts Declan had about Cranborne's relationship to the realm.

The entire hall was silenced as the king raised his hands. "It is with great pleasure that we gather to honor Viscount Cranborne. His efforts assisted us in signing the peace treaty with Spain." King James spoke in a tone filled with respect. Reaching down, he grabbed his gold cup, lifting it high, and added, "To Viscount Cranborne."

Raising their own cups in response, men and women cheered—well, everyone but the healer. Declan did not blame her. He was surprised she held together as well as she did. As the viscountess joined her husband on the dais, Declan snatched the healer's wrist and pulled her toward a table, spotting Percy, Catesby, and Fawkes. The men stood immediately upon their approach.

"My lady, how wonderful to see you," said Catesby, giving the healer a slight bow. "Pray allow me to introduce Mr. Thomas Percy and Mr. Guy Fawkes."

She nodded politely. "Mr. Percy. Mr. Fawkes."

≈∂∞

MacGregor pulled out her chair and she gave him a puzzled smile. The rogue was obviously trying to behave as a gentleman, and for once, Liadain welcomed the kind gesture. She did not think her nerves could withstand much more.

"I was just speaking of your prowess with the bow, MacGregor," said Catesby, taking a drink of ale and studying Declan with a glazed expression.

She raised her brow and cast a glance at MacGregor, regarding him with curiosity. Why did that not surprise her? She began to wonder if there was anything the man could not do.

"MacGregor is so precise with his targets. Indeed, he is something to see," added Percy.

Fawkes raised his tankard in mock salute. "I have not yet had the privilege, but I have heard the same."

She smiled at the men. "I would love to see him shoot the targets."

MacGregor grunted and lowered his head. "Why do ye encourage them, healer?"

"A healer?" Catesby asked with a puzzled look.

"Then where were you this morn when I was in need of your aid?" asked Fawkes, placing his hand to his head. "I think you could have assisted Percy as well."

"I am afraid there is nay cure for overindulging in ale," she said.

The men laughed in response, and it was indeed a jovial mood—one that she sorely missed. She could not even remember the last time she had enjoyed herself.

"His Majesty hosts a bow tournament on behalf of Cranborne on the morrow. I understand coin will be awarded to the victor. Are you interested, MacGregor?" asked Catesby.

MacGregor shrugged. "Aye. Percy, will ye be showing off your prowess then?"

Catesby choked on his ale, spitting some of it from his mouth. "My apologies, my lady," he said, wiping his chin.

"Of course. I want to watch your methods so I can learn more from the best. Your slight instruction has already greatly improved my aim," said Percy with a sly grin. "I shall soon be among the best of the archers."

Liadain listened as the men jested among themselves. As she thought of the differences between men and women, she couldn't stay the smile that played upon her lips. While the men bragged of sport and manly pursuits, the women merely spoke of other women. She was thankful she didn't have to deal with female conversation presently, but she was still subjected to learning everything she ever wanted to know about archery.

Needing a respite, she leaned into MacGregor and

brushed against his strong thigh. He was so warm. Reaching out, she placed her hand on his forearm. He was so hard. Hastily removing her hand, she stood, straightening her shoulders and clearing her throat. "Pray excuse me. I am in need of some fresh air."

MacGregor stood in one fluid motion. "I will take ye."

Shaking her head adamantly, Liadain spoke in soft tones. "Nay, please stay with the men. I only need but a moment. The heat is a bit overwhelming. I will stand in the entry to the garden, and ye can see me from here. I will be fine. Truly."

"Come now, MacGregor. She will be fine. You can spot her from here. Besides, it's not as though you're shackled to her," announced Percy in a haughty English tone.

Turning, they both cast Percy an irritated look.

Attempting to drink from his tankard, Percy looked over the top of the rim. "What?"

MacGregor shook his head and a shadow of annoyance crossed his features. Turning back to Liadain, he gently brushed her arm. "I shall be here if ye need me."

She turned away, but not before she heard MacGregor tell Percy that he was an arse. At least men spoke bluntly about what they were feeling and moved on. Unlike women.

Placing her back against the door to the garden, Liadain tried to absorb the fresh, cool breeze. Why were these festivities always so unbearable? She missed her Highland weather.

A short, portly man turned and headed toward her. Taking a deep, unsteady breath, she stepped back.

What was his name? Damn. It was too late to make her escape.

"It is a pleasure to see you again, my dear."

Smothering a groan, Liadain pulled her hand instinctively out of his reach. A wet kiss on the top of the hand was not something she wanted to repeat, especially from that beastly lord. They exchanged a polite smile and then she quickly turned her head away from him. It worked. Fortunately, he walked past her and she was not subjected to his improper behavior. Once was more than enough.

"You have the right idea. This heat is unbearable," an older woman standing beside her said with a smile. Her eyes held a certain kindness. She was slim with a regal quality about her.

"'Tis verra warm."

The woman looked at her, surprised. "You are from Scotland?"

"Aye," Liadain answered cautiously.

The woman patted her on the arm. "I don't mean to be so forward. I just adore the Scottish tongue. My husband was from Scotland." When Liadain hesitated, the woman spoke lightly. "My apologies. I am Lady Caroline Armstrong. My husband has recently passed and I am feeling a little melancholy. I find myself sorely missing Mangerton, my home."

"Please accept my condolences. I am sorry for your loss. My brother has recently passed as well. He was the Earl of Argyll." As if something clicked in her mind, Liadain's face lit up. "Armstrong? Are ye by chance a relation to Lady Rosalia Armstrong?"

A strange look appeared on Lady Armstrong's face.

Her mouth dropped open and a soft gasp escaped her. "Rosalia? She is my daughter. How may I ask are you acquainted with her?"

Nervously, Liadain shifted her weight. How exactly was she to respond? *My brother took her against her will and threw her in our dungeon.* She had to think of something quickly. Not adept at spinning lies, she would stick as closely to the truth as possible. "I had known her from her time at Glenorchy."

"Glenorchy? Is she still there? I know the last time we spoke she mentioned she was traveling there."

"I am nae sure, but I believe so. Your daughter is verra kind, if ye donna mind me saying as such."

Lady Armstrong smiled her thanks. "That is so kind of you to say. Her father and I would expect nothing less. Tell me, where exactly *is* Glenorchy?"

"'Tis in the Highlands."

"Of course *it is*," she said, almost as if she was correcting Liadain's speech. "Pray excuse me. It was lovely to have met you."

That was a little…odd. She thought for sure Lady Armstrong would have wanted to speak of Rosalia. For a moment, Liadain was actually excited that she had something in common with another woman at court. But the woman hastily took her leave.

"Did ye cool enough or would ye like to take a walk in the garden?" murmured a warm voice from behind her.

Liadain felt a lurch of excitement within her. Turning, she smiled in earnest. "I would love to take a walk with ye, MacGregor." As they moved out the door, she welcomed the cooler air that brushed against her skin. "I can feel the difference already."

"Aye, it was suffocating in there. Who was the woman ye were speaking with?"

Stopping suddenly, Liadain turned to face him with a devilish look in her eyes. "Ye will ne'er believe. In truth, I would have ne'er believed it had I nae heard it for myself. 'Tis a verra small world in which we live. Guess…"

He rolled his eyes, indulging her. "Mmm…Queen Anne."

She slapped him playfully in the chest. "Cease. Ye know it wasnae Queen Anne. Do ye yield?"

He held up his hands in mock surrender. "I yield. Ye clearly have me at a disadvantage, lass."

"Lady Caroline Armstrong."

MacGregor's expression turned unreadable and he stood motionless. He hesitated, measuring her for a moment, and then his eyes rounded in surprise. Thinking the man was clearly not listening, Liadain poked him in the chest with her finger.

"MacGregor, Lady Caroline. Rosalia's mother," she said in a tone that indicated the answer was obvious. His expression remained stilled and serious. Something was wrong. Reaching out, she touched his arm. "MacGregor?"

He peered down at her intently, and when he spoke, his voice cut through the silence, edged with steel. "Healer, ye just became acquainted with the *diabhal*." *Devil.*

Six

"*DIABHAL? CHAN EIL MI A' TUIGSINN.*" I DO NOT
understand. Liadain stammered in confusion.

Declan needed time to think. Rosalia's mother.
Here. At court. Was the fiery dragon here alone?
Doubtful. Furthermore, he could not help but wonder
if Dunnehl was with her. There were too many questions that he wanted the answers to.

"Come with me." He needed to know what the
healer had said to the fiery beast—and quickly. He practically dragged her to a secluded bench in the garden.

Her eyes widened with uncertainty. "MacGregor,
ye are frightening me."

Declan gently caressed the back of his hand across
her cheek. "Donna be frightened, but this is verra
important, lass. I need ye to tell me everything that ye
said, even if ye think 'tisnae important." Lowering his
hand, he gave her a reassuring smile.

"When I heard her name, I thought of Rosalia
and I asked if she was a relation. At first, she seemed
almost startled. Then she declared that Rosalia was
her daughter. I believe she asked me how we were of

acquaintance. I stumbled for the truth and didnae want to admit that Archie…"

"I understand. So what exactly did ye say?"

"I merely conveyed that I had known Rosalia from her time at Glenorchy."

Declan involuntarily groaned and rubbed his hands over his face. Placing his elbows on his knees, he cast a troubled glance. "What else did ye say?"

Hesitating, she eyed him with concern. "She wondered if Rosalia was still at Glenorchy because the last she had heard from her daughter, she was still traveling. I told her I wasnae sure, but I thought so. Then she asked where Glenorchy was. She ended the conversation rather abruptly and then took her leave. That was all. Please, MacGregor, what did I do? Ye must tell me."

Sitting up, he ran his hands through his hair and sighed. The healer was not at fault. How could she have known? The English dragon now knew Rosalia's whereabouts. How dangerous could this be, and what trouble could the woman bring to his clan? Feeling the healer's gaze upon him, he stretched his back and rolled his neck.

"MacGregor," she said with impatience.

"Ciaran and Aiden were attending court at the end of last summer's solstice. On their way back to Glenorchy, they found Rosalia dressed as a stable lad. She had cut her hair and was bruised from head to toe. At first, they didnae know she was a woman, but obviously they found her out. From what Ciaran said, the Armstrongs' coffers were empty and Rosalia was to wed an English lord."

Declan explained, "Rosalia refused to wed this

man and her father beat her horribly for her insolence. From my understanding, that wasnae the first time for such a thrashing. She had suffered many years of abuse at her own family's hand."

He paused. Perhaps he should ask the healer for a remedy for his aching head. He continued, "Ciaran brought Rosalia to Glenorchy and cared for her wounds. 'Tis how she came to be at Glenorchy. Eventually, he was to escort her to Glengarry to her *seanmhair*." *Grandmother.* Declan shrugged.

"Since we are still here, I donna know if Ciaran did or nae. I cannae imagine my brother would ever... ne'er mind my words," he said, shaking his head. "A few months past, the stable master and cook from Mangerton arrived at Ciaran's gates to report that the English lord Rosalia was to wed had killed her father."

The healer gasped. Reaching out, she clutched his hand. "I didnae know her father was killed. 'Tis tragic."

He shook his head. "Nay, healer. What is tragic is that Rosalia's mother took her leave with the English arse freely."

"*Freely?*"

"Aye. Rosalia's father was Scottish, but as ye know, her mother is English. Rosalia said that her mother didnae love her father and detested everything about Scotland. Well, she found her means of transport back to England and she clearly took it. Now she knows where Rosalia is, and I donna know if she will bring trouble to Ciaran's door."

"Mayhap Ciaran has already taken his leave to Glengarry and Rosalia is safe."

"Aye. And what if they didnae?"

❦

Liadain stared pensively into the darkness. Rosalia had run to escape abuse, and now Liadain had brought it straight to her door. Hell, she pretty much had opened the door and let it in. What was she thinking? She was a healer. She was to help. She was not meant to hurt others or to place them directly in harm's way.

"There has to be something I can do to fix this. Just tell me, MacGregor. I will do anything."

"I need to inquire if the English dragon is alone at court or if she is here with Dunnehl."

"Dunnehl? Please donna tell me he was the English lord Rosalia was to wed, because he is here."

He paused. "How do ye know this?"

Liadain was thankful for the darkness. It was the only way she could escape his scrutiny—although she could feel his eyes upon her. She shifted restlessly on the bench.

"Healer?" he demanded.

"Please, MacGregor, I donna want to battle with ye. We have more than enough to be concerned about."

"I told ye. I need to know all of it. Now," he ordered.

She did not understand why he would want to know the particulars of her encounter with Dunnehl, but the man sat wordlessly and she discerned that he was not going to give up any time soon. "When ye took your leave for the village, I supped, and as I walked back to my chamber, he approached me."

There was a heavy moment of silence.

If MacGregor required the entire truth, she would have to enlighten him about Dunnehl's churlish behavior, not thinking it would make much of a difference anyway. But she was uneasy about elucidating the details to MacGregor. She would just blurt it out quickly, like ripping a bandage off a wound.

"Dunnehl introduced himself and planted a kiss—a verra wet kiss—on the top of my hand. I tried to excuse myself and told him I would be retiring. At first, he restrained me and wouldnae let me pass. He then asked if I would be retiring alone. There. Ye have it all. There is nay more to speak of."

MacGregor stood but did not move. He was silent and all she could hear was the sound of laughter in the distance. That was why she jumped when she heard the sound of his voice. "Is that all, healer?"

Liadain rose and reached out, touching his hard back. He flinched but did not turn toward her. Positioning herself in front of him, she grabbed both of his arms. "MacGregor, there is nay more to tell."

"Did he hurt ye?" he asked, his voice hard. "I will have the truth."

"Dunnehl? Nay."

MacGregor grabbed her by the elbow, leading her out of the garden. How he could see in the darkness was beyond her, but he clearly knew where he was headed. "I need to think upon this. I will escort ye back to your chamber and we will speak on the morrow."

For once, Liadain agreed with him. If she could retract her words she would, but the damage was already done. She had certainly made a mess of things. Not wanting to make matters worse, she would wait until MacGregor told her what to do.

⁓

Declan's thoughts raced as he walked the healer back to her chamber. He would need to find a way to warn Ciaran, but how, when he trusted no one? Even more disturbing was the picture that continued to display in his mind, torturing him.

Dunnehl placed his hands on her.

The thought gnawed at him more than he cared to admit. He had not been there to protect her. After all, that was the sole reason he remained at court. He had failed her.

Sure enough, he had made another wrong choice. He had willingly traveled to the village—yet again desiring drink more than fulfilling his responsibility to the lass. Perhaps Ciaran was right and one day Declan's recklessness would harm another. The truth to that fact pushed upon him like a heavy weight. The situation could have been much worse, and he would not have been there to safeguard her.

They reached the hall to her chamber and had yet to say a word to each other. Casting a sideways glance, he saw that the healer's gaze studied the floor.

"Ye arenae at fault and I donna want ye blaming yourself," he said softly.

She nodded and looked away from him.

They passed two chambermaids in the hall and his eyes widened. One maid mumbled something he could not quite hear under her breath, while the other clearly made a dramatic attempt to step out of their path. The healer was still deep in thought and did not pay the women any heed.

As they reached the healer's chamber, a loud gasp escaped her. Her eyes shot up in surprise and she scrunched her features.

"What is that *smell*?" asked Declan as a pungent aroma filled the air.

Her door was ajar, the putrid scent coming from within.

He pushed open the door and immediately covered his mouth and took a leap back. "God's teeth! It smells as though someone has surely died," he choked out.

Reluctantly entering the lass's chamber, Declan glanced around. The room had been ransacked, with clothes, books, and some kind of herbs thrown in disarray. Cut-up plants were tossed all over the floor and the bed.

She followed him in. "'Tis carrion flowers. Why would someone do this?" she asked, covering her mouth and nose with her hand.

That was a reasonable question, but not one he wanted to contemplate while in the middle of the rancid odor. *Damn!* That was the foulest stench he had ever encountered. "Try to grab whatever 'tis ye need for this eve with much haste."

The lass did not hesitate. Her belongings were tossed about, but she quickly gathered what she needed, making a mad dash to the door.

Declan did not need prodding to follow. As if his arse were afire, he shot through the door, pulling it closed with haste behind him. They both walked with purposeful strides to the end of the hall. "Breathe," he ordered.

Her breath was uneven. "'Tis truly terrible. My eyes even weep," she said, rubbing her eyes and blinking back the tears. "I donna understand. I donna know if I should be frightened or verra angry. Why do ye think someone would do this to me?"

There had been something odd about the behavior of the two maids in the hall, and an unsettling feeling gnawed in his gut. But he wasn't about to cause the lass more worry. Until he knew for certain, he would keep such things to himself. "Whatever the reason, ye cannae stay in your chamber this eve. Do ye have a woman ye can stay with?"

"I suppose I could stay with my maid."

He folded his arms over his chest. "With a bunch of feeble lasses? Aye, they would certainly offer ye protection. Ye are a lady and cannae share quarters with the maids. Ye donna know of another woman?"

"Umm…I havenae actually attempted to make an acquaintance of any of these women at court, lest ye count Lady Elizabeth or Lady Caroline. Frankly, I donna believe I would wish to stay with either."

"Then we can take our leave to the inn."

Her voice rose in surprise. "I am a ward of the court. Are ye going to interrupt His Majesty and ask permission to escort me to an inn because some daft fool ransacked my chamber? The king would place me under constant guard. I would be—?"

"I cannae say that I blame ye." Hesitating, Declan knew he could not leave her unattended. He wouldn't leave her to sleep with the maids and pray they could fend off an attacker with a broom. And he most certainly did not want to alert the king. No matter that he had left her once before; he would not fail her again. The lass was his responsibility. Just this once… he would have to break his most sacred rule.

God help him.

He did not make this decision lightly. "We have

nay choice. I will pay someone extra coin to clean your chamber and make certain they keep their mouth closed. And ye will stay with me."

Her eyes widened with shock. "Och, nay, MacGregor. 'Tisnae proper," she said firmly.

Closing the distance between them, he cast a roguish grin. "What is the matter, healer? Ye donna trust me?"

❧

How was Liadain to say that she did not trust herself? Sleeping in the same room as MacGregor—she shivered at the thought. She could not deny the spark of excitement at the prospect of sharing such personal space, but her cynical inner voice cut through her private musings.

She was nothing to him.

Liadain shifted from foot to foot. "MacGregor, we cannae reside in the same chamber. We clearly cannae."

He simply raised his brow. "'Tis late, healer, and ye donna take any of my suggestions. Where do ye plan to sleep?" He paused. "If ye willnae seek Lady Cranborne, ye have nay choice. Ye will stay with me. Ye can trust me. I will sleep on the floor."

"*Trust* ye? 'Tisnae about trust, MacGregor. 'Tis just nae proper that we share quarters."

Folding his arms over his chest, he stood to his full height, towering over her. "I am nae going to stand here all eve and debate what is proper or nae when I only look after your safety. Suit yourself, healer." He turned abruptly and strode away from her.

She quickened her steps to catch up with him. "Wait! Where are ye going?"

Turning, he threw up his hands in the air. "I told ye. I seek my bed. If ye are too stubborn to stay with me, mayhap I will seek a willing lass or *two*." He turned up his smile a notch.

The man knew he had her cornered. What was she to do? Ask Lady Cranborne? She wanted to stay as far away from Robert as physically possible. She was completely irritated, and MacGregor irked her more than anything.

Before she realized what she did, she threw her sack at him, hitting his massive chest with a thump. "Ye will sleep upon the floor," she insisted, poking him in the chest.

MacGregor's smug expression lasted the entire way to his chamber. Pushing open the door, he gave her a roguish grin. "Welcome to my chamber, my lady," he said in a silky voice and gestured her in.

"More like the lion's den," she muttered, brushing past him.

Liadain wondered how she could be expected to stay here. The room even smelled of his spicy scent. She would just need to keep reminding herself that he was a rogue—a very handsome one, but a rogue nonetheless.

He dropped her sack on the bed, grabbed a blanket, and spread it on the floor. Not speaking a word, he started to remove his courtly attire.

She looked away. Perhaps it was her uneasiness, but the room was getting extremely warm.

"I hope ye donna mind, but I donna wear clothes to bed." His voice was a soothing murmur that sent a tingling shimmer down her spine.

Not able to stand the awkwardness, she slapped her

hands over her face and groaned. "MacGregor! Will ye *please*?"

"Pray untwist your knotted self, healer. I don my plaid."

Hesitantly, she lowered her hands and cast him a quick look. His chest was bare and a plaid grazed his hips—very low on his hips, but he was more or less covered.

The man was massive, filled with self-confidence, and he had a ruggedness and vital power that she couldn't deny. She needed to keep telling herself that even though he was certainly fair of face, he was sinful enough to make any woman—well, every woman— fall under his spell.

He nodded to her sack. "Undress, healer. Surely ye willnae wear your gown to bed. I will turn. Let me know if ye need assistance," he spoke with an obvious hidden meaning. MacGregor lowered himself to the floor and turned his back—his very broad back.

Liadain froze, staring at the delicious sight before her. If there was ever a perfect specimen for a man, it would be MacGregor.

"I donna hear ye changing your clothes. Mayhap ye do need my help, eh?" He smirked.

He was so arrogant. Looking around for the first thing she could find, she tossed her pillow at him.

He grunted. "Why is it ye keep throwing things at me?"

"If ye would cease acting as a rogue, mayhap I wouldnae need to throw things at ye."

"I am nae acting."

She gritted her teeth. "MacGregor!"

A warm chuckle answered her. With some careful

wriggling, Liadain was able to remove her gown on her own. Hastily, she donned her nightrail and climbed into bed. Pulling the blankets up to her chin, she cleared her throat.

"Do ye want me to blow out the candle?"

"Nay. Leave it lest ye trip over me," he said, turning over and tossing her the pillow. "Do ye know why someone would do that to your chamber, lass? Mayhap they were searching for something."

She shook her head. "What could they be looking for? I donna have anything of importance—only my herbs."

"Donna fret upon it. Just sleep now, healer. Ye are safe."

Liadain smiled at his attempt to reassure her. Turning on her side, she closed her eyes and there was a heavy silence. How could she possibly sleep knowing the man was on the floor barely clothed? As she rolled onto her back, her eyes flew open and she intently studied the ceiling for some time, watching the light flicker as shadows danced against the wall.

She tried to force her emotions into order, but they were not listening at all. This was ridiculous. Hearing his gentle rhythmic breathing, she knew he slept. She swore men could sleep anywhere at any given time. Did nothing bother them? Did they never lose sleep?

Probably not.

Lifting herself up on her elbows, she stole a lingering glance at him. His arm rested atop his head, blocking her view of his face. His plaid had separated and she could see part of his bare thigh. Blood coursed through her veins like a raging river, and her heart thumped erratically. Even knowing he was a complete and utter scoundrel did not cause her impure thoughts to cease. She began to wonder just what she wanted of him. Flopping back down, she let out a loud, frustrated sigh.

"I could always join ye and it wouldnae be such torture, lass."

He was awake!

"Ye are fine right where ye are," she said, speaking the first words that came to mind.

"Aye, but are *ye*?"

Sitting up, she punched the lumps out of her pillow and sank back down on the bed, turning away from him—out of sight, out of mind. This was going to be the longest night of her life.

Seven

Declan awoke with a start. Someone called to him from the other side of the door, their impatient pounding driving him mad. It was too early for such madness. All he knew was that it had better not be that witless Percy in a drunken stupor.

"MacGregor," whispered the healer from the bed.

Slowly pulling himself to his feet, he rubbed his aching back. "I am coming. Will ye cease?" he shouted at the door.

"MacGregor!" called the healer, her voice full of alarm.

Casting a quick glance, her saw that her raven tresses were tousled, hanging over her shoulders as she clutched the blankets to her chest. For a brief moment, he could almost imagine his fingers running through the loose tendrils. He wondered if they were as soft as they looked. *Damn*. He had never seen her more beautiful.

The healer's voice broke through his musings and she eyed him with concern. "MacGregor?"

Declan's eyes roamed over her and he winked at her

boldly. "Ye worry overmuch, healer." Approaching the door, he opened it slowly, positioning his body to block the view to the bed. Cranborne's hand was midair.

Declan raised a brow. "Cranborne."

The man nodded in greeting. "MacGregor, my apologies for disturbing you, but I cannot find Lady—"

"Then why are ye here?" Declan asked impatiently. The man was clearly preoccupied with something. His clothes were in total disarray and his hair was standing on end.

As if Cranborne sensed Declan's scrutiny, he ran his hands through his hair and sighed. "I went to her chamber and no one answered. I thought you may have seen her or know where she is. My wife is unwell. Something is wrong and she has not felt the babe for some time. I *need* to find Lady Campbell."

Declan heard a loud gasp behind him as Cranborne held an unreadable expression upon his face. With lightning speed, the man swung open the door, pushing his way into the room. Declan grabbed him with a firm grip, but it was too late. The damage was already done.

"Viscount Cranborne?" The healer colored fiercely. If she tugged up the blankets any further, they would be completely over her head.

Cranborne froze and Declan released his arm. The man whipped his head around and glared at Declan, a probing question coming into his eyes.

"'Tisnae as ye think. Her chamber was—"

"I don't have time for this now." Cranborne turned back to Liadain. "Elizabeth is unwell and has not felt the babe since last eve. She is asking for you. Could you please come at once?"

"Of course. I will meet ye in her chamber. Give me but a moment."

There was a heavy silence.

Cranborne pursed his lips as though he was about to speak, but simply gave a brief nod and walked out. The door was not even closed when the healer flipped back the blankets and sprang from the bed with purpose.

"Turn around, MacGregor. I need to dress with much haste."

He turned away from her. "After ye care for his wife, I will speak with him regarding your chamber and that this," he gestured with his hand, "wasnae as he thinks." He heard rustling from behind him.

"I donna have time to worry upon your pride or mine. I must see to the babe," she said hurriedly.

"I will come for ye there. I donna want ye wandering off without an escort, especially after last eve. I will also make certain that your chamber is cleaned of the beautiful flowers that someone so kindly left for ye." A feminine laugh answered him and he turned when she brushed up against his arm. The healer graced him with an enchanting smile, and he rewarded her with a larger smile of his own.

"I truly thank ye for last eve. Ye were a gentleman." Standing on tiptoe, she brushed a soft kiss on his cheek. "I shall see ye later."

Declan felt his heart lurch. For a brief moment, he was somewhat shaken. What the hell was *that*? He nodded and mumbled the first words that came to mind. "Aye. Make her well."

She moved impatiently toward the door. "I will try my best."

❧

Liadain raced to Lady Cranborne's chamber and prayed that all would be well. Even if Liadain did not currently view Robert in a favorable light, Elizabeth was certainly not to blame. The health of Elizabeth's babe was far more important than Liadain's own feelings or lack thereof for Robert.

When she reached the hall to Elizabeth's quarters, Liadain hurriedly passed a man and smiled in greeting. Was it her imagination or had he deliberately stepped away from her? Spinning her head around, she spotted him folding his hands as if he said a prayer. What was that about? She did not think they had ever been introduced.

Shaking off the odd encounter, she was greeted at the door by Robert, who hastily ushered her in. He was clearly shaken and concerned about his wife. Lady Cranborne was abed, her color pale as the fresh morning snow. Liadain approached the bed and offered her a comforting smile while Robert stood close to Elizabeth's side.

Reaching out, Lady Cranborne clutched Liadain's hand. "Thank you for coming. I am so worried about the babe. I have not felt him since last eve."

"I donna mind that ye called for me, but why didnae ye seek the midwife, Elizabeth?"

"I have been ill for months and you are the only one who helped me. I much prefer you are here," she said with resolve.

Elizabeth's head was clammy with a cold sweat. Liadain grabbed a cloth next to the bed and dampened it in a large bowl. Gently, she wiped Elizabeth's face. "It will be all right. Are ye in pain?"

"I have a slight ache in my stomach," she said, instinctively placing her hand over her rounded belly.

Liadain nodded and cleaned her hands in a bowl of water. "What kind of ache? Is it a sharp pain or a dull pain?"

Elizabeth shrugged. "It comes and it goes, but when it comes, it is a sharp pain and then turns dull."

"I just want to take a look. Viscount Cranborne, will ye please stand back?" Liadain waved him out of the way. As she lifted the blanket, she saw that Elizabeth's nightrail was soaked and there was a trace of blood.

"Dear *God*," exclaimed Robert. Elizabeth tried to sit up to catch a glimpse of what had caused her husband's sudden frenzy.

Liadain hastily flipped back the blankets and cast Robert a look of disapproval. Turning toward Elizabeth, Liadain gently coaxed her back down upon the bed. "Ye must be still. Viscount Cranborne, I need a word with ye," she ordered as Elizabeth called out in pain.

"Elizabeth!" screamed Robert, pushing Liadain aside and grabbing his wife's hand.

Liadain slapped him in the arm. "Ye arenae helping your wife," she said through clenched teeth. "Take your leave and seek the midwife. Please do as I ask."

Reluctantly, Robert left his wife's side. When he opened the door, sounds gushed in from the hall as he dispersed the small crowd that had started to gather.

The door closed and Liadain cast a glance at Elizabeth. The poor woman's face was pale and pinched. "It will be all right."

"Please tell me what is wrong. I need the truth." Elizabeth's eyes widened with concern.

"There is some blood, but there isnae yet a need to fear. I must take a closer look at ye."

Closing her eyes, Elizabeth nodded in consent. Liadain again pulled back the blankets and lifted Elizabeth's nightrail. She examined Elizabeth and felt for the babe's head. It was not as low as a head usually was for the birth of a child. Due to the bairn's position, Liadain deduced the woman had ample time before the wee one was ready to make his grand entrance into the world.

Without warning, Elizabeth jerked and her hands flew to her stomach. "I feel the babe!"

Liadain nodded. "Aye. Sometimes when it gets close to time for the bairn to come, he tricks ye into thinking he is ready, but he isnae. Be sure to drink plenty of water. I am nae sure why it helps, but it does. We will get ye cleaned up and change your linens, but I think ye need to remain abed for a few days and rest. If ye do that, I think ye and your wee one will be fine. When was the last time ye drank?"

Elizabeth looked puzzled. "I'm really not sure. Last eve?"

Liadain approached the bowl of water and cleaned her hands. She lifted the pitcher and poured some water for Elizabeth, aiding her to drink. When Elizabeth finished, she placed her head back down on the pillow while Liadain filled the cup again. "I want ye to try to drink all of this as well."

The door swung open and the color drained from Robert's face. "The midwife was escorted to see Lady Somerset. Tell me what I can do."

"Your wife and bairn are fine. The babe isnae yet ready to come. I suggest the viscountess remain abed for a few days of rest." Liadain wiped the sweat from Elizabeth's brow.

"We will do whatever you recommend. I am so thankful you are well, dearest."

"Your child is very stubborn, Robert," said Elizabeth, dryly.

He chuckled in response.

"Please wait in the hall until we change the linens. Then ye will be able to spend some time with your wife," said Liadain, gesturing Robert out the door. When he did not respond or move, she quickly added, "Ye donna have anything to worry about. They are fine." She gave him a reassuring smile and turned around as the door closed.

Elizabeth grabbed Liadain's hands as tears streamed down her face. "Thank you. Truly. I don't know what I would do if I lost this babe. Robert would never forgive me."

Something moved out of the corner of her eye. Liadain swung her head around and saw Robert standing silently in the corner of the room, his eyes darkened with emotion. Liadain turned toward Elizabeth and smiled warmly. "Viscount Cranborne loves ye."

❧

After an unsettling morning and paying off a few maids to clean the healer's chamber, Declan eventually proceeded to see how Lady Cranborne fared. Although Cranborne was clearly an arse, Lady Cranborne should not be blamed for her husband's mistakes. Declan would not wish ill feelings upon her or the bairn she carried.

When he reached the hall, he found Cranborne pacing. "How are Lady Cranborne and the babe?" Declan asked.

An expression of relief passed over the viscount's face as he stopped in front of Declan. "Thanks to Lady Campbell, they are well but my wife will need to spend some time abed. Lady Campbell is in there with her now."

Declan nodded and there was an uncomfortable silence, neither of them wanting to converse on the inevitable. This may not have been the most appropriate time, but Declan could not have Cranborne thinking the worst. That was why he thought to be the bigger man.

Folding his arms over his chest, he stood to his full height. "I need to speak with ye about this morn."

Cranborne mirrored his stance. "I thought you might."

"Last eve, someone entered Lady Campbell's chamber and ransacked her belongings. I donna know if they found what they were looking for, but they were kind enough to leave cut-up carrion flowers all over the floor and her bed."

Cranborne's eyes widened. "What could Liadain... er, Lady Campbell possibly possess that someone would want, and who in God's name would spread carrion flowers throughout her chamber?"

"'Tisnae anything I havenae already asked myself." Declan paused and cast him a pointed look. "She couldnae stay in her chamber, and *that* was the reason she shared mine. I slept upon the floor."

"You mean to tell me there was no other female

acquaintance she could have sought out?" His expression was clearly one of disapproval.

"And who exactly was she to seek out, Cranborne? Your *wife*?" Declan raised a brow.

"It was improper and you know it."

Did everyone in his life feel compelled to lecture him? "I wasnae going to leave her unattended or with someone I donna know."

Cranborne shook his head. "I understand your reasoning, but I'm sure I was not the only one to know she shared your quarters last eve. Have you no regard for her reputation?"

Declan stiffened and his eyes narrowed. "I slept upon the floor. It wasnae as if I ruined her or the like. I believe that task already fell to ye," he spat, giving Cranborne a knowing look. At least the man had enough sense not to push the issue further.

The door swung open and both men gaped at the healer. "I thought I heard voices out here. Ye may see to your wife now, Viscount Cranborne."

"You have my thanks."

Stepping out into the hall, she shut the door behind her. "MacGregor."

"Cranborne's wife and bairn are well, thanks to ye. Ye did well, healer."

She waved him off. "It was hardly me, but they are well. I must go to my chamber and change," she said, pointing to her soiled gown.

"I will accompany ye. Ye didnae have time to break your fast. Would ye like me to get ye something to eat?" he asked as he escorted her through the halls.

She smiled her thanks. "Nay. I will eat later. Are ye

nae supposed to be shooting arrows in the tournament this day?"

A few men passed them while deep in conversation, and their eyes widened when they spotted the healer. One of the men spoke a prayer under his breath but loud enough for Declan to hear. This was the second time for such a coincidence, and Declan did not believe in chance occurrences.

Casting a quick glance at the lass, he saw she was oblivious to her surroundings and simply waited for him to respond. "Aye. After the midday meal. Would ye like to come and watch?"

She playfully elbowed him in the arm as the other men moved on. "I might even be persuaded to cheer for ye."

"Now what would I have to do to persuade ye to do that, lass?" he asked.

Color stained her cheeks. "Would ye cease speaking as if I am your latest conquest? Ye know it will ne'er happen, and frankly, it annoys me."

Declan stopped abruptly. "Donna say *ne'er*, healer," he whispered.

She tapped him playfully in the arm and rolled her eyes. When they reached her chamber, she hesitated, her mouth dipping into a frown. "Do ye think 'tis safe? I donna know if my senses could bear it."

"I saw to it. 'Tis clean now."

"Thank ye."

As the healer pushed open the door, he laughed as they both gulped for air at the same time. Everything in the room was in its rightful place. In fact, there was no evidence that anything had ever been amiss.

Releasing his breath, Declan chuckled. "'Tis safe to breathe now, lass. I cannae even smell the dreaded plants."

"Praise the saints for small favors. What did ye bribe the maids with to have it cleaned so quickly?" She shook her head. "Ne'er mind. I donna want to know. I think I am able to manage now on my own. Ye can wait outside."

Closing the distance between them, he peered down at her intently. "'Tisnae as much fun if I wait outside," he murmured with a wanton purpose. His hot gaze slid over her body.

Her breath quickened and her tongue darted out to wet her lips. "MacGregor, I donna understand ye."

"'Tis naught to understand, healer."

"Why do ye behave this way?"

He was about to answer when she held up her hand to stay him.

"'Tis as if ye are two completely different men. One man is an arrogant arse who is always chasing lasses, and the other man is kind and filled with compassion. I believe I am much fonder of the latter," she said dryly.

"Ah, lass, but I am one and the same. I will always chase the lasses with kindness and compassion." He winked at her.

"Ye insult me." She smacked him in the chest. "Ye treat me the same as the women ye bed, and unlike them, I donna welcome your advances. When will ye get it in your head that I will ne'er be one of the many women that have shared your be—"

Before he realized what he was about, his lips crashed down upon hers and Declan silenced her with a brutal, punishing kiss. How dare a Campbell invade his mind and render him witless? He would make sure she knew he was no gentleman and never would be. He knew she would be cross with him, but honestly, that would make it so much simpler to push her away. No woman ever consumed his thoughts, nor should any be allotted that privilege.

His mouth did not become softer as he kissed her and his tongue explored the recesses of her mouth. He pulled her roughly to him in a firm embrace. He wanted her to know what she did to him. No female had ever made him lose such control. Lady Liadain Campbell drove him completely mad.

At first, she tried to twist out of his hold. He held her firmly in place, waiting for her to further fight his advances. But then the very air itself changed. The healer gave in freely to the passion of his kiss.

❧

Liquid fire fueled Liadain's veins. Initially, she wriggled in MacGregor's arms, arching her body, fighting to become free. But he only gathered her closer, his firm hands locked against her spine. Instinctively, she placed her fingers against the corded muscles of his chest, and that was her undoing.

His grip tightened around her and the warmth of his arms was so male, so bracing. She buried her hands in his thick hair and returned his kiss with reckless desire. Her thoughts spun. It had been far too long. She missed the warmth and touch of a man. Blood pounded in her brain, leapt from her heart, and made her knees tremble.

She drew herself closer to him. God help her. Her desire overrode all sense of reason. She could feel the thrill of his arousal against her, and the knowledge made her feel even more wanton.

MacGregor's touch was purely divine. Her whole being flooded with pleasure.

Without warning, he pulled back. The smoldering flame she saw in his eyes startled her. "I will wait outside your door and donna say 'ne'er,' healer." He smiled provocatively and simply turned and strutted out with pure male satisfaction.

Liadain stared tongue-tied at the closed door. Her embarrassment quickly turned to raw fury. He was MacGregor…a rogue. What was she thinking? He was a master at getting whatever he wanted from women. She knew that and yet did not have enough strength within her to stop. Her emotions whirled and skidded as his words haunted her.

Donna say "ne'er."

She was an idiot.

Eight

As Declan waited with the men while the targets were prepared, the women gathered to watch the tournament. King James had already taken his seat under his brocade-adorned tent, patiently waiting for the game to begin. His brown hair was combed back and his beard was nearly as long as his chest. There was no question the man was the king, the way he portrayed such a regal air of command.

While the target was being placed in position, Percy slapped Declan on the back. "I hope your nerves don't get the best of you, MacGregor. His Majesty watches," Percy said, nodding toward the royal tent.

"I didnae think upon it, but thank ye for reminding me, Percy," Declan answered dryly.

Fawkes shook Declan's arm. "Good luck to you." He nodded to Percy. "And thank you for the entertainment."

Catesby laughed. "Percy, try not to make a fool out of yourself in front of His Majesty, my dear boy. Although, if our king requires a new court jester, you may yet be in luck."

Percy's face reddened slightly. "Very humorous."

His pride bruised, Percy lowered his head and walked off with Fawkes to lick his wounds.

Catesby nodded. "MacGregor, might I have a word?"

"Aye?"

The man looked uneasy. "There is no easy way to speak this, but I fear I must."

"What is it?" asked Declan, not sure he wanted to know the answer.

"There have been rumbles throughout court regarding Argyll's sister. Since you have an association, I thought you should know."

"And what exactly are these rumbles?"

"Some men say she is…" Pausing, Catesby looked around to make sure no one was within hearing distance. "Some men say she is a witch."

Declan smirked. "'Tis absurd. She isnae a witch." He waved Catesby off.

Reaching out, Catesby grabbed Declan's arm. "MacGregor, I speak the truth. Word spreads that she is a witch, and some are taking the matter quite seriously, I assure you."

Declan looked upon him with a critical expression. "Who speaks this? Tell me."

"I have heard it from many. They say Lady Cranborne was gravely ill and that once she drank the potion given to her from the hand of Argyll's sister, she greatly improved. Others have said Lady Cranborne lost her child, and when she was touched by Argyll's sister, her babe was brought back from the grave."

Declan folded his arms over his chest. "I told ye. She is a healer. Aye, she saw to Lady Cranborne and her health improved, but nae because she was given a potion by a witch or her bairn was brought back from the grave." He rolled his eyes and shook his head. "'Tis truly ridiculous."

"Ridiculous as it may be, you know how King James feels about such matters. If it would ever get back to him—"

"Men and women alike shouldnae speak of what they donna understand. Some plants and herbs have healing properties. Because she knows how to use them, that doesnae mean she is a witch."

"I know that and you know that, my dear boy, but others do not. They fear what they do not understand. I only tell you this so that you keep a watchful eye on her. If the king should ever catch wind of this…" Lowering his voice, Catesby added, "You know he travels to Norway and leads the witch hunts. What do you think he would do if he found one was under his own roof?"

Declan knew this unjustified labeling was truly absurd. The lass might certainly be an enchantress, but she was no witch. "Thank ye for the warning. And Catesby, I would expect ye to halt such rumblings if they are ever upon your ears. Donna encourage this madness."

Catesby looked offended and placed his hand over his heart. "Of course, my dear boy."

Deep in thought, Declan ambled back across the field. The tournament was about to begin and he wanted to make sure the healer was well. If these words were spreading through court, he knew someone would be daft enough to believe such untruths and the matter could quickly transform into a more serious issue. He wouldn't give any more fuel to the accusations, but he would make certain that the lass temporarily ceased her healing.

He searched for the healer in the crowd, finally spotting his wee bonny witch speaking with Rosalia's mother.

❧

Liadain fretted. Where was MacGregor when she needed him? She'd avoided him after their unsettling encounter outside her bedchamber, but now she desperately wanted him by her side. Lady Armstrong had spotted her and headed straight for her.

It was too late to make her escape.

She pasted on a bright smile. "Lady Armstrong. A pleasure to see ye again."

Rosalia's mother returned a smile that did not quite reach her eyes. "A pleasure to see you as well, my lady. It is a great day for a tournament. Is it not?"

Liadain nodded and looked away uncomfortably. "Aye."

"I must apologize that we did not get to speak more last eve. How much longer will you be staying at court? Will you be traveling home soon?"

As Liadain turned, Lady Armstrong's probing gaze sent a chill down her spine. "I am nae sure."

Lady Armstrong's features were deceptively composed. "Tell me. Was my daughter well when you saw her last?"

Liadain clenched her fists tight at her side. "Rosalia was well." She frantically glanced through the crowd, searching for MacGregor. Clearly Rosalia's mother was prodding for information about her daughter, and Liadain did not want to make matters worse by saying something she should not. When a familiar voice spoke from behind, she immediately stiffened.

"I see you have met the Earl of Argyll's sister, Lady Armstrong."

Liadain said a silent prayer. Could this be any worse? She needed rescuing—fast.

"Lord Dunnehl. How fortunate that we bumped into each other. Lady Campbell and I were just speaking of my daughter," said Lady Armstrong, placing her arm on Lord Dunnehl's.

Liadain did not fail to notice the silent message that passed between the two of them at the mention of Rosalia. The strong feeling in the pit of her stomach led her to believe this was not going to end well. Lady Armstrong's eyes lit up in surprise as Liadain felt a warm, strong hand at her back. She would recognize the warmth of that touch anywhere.

MacGregor.

"The tournament is about to begin. Viscount Cranborne has arrived," MacGregor said in an unreadable tone.

She glanced up at him and cast him a thankful look. Turning, she said in a soft tone to Lady Armstrong, "Pray excuse me." She had taken a step away when a hand reached out to stay her.

Rosalia's mother smiled in amusement. "But you have not yet introduced us."

MacGregor paused, glaring at Lady Armstrong's restraining grip upon Liadain. Without warning, he reached out and positioned the woman's hand back on Lord Dunnehl's arm.

"Nay, she hasnae." He placed his arm protectively around Liadain's back, urging her to step away. "Come. *Tha mi duilich.*" *I am sorry.*

Lord Dunnehl smirked. "Highland *barbarian.*"

Liadain held her breath, praying MacGregor did not hear Lord Dunnehl's words. The beastly lord was obviously trying to provoke him. All she needed was to have MacGregor raise his sword against Dunnehl and slay a peer of the realm in front of the king. She couldn't help but cringe when MacGregor stiffened and slowly turned around, his face a glowering mask of rage.

Hastily, she pulled his rock-hard arm close to her side. "Donna. Ye will only make matters worse. *Cha leig thu leas.*" *Do not bother.*

A muscle ticked angrily in his jaw. "That English arse—"

"Is clearly an English arse. There is nay changing him and ye will only make matters worse. Leave off, I beg ye." He weighed her words carefully. When he finally nodded his head in consent, Liadain breathed.

"The men line up for the tournament. Please remain where I can see ye," he ordered.

MacGregor did not need to tell her twice.

❧

Entering the royal tent, Viscount Cranborne greeted the king with a warm smile. "Majesty," he said, giving his king a low bow.

"Ah, if it isn't Viscount Cranborne. Come. Have a seat," King James said, gesturing to the chair beside him.

He nodded. "Thank you, Your Majesty. My apologies for the delay. I thought my wife was to give birth to our child, but it turned out to be false."

"No need for apologies. And your wife is well?"

"She is."

The king slapped Robert upon the shoulder. "I am glad to hear it. The games are about to begin. And you are certain you do not wish to partake in the tournament yourself, Cranborne?" he asked, leaning in closer.

"I am sure. I enjoy watching just the same. The fact that you even hold such games in my honor is reward enough."

Robert's palms were sweaty and his heart started beating rapidly. He needed to broach the topic delicately. He had proven adept at handling himself in Spain. He could do this. It was time to step up and play the game of men.

"I understand the champion will receive a sufficient amount of coin."

The king smirked. "Are you changing your mind, Viscount Cranborne?" he asked, eyeing him quizzically.

"I do not change my mind. I only suggest that perhaps if the stakes were raised, they may further advance Your Majesty's objectives as well."

Robert became increasingly uneasy under the king's scrutiny, and a warning voice whispered in his head to tread carefully. When something flickered deep in the king's eyes, Robert feigned sudden interest in the tournament.

"What did you have in mind, Cranborne?"

Highland barbarian.

Declan would show Dunnehl a Highland barbarian when he shoved his broadsword up the lord's English arse…

He watched Percy step up to shoot his first round in the archery contest and wipe the sweat from his forehead. Lifting his bow, he visibly trembled, studying the target. In fact, he examined it so long that Declan could have made another target before Percy even took the shot. Finally, the man released the arrow. With a critical eye, Declan watched it whiz through the air, missing the goal entirely by several feet.

Percy shook his head. "The competition is not too great, MacGregor. I don't think you'll have a problem."

Declan gave him a manly slap to the shoulder. "Head high, Percy." Declan moved into position and adjusted the arrow. Lifting the bow, he aimed and released his shot.

Dead center.

The crowd cheered and the king yelled, "Well done, MacGregor!"

Declan nodded his thanks and then stole a glance at the healer. When their eyes met, her expression brightened and they shared a smile. He knew that she was proud of him, and it warmed his heart that she would be.

The crowd was silent as the next man raised his bow and released his arrow, making the mark. Praise the saints for some competition. Declan was tired of shooting with Percy and Catesby. No one had challenged him for a long time, and it would be good to engage in some healthy sport—especially one he excelled at.

Three men, including Declan, had made it to the final round. They waited patiently while the targets were moved back several additional yards.

Feeling a soft tap on the shoulder, Declan turned around as the healer graced him with a smile. "I just want to wish ye luck. Although I donna think ye need it. Ye are doing verra well, MacGregor. I am truly impressed."

He peered down at her intently. "'Tisnae the only thing I do verra well, healer."

Folding her arms over her chest, she twisted her head and pursed her lips. "Ye know, I find when most men flaunt their abilities 'tis only because they are sorely lacking…" She nodded to his manhood and then looked up at him with a raised brow.

He stilled his expression. Leaning in a hairbreadth away from her ear, he spoke in a low, silky voice. "When ye kissed me, ye didnae think I was sorely lacking." His tone made her flush, as he knew it would.

"When I kissed ye? Ye kissed *me*," she murmured haughtily before she turned and bolted away like a scared rabbit. With a springy bounce, she disappeared into the crowd. Just as well. He needed to return his attention to the tournament.

The first man was ready to shoot for the second round. The crowd gasped in excitement as the arrow landed several inches above the mark. Now this was definitely turning into a competition, and Declan could not stay the smile that played his lips.

The next contender stepped forward and raised the

bow, then studied the target and released the arrow. Again, admirable aim, hitting the center mark with astounding accuracy.

The man turned toward Declan and gave a brief nod. "Good luck to you."

"Thank ye. Great shot." Stepping forward, Declan adjusted his stance and raised his bow. Calculating the target, he released the arrow, watching it sail through the air and hit the mark.

Dead center.

The king clapped in excitement and approached the men with Cranborne in tow. "Very well done. It has come down to the two of you—MacGregor and Graham. You both have very fine skill. I would wish to reward you both, but only one can be the victor. Let's put your skill to the test, shall we? Move the targets back an additional twenty yards," he ordered.

Everything fell silent.

The king's voice carried a unique force. "I am a man of my word. The victor will be rewarded, and I assure you the prize makes for a more enticing competition. You will both shoot only once. The closest to the center mark will be deemed the winner. I will bequeath the champion…Castle Campbell and the lands to the east."

The crowd roared with delight and Declan could barely think above the noise.

The king held up his hands for silence and a hushed stillness enveloped the crowd. "What say you?"

Declan froze into blankness. Castle Campbell? He did not believe in coincidences. Why would King James offer the neighboring Campbell lands as a prize?

Ciaran would be most pleased and the MacGregors would gain a piece of their enemy's lands. The bloody Campbell was probably rolling over in his grave right now. A thought suddenly popped into Declan's mind.

What if he won?

His mind raced. Ciaran had no interest in Castle Campbell and would be concerned with only the surrounding lands. Declan would have a home of his own and could finally be rid of his annoying brothers. This was indeed the opportunity he had been waiting for—a chance of a lifetime. The king waited for the men to answer.

Graham quickly accepted and the king shook his head in approval.

"Very good," the king said, slapping Graham heartily on the back. Turning, he nodded to Declan. "And what of you, MacGregor? What say you? Do you accept the wager?"

Declan could feel all eyes upon him, and he swallowed hard, trying to manage a feeble answer. He knew he had a God-given gift, but he had never tried to shoot at that distance. What if he failed? Better yet, what if he won?

The king cleared his throat. "MacGregor, I will have your answer."

"Aye, Your Majesty. I accept the challenge."

Nine

DECLAN HAD TO BE DREAMING. CASTLE CAMPBELL WAS a rather steep reward for a mere archery contest. If he won, would the king expect something in return?

Turning, he searched for the healer in the crowd, but he could not see her through the masses. He wondered if she had heard the prize for winning the competition. The boards were now in position, and it was decided that Graham, the other contender, would shoot first. Declan was anxious to see how the man held up under the pressure.

As Graham released his shot, Declan held his breath. The arrow landed only a few inches to the right of the mark. The man closed his eyes and tilted his head back, no doubt saying a silent prayer of thanks.

The crowd roared with excitement.

Graham inclined his blond head in acknowledgment and watched as Declan analyzed the mark of his feathers on the target. He stepped forward and raised his bow with quiet assurance, assessing the target. Before he could draw a breath, he released the arrow. Then with deliberate casualness, he turned away and simply lifted his brow.

Graham paled.

"Graham shot to the right and MacGregor shot to the left. Both arrows are exactly the same distance from the mark," shouted a man, examining the board.

King James smiled. "You both realize the winner is the one who hits the closest to the center mark. There are no ties. It appears we have a competition! Move the boards back twenty yards!"

The crowd applauded.

Declan briefly closed his eyes and calmed his racing thoughts. Castle Campbell was within his grasp and he could not, would not, falter. Once the healer was no longer a ward of the court, he would depart and not look back. Declan could not wait to observe his brother's expression when he returned to Glenorchy with such a treasure.

The men called out when the targets were in position. After another prayer, Graham stepped into place and took aim. His arrow whizzed through the air and hit the board with a thump, only an inch above the goal. Elevating his bow triumphantly in the air, he cast Declan a smug look.

Declan stepped forward without hesitation. While the crowd still rallied for Graham, Declan lifted his bow and hastened his shot, releasing it within seconds.

The crowd fell silent as they waited to hear the winner declared. .

"Graham shot slightly above the mark and MacGregor's arrow is below...*exactly* the same distance to the mark," shouted the man, again examining the board.

The king threw back his head, his laugh rippling

through the air. Graham did not find the situation as humorous, and with widened eyes, stared at Declan wordlessly.

"You both know that we are only able to crown one winner. If you two keep this up, we will be here all eve," King James jested.

"If Graham is willing to yield and admit I am the better shot, we will nae need to be here all eve," said Declan in a confident tone.

As the targets were once again moved back, Declan noticed the tense furrows on Graham's brow and the sweat pouring down his face.

Graham grabbed his arrow and moved into position. Briefly closing his eyes, he murmured something under his breath. His eyes flew open and he shot—closer than all of his prior attempts, nearly hitting the mark.

Shouts of congratulation rang out among the crowd.

He approached Declan with an arrogant swagger and gave him a knowing grin. "Do ye wish to yield now, MacGregor, and admit I am the better shot?"

Declan chuckled, slapping him upon the shoulder. "I ne'er yield," he said, ambling around him with confident strides.

Raising his bow, Declan briefly studied the location of Graham's arrow on the board and then quickly released his own arrow, aiming higher than his previous attempts. The arrow soared through the air and then plummeted with lightning speed. The tip of Declan's arrow struck Graham's on the board, cutting off Graham's arrow's feathers and hitting the center mark with outstanding accuracy.

Standing in awe, Graham watched pieces of his arrow's feathers drift slowly to the ground.

"MacGregor hit the mark!" shouted the man inspecting the board.

"Very well done!" the king bellowed as he approached. Pulling out a purse, he tossed the pouch to Graham. "You did well."

"Thank ye, Your Majesty," Graham said with a slight bow. Standing to his full height, he held out his arm to Declan. "It was a fair game, MacGregor. Please accept my congratulations."

Declan clasped his arm. "Ye are one hell of a shot, Graham."

"As are ye."

"Congratulations, MacGregor," said Cranborne, giving him a nod.

"Thank ye."

"MacGregor, I'll speak with you on the morrow," murmured King James before he turned on his heel.

Castle Campbell was his!

Never did Declan think he would ever be able to achieve such stature. He'd be the master of his own home. No longer would he be scolded and reprimanded for living his life the way he saw fit. He would answer to no one but himself. Luck was most definitely on his side—or the gods—but either way, he would take it. The healer's voice pulled him from his thoughts.

"I saw your last shot. Ye are quite skilled with a bow. I assume your reward was well worth your efforts," said the healer.

Declan laughed richly. "Ye could say that. Ye didnae hear the prize, then?"

"Nay, I was too busy cowering from Lady Armstrong and Lord Dunnehl."

He clutched her hand in his, not exactly sure how to broach the subject of his winnings. "Walk with me." Inclining her head, she walked leisurely beside him as they headed toward the gardens. "I need to speak with ye about a few things. And I need ye to listen. There are tales spreading throughout court. Tales…that ye are a witch."

Stopping dead in her tracks, she glanced up at him. "A *witch*? *Chan eil mi a' tuigsinn*," she said. *I do not understand*. "'Tis truly ridiculous."

He glanced around cautiously. "Lower your voice." When they made it to the hidden bench in the garden, Declan gestured for her to sit. "I said the same, but it still doesnae change what is being spoken."

"Who speaks such untruths? Tell me." She eyed him with concern.

"I donna know. Catesby said as much before the tournament, and I would ne'er have believed him, had I nae seen it for myself."

The healer gave him a puzzled look. "What do ye mean?"

"A few times I have seen men and women looking upon ye with uncertainty and clearly making every effort to step out of your path…while warding off your evil intent," Declan explained.

The healer shook her head. "Why would they think I was a witch? They donna even know me. Do ye think that was why the carrion flowers were spread in my chamber?"

"Catesby said there are rumors that ye healed Lady

Cranborne with a potion and then ye brought her babe back from the grave."

She gave a false laugh. "The *potion* was only some healing herbs that anyone could gather in the forest and Lady Cranborne's babe wasnae dead. I cannae wait to be rid of court." She threw up her hands, exasperated.

Declan placed his hand on her shoulder and they shared a smile. "I know it, but until then, I ask that ye are careful. Donna openly speak of your healing and be aware of your surroundings and who is listening." When she rolled her eyes, he quickly added, "Lass, I donna think ye are treating this subject with the importance ye should."

"MacGregor, I will be watchful of what I say, but honestly, who would believe such a tale? I am the Earl of Argyll's sister. Ye know me and so do Viscount and Viscountess Cranborne."

"And King James leads the witch hunts in Norway. Ye are only familiar with what the bloody Campb... er, Argyll wanted ye to know. Ye need to grasp what I speak, healer. Those accused of witchcraft are burned, drowned, stoned, or hung only because a man says 'tis so."

"I donna understand how men and women can be so completely daft."

"I donna think that will ever change, lass. I often wonder that myself. But until then..."

She held up her hands in mock surrender. "I give ye my word. I will be vigilant." She rose from the bench and smiled. "If ye will excuse me, I escape to my chamber."

"I will escort ye."

How the hell was he going to tell her about the prize? He needed to think.

Just as they rounded the tree, Cranborne spotted them. The healer swore under her breath and then widened her smile.

Declan tried to mask a guilty look. What possible excuse could he offer for taking the healer behind the bushes alone? Damn. For the second time, he found himself in this predicament.

"Lady Campbell…" Cranborne's coolly impersonal tone broke the stillness.

The healer stiffened at his side and Declan stepped between them. "Listen, Cranborne." There was a cold edge of irony in his voice. If the man accused him of another improper dealing with the lass, he might see Declan's fist.

"The babe comes and Elizabeth is calling for you. Could you please come with me at once?"

"Of course."

❧

"Push, Elizabeth."

Elizabeth screamed out in pain. "I can no longer push. I simply cannot," she cried. Her face was pale and pinched as her maid wet a cloth and gently wiped her brow. "I think I'm dying."

"Ye arenae dying. Ye can do this. Now I want ye to take a deep breath and then give me one more strong push," Liadain ordered as the bairn's head was crowning.

"I can't. Why would Robert do this to me? Why? If he *ever* touches me again, I swear…" Elizabeth cried.

"Elizabeth," she spoke calmly. "Ye are in child-birth. 'Tis normal to have such feelings and ye can kill the viscount later, but right now, I need ye to push."

"I can't," she moaned, turning her head from side to side.

"The only way to cease the pain is to bring the babe into the world. Now push, Elizabeth, push!" When she had made one more straining attempt, the bairn's head was through. Liadain gently pulled him out. She barely had to lift him before the babe gasped for air on his own and began to wail. "Ye did it. Ye have a bonny son."

Elizabeth cried out joyfully.

Liadain reached for the knife and cut the cord. Grabbing a towel, she wiped off the bairn and then swaddled him in a blanket. He had a full head of honey-colored curls, and his eyes were the color of the bluest sky. He was a delightful little treasure. She carefully placed the bundle in the arms of his mother. She never ceased to be amazed at the look of pure wonder upon the faces of new mothers. Every child was simply a miracle. All her pain forgotten, Elizabeth smiled in delight at her new son.

"Would ye like me to seek your husband now? If ye arenae still planning on sending him to his maker," Liadain said, raising a brow.

Elizabeth nodded, her gaze never parting from her son.

Liadain swung open the door to find Robert clearly distraught. "Elizabeth?"

"Is well and so is your bairn." She gestured him into the chamber and Robert immediately looked relieved. With brisk steps, he moved to Elizabeth's side and smiled at her tenderly.

"We have a son, Robert."

He closed his eyes, but not before a lone tear escaped down his cheek. He pecked a kiss on the top of his child's head and then kissed Elizabeth tenderly.

Not wanting to impose on their private time together, Liadain cleared her throat. "I will be taking my leave."

"Wait, Liadain!" Elizabeth called out. "Robert, could you please hold your son?"

He chuckled at her question. "Dearest, you do not need to ask me that twice." Robert picked up his bairn and gently rocked him in his arms, walking toward the window and making cooing noises under his breath.

"Liadain, please come here," said Elizabeth, extending her hand.

Liadain grabbed her hand and smiled.

"I cannot thank you enough for all you have done for me…for us. I don't know what I would have done without you. You were truly sent from the gods and for that I am grateful. If there is anything that you ever require, please don't ever hesitate to ask. I owe you much."

"Ye owe me naught. The health of ye and your bairn are reward enough."

She cast a glance at Robert holding his child tenderly. The sun bathed their features in a shimmering light. Perhaps if events had played out differently, that could have been their son, their moment. With a subtle ache in her heart, Liadain knew the past was best left that way.

Suddenly she felt so utterly exhausted that even her nerves throbbed. Murmuring her good-byes to the new family, she retreated to her room to get a few hours' rest. After pulling off her dress and sliding under the covers, she was sound asleep in a matter of seconds.

What was that tapping noise? She stirred. Perhaps the unwelcome disturbance would cease and she could resume her blissful unawareness—well, she could if that incessant banging upon her door would stop. *Now.* She rolled over and grabbed her pillow, attempting to block the maddening pounding.

"M'lady?" called someone from outside her door.

Removing the pillow, Liadain raised her head. Perhaps he would take his leave if she remained perfectly still.

"M'lady?" the voice called again, more impatiently.

Liadain silently cursed. "Aye?" she answered reluctantly.

"His Majesty requests your presence and I am to escort you."

Ten

DECLAN BROKE HIS FAST AND REVELED IN THE KNOWLEDGE that he would shortly be granted an audience with His Majesty. Castle Campbell. *His*. It was only a matter of time. And unlike the bloody Campbell, he had not needed any manipulation or political aspirations on his part to gain such a worthy prize. He had won the tournament simply on skill and he was rather proud of himself.

Finishing what was left of his biscuit, he was reminded of Ealasaid's cooking. He had to admit, a part of him—a small part—sorely missed home. He wondered if his clan would have new respect for him now that he would be master of Castle Campbell. He had just risen from the bench when a young page approached him.

"His Majesty summons you."

As Declan walked through the halls of court, he could not ease his pounding heart. He was elated; his life held new meaning. He only wished his father and mother had lived to see his success. Holding his head high, he entered the king's solar.

"Your Majesty," said Declan cheerily, giving his liege a low bow.

King James sat behind his massive desk and chuckled at Declan's lightheartedness. "Please sit, MacGregor. Your skill with a bow is truly to be admired. That was an excellent shot."

Declan sat down in the chair and leaned back, relaxing in the gentle companionship. "Thank ye, Your Majesty."

King James shuffled through a pile of papers and pulled one out of the stack. For a brief moment, he studied the document. "I have summoned you to discuss the particulars of your recompense."

Sitting forward on the edge of his chair, Declan was barely able to contain his anticipation. This was the moment he had been waiting for.

"Ciaran MacGregor shall hold a portion of the Campbell lands. Declan MacGregor, Castle Campbell is yours…with Argyll's sister as your wife."

Declan was too stunned to offer any immediate objection. What the hell just happened? Had he been commanded to wed…*the healer*? Was his liege mad?

When the king cast him a puzzled look, Declan realized his mouth had fallen open. Trying quickly to recover his wits, he hunched over and rested his arms on his thighs. He needed a moment—or several days—to comprehend his liege's words.

"MacGregor?"

"My apologies, Your Majesty. I am trying to understand," said Declan, lifting his head and running a hand through his hair.

King James's eyes flashed a gentle but firm warning.

"What is there to understand? You thought that I would just hand over Castle Campbell and expect nothing in return?"

"The reward for the tournament was Castle Campbell—naught more," Declan blurted out, a little harsher than he intended.

"And you are being justly rewarded. You seem to have taken an interest in Argyll's sister and—"

Declan could barely rein in the frustration that coiled within his body. "Your Majesty, I can assure ye I have nay interest in Argyll's sister. I cannae wed a Campbell."

"Pardon the intrusion, Your Majesty. Viscount Cranborne has arrived," said the king's page.

Cranborne?

"Your Majesty," said Cranborne as he entered the room and gave a low bow.

King James gestured for Cranborne to rise. "Sit and join us." Cranborne tugged at his doublet and took his seat, uneasy under Declan's scrutiny.

If Cranborne had a hand in this, there was no doubt in Declan's mind that he would be hanged for killing a peer of the realm. The man's guilt was further confirmed when he hastily looked away under Declan's gaze.

Declan seethed with mounting rage.

"I was explaining to MacGregor the conditions of our agreement," the king explained to Cranborne.

"Of *your* agreement?" Declan asked Cranborne, his voice cold.

His Majesty smirked and shook his head in disgust. "All that reaches my ears is discord between the

Campbells and MacGregors, and the Highland squabbles that grow ever so tiresome. The lairds continue to fight among themselves with no regard for my command. I have decided to heed Cranborne's recommendation."

King James leaned forward in his chair and spoke in a grave voice. "Your clans have been warring for years. I cannot think of a better example to be set than by the two of you. You gain a portion of your enemy's land but, in doing so, must wed Campbell blood. The Highland lairds may think twice before they act and cease with these trifling quarrels. Make no mistake, I *will* be obeyed."

～

Liadain sat up abruptly, instantly wide awake. "Give me but a moment." She sprang out of bed and hastily donned a clean gown. She was shaking, aware her day of reckoning could not be postponed forever. She had to fight a battle of personal restraint not to flee. King James had made up his mind. Why else would he summon her?

Attempting to tame her unruly locks, she fumbled to secure the loose tendrils with a couple of pins. That would have to do. With a deep, penetrating breath and a not-so-steady hand, she opened the door.

His Majesty's young page stood before her. "M'lady."

As she was escorted through the halls, she could not stop herself from feeling a shiver of apprehension. She wiped her palms on her dress. Being a ward of the court, she would inevitably be forced to wed. But what if the king arranged for her to wed someone as unsavory as Lord Dunnehl? Liadain tried to swallow the lump in her throat. No matter King James's feelings toward her deceitful brother, she was still the sister of an earl. Surely that should count for something.

The young page approached the massive wooden doors, and as soon as she passed the guards, her nervousness was back to grip her. Stiffening her spine, she held her head high as she entered King James's study. She would accept her fate with grace and dignity.

Rows of books graced several shelves, and a huge wooden desk took up the entire end of the room. A long table with at least ten chairs stood in the center of the study and there was still ample room to move around it. Heavy drapes hung over the windows and there was an open view to the fountains. The study was truly one of the many magnificent rooms at court.

"My lady," King James said.

Whipping her head around, she realized she was rudely gaping. She lifted her skirts gingerly to the sides and bowed her head, bending in a deep curtsy. "Your Majesty."

"Please rise."

"Thank ye, Your Majesty." As she rose, she caught something out of the corner of her eye.

What were *they* doing here? Her nerves had been too on edge to notice them before. Why would King James have MacGregor and Robert present to hear her fate? Robert's gaze came to rest on her questioning eyes while MacGregor kept his eyes forward.

"Please sit," said His Majesty, gesturing to a chair in front of his enormous desk.

Everyone sat silently for a moment and Liadain tilted her head to one side, stealing a slanted look at

MacGregor. He sat very still, his eyes straight ahead. In fact, he did not move at all. The man was always composed, but she sensed something was amiss. Perhaps King James had rescinded his reward for the tournament. She hoped that was not the case. MacGregor had won the contest fairly and she would be the first to say as much.

The king sat forward and studied her intently. "I want you both to wed."

Liadain gasped as she tried to fight for collectedness. Was he mad? Why would King James pair her with MacGregor? In fact, where would he get such an idea? Only one thought came to mind.

Cranborne.

She was so disgusted that she could not even look at Robert. No wonder MacGregor appeared distraught—he must be furious. She had to convince the king to change his decision by any means necessary.

"Your Majesty," Liadain's voice trembled with uncertainty. "I beg ye to see reason. There is nay advantage to this union. MacGregor is but a third son and I am still the sister of an earl."

King James pursed his lips. "Ah, the sister of Archibald Campbell, seventh Earl of Argyll." His eyes narrowed and he spoke in clipped tones. "Your brother disobeyed my orders. Your brother sought for himself and his own personal gain. Your brother was full of greed and deceit. So yes, let us speak of how you are the sister of an earl."

She paled and shuddered.

The king studied her. "Since you have no other relation, and Cranborne and Argyll were of acquaintance,

I had asked him to see to your welfare. I have also decided to heed his recommendation."

Liadain cast Robert a disgusted look. At least the man was wise enough to cower under her wide-eyed stare.

King James leaned back in his chair and spoke in a tone that forbade any further question. "Since Ciaran MacGregor now holds a portion of Argyll's lands and Declan MacGregor won Castle Campbell, the Campbells and MacGregors will be joined—by marriage. You should be in high spirits, Lady Campbell. You are going home."

Silence enveloped them.

"Cranborne, see it done this day. MacGregor, you are free to take your wife and your leave after the exchange of vows." The king rose, as they were clearly dismissed. "Now if you will excuse me, I have other pressing matters to which I must attend."

Liadain sprang to her feet. She lifted her chin and boldly met the king's gaze. "Your Majesty, I cannae wed this man," she said sharply, abandoning all pretense.

MacGregor reached out to touch her arm in warning, and she pretended not to understand his look.

King James laughed as if sincerely amused, his expression one of complete unconcern. "I have given you a command." He waved his hand in a gesture of dismissal, firing her ire even more.

Tears of frustration welled in her eyes. Robert placed his hand upon her shoulder, but she quickly shook it off and spun on her heel. She walked out of the study silently, stepping firmly with each step sounding, until she was abruptly caught by the elbow and firmly held back to slow her pace.

"Unhand me," Liadain said through gritted teeth.

"Let me explain," said Robert hastily.

"What is there to explain? Your *recommendation* sealed my fate. Ye had nay right to intervene."

"Aye, healer. Let him explain before I remove his head from his shoulders," bit out MacGregor.

Glancing around the hall, Robert spoke in hushed tones. "This is not the place to have such a conversation."

"Fine. We can speak in my chamber," Liadain said haughtily. Not waiting for either man to catch up, she stormed off to her room. She threw open the door and entered like a whirlwind, not even waiting for the door to close. "What the hell, Robert?"

"Liadain, watch your tongue," he reprimanded.

Without warning, MacGregor pummeled Robert against the stone wall with a heavy thump. "Aye. What the hell, Cranborne?"

Robert tugged at MacGregor's arms to release himself, but the massive man simply did not budge. "Word spreads throughout court that Liadain is a witch. If these untruths fall upon His Majesty's ears, she will face judgment, and you know what happens to those accused of witchcraft. There is no fair trial. Since Archie and I were of acquaintance, the king placed me in charge of her welfare and I saw it fit to remove her from court—immediately…for her own safety."

"By marrying her off to me?" MacGregor bellowed. He shook his head in disgust and gave Robert another shove before he let him go.

Robert adjusted his clothing, keeping a watchful

eye on MacGregor. "I see the way you look at her and thought—"

"Ye see the way I look at her for being a pain in my Highland arse?" MacGregor shouted.

Liadain was not overjoyed either, but the man did not have to put it that way. As if she wanted some arrogant, self-centered, could-not-keep-his-cock-under-his-kilt rogue for a husband.

How dare he!

Rancor sharpened her voice. "Bastard."

MacGregor walked forward, stopping in front of her. He leaned in so close that she could feel his breath upon her lips. "I am nae a bastard, healer. Lest ye forget, I am only a third son."

The true meaning of his words stabbed at her heart. She had unintentionally hurt him. This was a huge mess. She did not intend to denigrate him and she would have said anything to have him released from this union.

She had watched Archie for so many years, realizing everything her brother did was always with motive and reason—advancing his own gain. Liadain had thought by merely pointing out there was no advantage to this marriage…It was pointless to explain. MacGregor had already begun to pace.

She rubbed her temples, trying to alleviate the pain in her aching head. "Robert, ye did this. I am asking ye to undo it."

His mouth dipped into a frown. "I cannot. His Majesty has spoken. You will have to wed. It cannot be undone."

"Cranborne, I should run ye through where ye

stand," MacGregor snarled. "After all ye have done. *Ye* took her innocence. It should be *ye* before the altar."

Robert held up his hands. "I understand your anger, but the fact remains, you must wed. I will meet you in an hour in the cathedral," he said solemnly, walking out and closing the door behind him.

The shock of defeat held Liadain immobile. She closed her eyes, feeling utterly miserable. "My apologies, MacGregor." Her eyes flew open when she heard the door close. She was left alone with nothing more than her misery to accompany her.

Having less than an hour of freedom remaining, she sat down on the bed. On one hand, there was no more uncertainty about her future. She supposed it could have been much worse—Dunnehl perhaps. All that time she had spent worrying on the unknown. Who would have thought she would be returning to her own home?

Forcing herself to settle down, she began to think this might not be as awful as she had initially believed. And she was going home.

Imposing an iron control, she rose to dress more appropriately. She donned a moss-colored gown with gold trim. When she took down her hair, waves of raven tresses fell down her back. She glanced into the looking glass and pinched her cheeks for color. That would have to do. Taking a deep breath, she opened the door and walked out on her own accord. That was a start.

She wandered the halls and ended up in front of MacGregor's chamber. Perhaps if they could have a few words before the ceremony, she could alleviate some of the tension between them. She knocked on his door and waited. When no one answered, she pushed open the door.

A single candle lit the room. MacGregor's tartan of red and green was thrown carelessly upon the bed, and his bow leaned in the corner. She had started to back out of the room when a thought struck her. She grabbed the tartan from the bed and closed the door.

Robert greeted her on the steps of the cathedral. "MacGregor is already within," he said, escorting her in by the elbow. "You look lovely."

Her only response was a wicked glare.

Rows of pews lined the floor. The cathedral ceilings depicted Christ held by archangels. Several statues of the Holy Mother were displayed alongside the pilasters. It was all rather beautiful and grand. A lone figure stood at the altar—MacGregor. He did not bother to turn around upon her approach.

Liadain stepped up beside him. There were no flowers, no rings, no songs of praise and glory, and besides the priest before them, only Robert was in attendance. This was not how she had imagined her wedding day. Although she did not have a clan pin to attach to MacGregor's tartan, she had hoped that wrapping it around her shoulders would show a strong gesture of peace for the beginning of their marriage.

But MacGregor had yet to even turn her way. He remained as still as a statue. He did not bother to cast a single glance at her—even when he spoke his vows. She had to make a truce. She gently touched his arm. Nervously, she moistened her dry lips. He raised his eyebrow questioningly, looked down, and then his expression darkened.

~∞~

The healer gazed upon him with her head held high, proudly displaying *his* plaid—the MacGregor tartan. Declan was breathless with rage. A damn Campbell wore his clan colors. This woman asked too much of him and was clearly daft. Well, she was a bloody Campbell. What else did he expect? Not only was he forced to take the chit to wife, but now she expected him to accept her willingly in the clan. She was clearly mistaken.

Her speech to King James continued to hound him. Declan was not thrilled at the prospect of marriage either, but the healer's words stung. How kind of her to remind him that he was insignificant and would never amount to anything. In truth, he did not want to wed at all. Women already flocked to him in droves. Besides, having Ciaran and Aiden constantly reprimand him was bad enough. The last thing he needed was a nagging female added to the mix.

He assumed the healer spoke her vows because all he heard was the priest announcing they were man and wife. His eyes came up and he studied her face. Tears swam in her eyes. He was glad to see she was just as tortured as he was. He must be such a disappointment to Lady Liadain Campbell, being only a third son and all.

"Pack your bags. We leave on the morrow," Declan said, his voice emotionless.

He kissed the lass quickly on the cheek and left

her standing alone at the altar. He stormed down the aisle, his fate sealed. Cranborne called his name, but he didn't acknowledge the arse. Viscount or not, the man could go straight to hell for all he was concerned.

As he thundered through the halls of court, Declan realized he would not miss a damn thing about this cursed place. Everyone could take their pretenses and their politics and shove them up their bloody arses.

Finally reaching his chamber, he whipped open the door and banged it shut. Approaching his sack, he grabbed his brother's ale and pulled it out. Enough of this watery piss these English let pass for ale. He required a man's drink, now more than ever. He took a long, hard drink, the fiery liquid burning his throat. He reveled in the numbness it brought. He would stay this way until it was time to take his leave on the morrow or he would simply pass out—either way, he cared not.

❧

Liadain tossed and turned well into the night. MacGregor had avoided her for the remainder of the day, and he'd practically spit in her face for attempting to make peace between them.

She understood his hostility, but on the other hand, the man had to discern that she had no choice or voice in the matter. The fact that he would blame her for this marriage was ridiculous. Surely, he could see that—well, eventually she hoped that he would.

As she lay abed watching the shadows of her candle dance on the ceiling, she resigned herself to the fact that her new husband would not be coming to her bed. So why was she even agonizing over it? She threw off the blankets and wandered around the room aimlessly.

Living most of her existence with Archie, unnoticed and alone, had been difficult, but how cruel it was to have the second part of her life beginning very much the same. She and MacGregor had to find a way to reach a compromise. She refused to have it any other way.

She threw on her cloak over her nightrail and walked quietly into the hall, gently closing the door behind her. The rogue had had all day to come to his senses, and enough was enough.

Her knock on MacGregor's door seemed much louder this late in the eve. When no one answered, an unpleasant thought came to mind. What if her new husband had taken his leave without her? She had almost given up when the latch lifted from the inside. She pushed open the door and walked in.

Liadain jumped as the door made a banging sound behind her and she was embraced by darkness. Turning around blindly, she fumbled for the latch on the door. Something cold and sharp poked her throat.

"Donna move lest I spill your blood," slurred MacGregor, his breath reeking of ale.

"'Tis me." She froze in place and the blade remained at her throat for a moment too long. When MacGregor moved, she felt a sharp pain and gasped.

He lit a candle as she raised her hand to her throat. A small stain of blood brushed her fingers. When she cast him a quick glance and he did not notice, she thought it was in her best interest not to mention that he had cut her.

He stumbled into a chair and grabbed what she presumed to be ale. He gulped a healthy amount, then wiped his mouth with the back of his hand, his expression one of disgust.

"Is this what I can expect of ye? Roaming the halls late in the eve and sneaking into a man's chamber?" he asked with heavy sarcasm.

She straightened her spine. "I wasnae sneaking into any man's chamber. I came to speak with my husband."

His eyes blazed with sudden anger, and a cold, congested expression settled upon his face. "What the hell do ye want?"

"Please donna speak to me that way." She approached the bed and sat down hesitantly on the edge.

He smirked and took another drink of ale. "What do ye want, *healer*?"

"My apologies that—"

"Ye shackled me?" he slurred.

Her fingers tensed in her lap and she fought to maintain from throttling him. "MacGregor, I cannae change King James's command."

"King James's command? Donna ye mean to say your past lover's *recommendation?*"

She was glad the semi-darkness hid the flush on her cheeks. "'Tis done. I cannae change the past. I thought mayhap we could start anew."

"I donna want to start anything."

"MacGregor, please see reason."

"See reason?" he bellowed, throwing his hand up in the air.

She began to think this was not one of her best ideas. He was clearly in his cups, so there was no discussing this intelligently with him. She jumped to her feet. "My apologies. I thought we could speak. I was wrong. I will be retiring to my chamber."

"Why did ye even come here?" he snarled.

She paused. "In truth? When ye did not come this eve, I thought to make amend—"

He threw back his head and laughed, hoarsely and bitterly. "Ye actually think that I would come to your bed, healer?"

A war of emotions raged within her. "'Tisnae what I meant."

"I donna need to take ye on your wedding night…" Pausing, MacGregor took another drink of ale and then his mouth twisted into a cynical smile. "Ye have already been taken."

Eleven

THERE. THAT OUGHT TO DO IT. ANOTHER NAGGING female removed from his presence. *Women*. They were good for one thing at best, and as long as they kept their mouths shut, he cared not.

Declan took another gulp of ale and stared blankly at the closed door. Knowing the lass was not to blame for her brother's treachery did not lighten his mood. Nor did it change the fact that she was the woman who had forced him to the altar—a Campbell by blood—well, a half-Campbell. Frankly, it did not matter. A Campbell was a Campbell.

The ale had begun to make his senses spin. He knew he had better seek his bed and gain a few hours' sleep before he traveled to Glenorchy—*home*. He pulled himself to his feet and swayed. Pausing to steady his body before he keeled over, he staggered over to the bed and collapsed. He swore he had just fallen into blissful splendor when he dreamed that a pesky voice was calling to him.

"MacGregor!"

Declan felt a firm push on his shoulder, the

realization washing over him that he was no longer slumbering. He moaned into the pillow. "What the hell? Cannae ye see I sleep?"

"MacGregor, I need a word," the irksome voice reiterated.

"God's teeth, Cranborne, ye cannae leave a man in peace. I married the wench. What else do ye want from me?" When Declan made no attempt to move, Cranborne gave him another hard shove. "All right! Cease your prodding!"

Declan rolled over reluctantly and then sat up, running his hand through his hair. "Ye have my attention. What the hell do ye want now?"

Cranborne stood over him with his hands on his hips, a probing look coming into his eyes. "Liadain's care of Elizabeth has fallen back upon my ears and more question me of witchcraft. Are you still planning on taking your leave this morn?"

Concern for the healer's safety was like a splash of cold water in Declan's face. "Aye." He rubbed his hands over his eyes.

Cranborne walked across the room and sat down in the chair. "I know this was not what you wanted."

"Ye think?"

"Liadain was not at fault. She should not be held responsible for Archie's actions, nor should she be blamed for your union. Archie and I were acquainted for years. I knew he was determined to make a position for himself within the realm. What I did not know about were the unconscionable attempts he would make to achieve such status.

A certain amount of tension remained in

Cranborne's voice. "After Liadain's mother died, she lived with her father and Archie, neither one of them caring for her welfare. She resided there unseen and overlooked. I didn't even know Archie had a sister. When I met her, she was so young and beautiful. It was hard for me to believe something so angelic could be a part of Archie's blood."

Declan shook his head. "Aye, so angelic that she would be forgotten. Ye deflowered her and promised her marriage, only ne'er to return."

"I have no excuse for my behavior. I speak the truth when I say that traveling to Spain changed me. It forced me to mature—quickly. I truly had every intent to come back to Liadain…and then I met Elizabeth. What can I tell you? The clouds parted, the sun came out, and I just knew we were destined for each another. I loved her from the moment our eyes met."

"Ye pledged your troth to Liadain."

"And for that, I am regretful. I should have written and explained myself. If I could change the past, I would, but I would never change the time spent with my wife. I love her and our son," Cranborne said solemnly.

"All this love for one woman?"

A soft rumble escaped Cranborne. "MacGregor, you surely have much to learn and obviously have never found love for yourself." A glazed expression came over his face. "When Elizabeth is near, the very air itself is calm and serene. The woman simply makes me joyful to be alive, and I'd do anything to protect her…Hell, I'd give my life for her." He looked back at Declan. "I cannot change your path and I merely look after Liadain's welfare. I need to make certain she is safe."

Declan raised his brow. "*Safe?* Shouldnae ye have thought of that before ye wed her off to me?"

"Whether you choose to deny it or not, I see the way you gaze upon her."

"I gaze at all women that way," Declan said dryly.

"I've watched you. I've seen you with Liadain—you care for her. You even remained at court to protect her. Once you resign yourself to the fact that she is indeed your wife, perhaps you will be able to see things differently. I understand that you were distraught after your vows, but you cannot treat her poorly."

"God's teeth, Cranborne, will ye speak your mind already?"

"I entrust her into your care…I need your word that you will not lay a hand on her. I know she is sometimes difficult and speaks her mind—"

Declan laughed as if sincerely amused. "On that, we are in agreement. I will not lay a single hand on her. Ye have my word."

Cranborne stood. "His Majesty would never have awarded Castle Campbell without Liadain's hand. I hope you both find…My apologies that this was not what either of you wanted, but you have my thanks for seeing to Liadain."

The man was gone before Declan could think of another cold retort. Cranborne was truly daft—as if Declan would ever strike a woman. His mother would have castrated him. Cranborne need not worry. Touching the healer was the last idea that came to mind. He needed to take a piss. Where was the damn chamber pot?

❧

Liadain rose early, assuming MacGregor would want to take his leave immediately. She was exhausted, hollow, and lifeless. Moving around her chamber in a sleepless daze, she gathered her belongings, piling them upon the bed.

Her mind drifted back to the last words her husband had spoken to her. He was a vile beast. Granted, she had been a fool to believe that Robert loved her and would come back for her. She would even concede that she willingly gave herself to him under the promise of marriage. But…MacGregor had no right to condemn her for one mistake. It was not as if she had shared her bed with hundreds. The more she pondered that, the more it fired her blood. The rogue had bedded countless women yet chose to pass judgment upon her.

There was no sense biding her time in her chamber. Before she took her leave, she wanted to peek in on Elizabeth and her bairn to see how they fared. She walked through the halls of the court for the last time, casting demure smiles in greeting as she passed a few men and women. Thankfully, it was still too early in the morn and not many wandered about.

Liadain reached Elizabeth's door and knocked. When a maid answered, Liadain lowered her voice. "My apologies. I know 'tis too early to pay—"

"Ann, let her in. Liadain, come," said Elizabeth. Still in her nightrail, Elizabeth sat in a chair near the window, holding her bairn. She let out a long sigh of contentment and smiled. "I never tire of him."

Liadain placed her hand on Elizabeth's shoulder and glanced down at her son and smiled. "Nor should ye. He is such a beautiful bairn."

"Robert and I decided on a name. His name is William…after my father," Elizabeth said proudly.

"William. 'Tis a verra strong name for such a handsome laddie."

She sat down and watched Elizabeth cradling her child. An overwhelming feeling gnawed at her gut. How gratifying it must be to have a husband who loved you and wanted you, and a son who simply adored you.

"I will be taking my leave and I wanted to see how ye both fared," said Liadain.

A momentary look of discomfort crossed Elizabeth's features, and she cast her eyes to her bairn. "Robert spoke to me of your marriage."

Liadain looked away. "Aye."

"You are a beautiful woman and MacGregor is a handsome—well, he is very beautiful also." Elizabeth giggled. "Even if you do not have a love match now, perhaps it will grow into one in time."

"Elizabeth, with respect, I donna really want to speak upon it."

"I only wish that one day you will find what Robert and I share."

Liadain stirred uncomfortably in the chair. She wanted to see to Elizabeth's well-being but did not seek counsel—especially from the wife of the man with whom she had shared a bed. Unfortunately, Elizabeth did not take her declaration seriously and continued.

"When Robert and I met, I knew we would wed. We loved each other from the first time our eyes…" Elizabeth cleared her throat. "I do not think it possible to love him any more than I do. I know you don't want to speak of it, but have faith that everything will be all right. In time, you will grow to care for one another if you just give it a chance. Perhaps you will even be lucky enough to find that MacGregor is much the same as my Robert."

God help her. Why must she be tortured? If Elizabeth did not cease her commentary, Liadain was going to lose her contents. The gods must surely be laughing at her expense. As if wedding the husband spawned from the devil was not bad enough, now she was forced to listen as Elizabeth chatted about Robert's fine qualities.

Robert.

The same Robert who had offered Liadain promises of marriage. The beastly man who had deserted her, ruined her, and ultimately sealed her fate by bonding her to a Highland rogue who bedded any female who glanced his way.

The thought crossed her mind to open her mouth and enlighten Elizabeth as to Robert's true character—or lack thereof, but Liadain knew she was better than that. That was her father's foul blood rising up. And she refused to follow in her sire's or her brother's footsteps.

When Elizabeth cleared her throat, Liadain realized her attention had been elsewhere. "Thank ye for your kind words." Rising from the chair, she took a final glance at William. "It has been my pleasure to know ye, and I wish ye and William well. Good health to ye both," she said as she smiled tenderly.

"Thank you for all you have done. I owe you much," said Elizabeth. "Have safe travels."

Declan secured his bags to his mount, anxious to take his leave. The stables were quiet that early in the morn with only a few men mounting up for an early ride. He hoped the healer had managed to gain a few hours' sleep since he anticipated riding well into the night.

They needed to make haste. With the threat of witchcraft looming over the healer's head, he would not leave anything to chance. Besides, not only was he eager to divulge his winnings to his brother—well, his winning of the castle, not his bride—but Ciaran needed to be warned about Dunnehl and Rosalia's mother. Declan would not underestimate the English cur's cunning. Ciaran and Aiden would know what to do. They always did.

"I heard you were escaping the confines of court." Catesby made his way over to Declan's mount with Percy in tow. "I'm envious."

"Aye, 'tis true," said Declan, adjusting the leather straps on his satchel.

"With a new lady wife as well," interjected Percy, patting his horse on the rump and lifting his brow to Declan.

When he didn't answer, Catesby leaned in closed and lowered his voice. "You won Castle Campbell fairly. The king had no right to force your hand and shackle you to Argyll's sister."

Declan smirked. "He has every right. He is our liege."

"Be that as it may…he deliberately deceived you. I certainly hope you gave him a piece of your mind. You must be furious."

"'Tis of nay consequence. What is done is done."

"You know, MacGregor, there are some who believe His Majesty should be removed from the throne." Catesby and Percy studied him intently, waiting for his response. Something behind their eyes cautioned him to tread carefully.

Declan masked his expression and softened his voice. "And saying as much will cost ye your head."

"Only if such words fall back upon His Majesty's ears. I do not believe I am mistaken when I say that you look like a man who would keep such confidences to himself." Catesby lifted a brow.

This was the second time they had brought up this subject. "As long as it doesnae involve me, I donna care. Unless, of course, ye are planning on taking action and devising a plot to remove the king from the throne yourself." He mirrored their expressions.

Percy coughed nervously and Catesby lowered his eyes. "Of course not, my dear boy. That would be completely outrageous. Percy and I just heard of your marriage and wanted to wish you safe travel."

"Thank ye."

"Ah, here comes your beloved now," said Percy dryly. Upon the healer's approach, Catesby and Percy ambled away. The two of them were up to something, and Declan was relieved that he did not have to remain at court to find out what they were conjuring. The less he knew, the better.

The healer hobbled toward him with a large sack that he could immediately see was too heavy for her to carry. But when he reached out to take her bundle, she pulled away.

"I am perfectly able to manage myself, thank ye."

The stubborn lass stepped around him and approached her mount. Readjusting her grip, she hefted the sack unsuccessfully and it fell to the ground with a heavy thump. She cursed and her horse shied.

"Move away before ye hurt yourself." He did not give the healer a chance to respond before he tossed her bundle on top of her mount, tying off the leather straps. When he glanced down, she pulled her gaze away from him. "Are ye ready to ride?" he asked.

She simply nodded. When her eyes met his, he noticed a colored mark upon her skin. An angry, red line splayed across her ivory neck. Reaching out, Declan gently rubbed the injury and he did not miss her shiver under his touch.

When he pulled his fingers back, they were dry and free of blood. "When did ye cut yourself?" he asked.

"Mmm...let me think," she said, tapping her finger upon her chin. "That would have been the second time ye placed your dagger at my throat. Rest assured, there willnae be a third." There was defiance in her tone as well as a subtle challenge. Tossing her tresses across her shoulders, she boldly met his eyes.

He was too stunned to offer a response. When had he cut her?

"I donna—"

The healer's shoulder bumped against his chest as she grabbed the reins to her mount. She led her horse over to the mounting block, then climbed upon her horse's back.

Declan remained as still as a statue. He was too caught up in the fact that the lass had announced that his blade had sliced her—his blade, his hand. The gods knew he did not want to take the bloody Campbell's sister to wife, but he would never deliberately harm her. This bothered him more than he cared to admit. To be truthful, he felt like an arse. What could he possibly say to her now?

She waited patiently and could scarcely meet his eyes. Since his voice had deserted him, he realized it might be safer to mount up and keep his mouth shut. Perhaps they could converse later when his foot was not in his mouth. He prayed the gods might favor him with such a time. Until then, he had only one purpose: flee the madness of court.

Departing the gates of hell, Declan breathed a sigh of relief.

❧

Percy leaned back, sipping the liquid fire contentedly. He would not worry over matters that were simply out of his control. Frankly, he was tired of upholding this ridiculous pretense. Their plan would be in motion soon and he could finally get down to the business at hand.

Glancing at Catesby in the chair beside him, Percy shook his head. Catesby was nervously tapping his fingers on the desk and looked as though he was about to throw up. "Patience, Catesby."

An uncertainty crept into Catesby's expression. "It would be easy for you to say as much. What do you think he will say when we advise him that MacGregor—"

A short, stocky man headed toward them, his steps slowing as he cast a puzzled look. Percy did not exactly trust the man, but they held the same purpose. Pulling out the chair, the man took his place behind the desk. "What of MacGregor?"

Percy traced an invisible line on his cup. "He did not take the bait."

The man's mouth thinned with displeasure. "I thought as much. We have no choice but to implement another course of action. We must see Lady Stuart to the throne, and I will not permit some Highland *barbarian* to keep us from our purpose. I have set things in motion. In two months, King James will be addressing Parliament again after failing to win its support. On the eve of the state opening, we will make our move." He raised his brow and nodded to Percy. "Are you ready?"

Percy smirked. "Of course, I'm ready."

"You must know how difficult this has been for Percy to pretend he had no skill with the bow. He actually had MacGregor instruct him at one point," said Catesby. He chuckled, a bit more relaxed.

"Your chance to prove your skill will be here soon enough, and you will be richly rewarded for your service…once you kill the king."

Twelve

THEY HAD RIDDEN NORTH FOR A FEW HOURS, AND MacGregor had yet to utter a single word. Liadain chose not to fret over it. He was a man and a MacGregor—the combination of the two a stubborn mix.

A gentle breeze and the smell of pine tickled Liadain's nose. She glanced up at the cloudless sky and studied the sun's position. It was almost midday and the insufferable temperatures would soon be upon them. She hoped the shade from the surrounding forest would stay the heat, knowing nothing could darken her mood faster than sweat pouring down the back of her traveling dress.

"Will we be taking a rest soon?" she called to MacGregor's broad back.

Without turning around, the obstinate man continued on course and did not respond. For a moment, she did not think he would even acknowledge her. "I hadnae planned upon it. Why?"

"I need to stop."

"Now?"

"If nae now, soon."

To her surprise, he reined in his mount and tethered him to a tree. At least there was some hope that
he would not be sparring with her constantly. Praise
the saints for small favors. She watched him disappear
into the brush.

Liadain dismounted and secured her horse, glancing around for a secluded area to see to her personal
needs. Green, jagged thistles grew like the plague on
the opposite side of the path. The other side had dense
trees, but it did not appear to have as many prickly
plants that would damage her skirts. In the distance,
she thought she spotted a large pile of boulders and
rocks that would offer her some discretion. That
would have to do.

She stood behind the base of the mound. Fumbling
hastily to lift her skirts, she almost did not make it. How
truly embarrassing that would have been. As soon as she
squatted and started to feel some relief, she saw a pair
of black, beady eyes staring back at her from the stone
fissure. She bit back a scream and stood very slowly.

The snake poked out its repulsive head and slith-
ered down through the rocks, heading steadily toward
her—its forked tongue darting in and out. If she ran, it
would surely lash out and sink its fangs into her. Even
worse, what if it slid under her skirts? Hurriedly, she
bunched them together, lifting them up behind her
and never taking her eyes from the vile creature.

The beastly snake was almost upon her. She could
not breathe.

Somehow, she forced herself to find her voice and
shouted. "MacGregor!" Where was that dastardly
man? He was supposed to be her protector.

~

Declan's mind was numb, as it had been all morn. He could not stop seeing the images of his dagger piercing the healer's throat. He would never harm a woman—not on purpose. When the lass had asked him to rest, it had taken him a moment to realize that she was speaking to him. His thoughts were too consumed with guilt.

"MacGregor!"

Without hesitation, he ran back to his mount and grabbed his bow. Where the hell was she? His eyes searched frantically through the forest.

"MacGregor!"

With lightning speed, he bolted through the trees toward the sound of her voice. He spotted her still form and stopped. Cautiously, he raised his bow while searching the surrounding landscape. Once he knew for certain there was no viable threat, only then would he attempt to approach her.

He remained alert, trying to decipher what was amiss. The healer was frozen with her skirts lifted up, giving him a perfect view of her creamy thigh.

Tears choked her voice. "Please, MacGregor."

Following her wide-eyed stare, he recognized the reason for her distress. The culprit was making a beeline toward her. Lifting the bow, Declan took his shot, and as soon as the arrow made impact, he realized his mistake.

When the tip penetrated the reptile, the snake involuntarily jumped…right onto her foot. Her shrill screams rang through the trees and she jerked back several feet. To his surprise, the lass did not stop there.

She hiked up her dress even higher. She bounced up and down as though her feet were afire. Curses were thrown like stones as she swore like a man in the heat of battle. The shocking spectacle made any words that came to mind wedge in his throat.

The lass suddenly turned and raced back through the woods. Declan gaped as he caught glimpses of her bare, shapely legs fleeing through the forest trees.

What the hell was that? He threw back his head and roared with laughter. Who would have thought that the woman who resided under the same dangerous roof as the bloody Campbell was deathly afraid of snakes? Hell, she had lived with one. The idea was truly unbelievable. Honestly, he had never thought of her as faint-hearted.

He shook his head and walked back to the horses. He hoped the lass had enough sense to stop running and that he would not have to chase her down. Although the way she behaved, nothing would have surprised him.

The healer sat upon her mount, her back stiff and straight. When he approached, she cast her eyes away from him and shifted in the saddle.

"Why did ye run? The snake was dead."

"I donna like snakes. I donna, donna, donna. I really donna. It *touched* my foot," she blurted out and then shivered.

Declan tried not to chuckle, but one involuntarily escaped him. "I gathered that ye donna favor snakes, but 'tis dead." He extended his hand to her. "Come down and stretch your legs before we ride again."

She waved him off. "Nay, I am fine right where I

am," she said as she studied the ground. "I had more than enough stretching."

"There are nay more snakes, lass. Come down."

"Unless ye intend on pulling me from my horse's back, I am nae moving," she said stubbornly.

The words were out of Declan's mouth before he had a chance to stay them. "Ye know, they could as easily be in the trees above your head as they could be upon the ground." He patted her horse on the rump. He was teasing her, affectionately, not maliciously.

She paled and became watchful of the branches above. "Ye know? Ye may think ye are humorous, but let me assure ye that ye arenae."

"Suit yourself." Declan shrugged and turned away, wondering what other new discoveries he would learn about his wife on this journey.

❦

It was confirmed. Her husband was indeed a beast. Liadain had not missed the glint of humor in his eyes. Her traveling companion clearly thought he was comical. One thing was for certain: he did not know her at all.

Her embarrassment quickly turned into annoyance. She could admit she was by no means perfect, but MacGregor did not have to laugh at her discomfiture. It had been impossible not to hear the chuckle he tried to disguise. The rogue had better cease. The ride back to Glenorchy was a long one, and she could just as easily get under his skin.

After they had ridden several miles in hushed stillness, Liadain recognized that she had had enough.

Between the suffocating heat and the lack of conversation, she was completely miserable. If this was how it was going to be the entire way, she might as well pull out her dagger and yield now.

"Are ye nae going to speak to me at all?" she asked. "That will make for a verra long ride."

"I am speaking to ye," MacGregor said as if the answer were obvious.

There was a heavy silence.

"The heat is thickening," she stated.

"Aye."

"The pests are encircling my head," she said through gritted teeth. She managed to fan the tiny buggers out of her face, but that did not prevent them from buzzing around her ears.

"Aye," he replied without inflection.

"It should be cooler when we reach the Highlands." She spoke in an encouraging tone. But if he gave her another one-word answer, she swore her dagger would find its pointy end at the base of his throat.

"Aye."

"Ye are an arse, MacGregor." For a brief moment, she could have sworn he actually chuckled.

"Dè thuirt thu?" What did you say?

"Chan eil e gu difeir." It does not matter.

He seemed relieved to be released from the one-sided discussion. Left alone with her thoughts, Liadain pondered if her herbs survived or if someone had tended to the garden. Living with Archie was not the most ideal situation, but her brother had left her alone. As she studied her new husband, she could not help but wonder if he would do the same. No matter, at least she would be home.

MacGregor reined in his mount. "We will make camp here this eve," he said, leaving the path and entering a clearing. "There is a creek over there to water the horses."

She followed him and dismounted. Her legs buckled and she could barely stand. Pausing to reflect a moment before she made an effort to walk, she was a little surprised that he wanted to stop when he did.

Liadain knew she should quit examining the man's every action and just be thankful she was no longer made to suffer the arduous trail—well, her arse was certainly grateful. She grabbed her horse's reins and led her mount over to the water. The creek was only a few feet wide but probably about waist deep in the center. Flowing water gushed over the rocks, making trickling sounds that beckoned her. How refreshing it would be to strip off all her clothing and immerse herself in its cooling depths.

MacGregor stepped next to her. "I will tether the horses if ye want to wash," he said, reaching for the reins.

She wasn't about to argue. "Thank ye." He had barely moved out of her way when she could no longer wait. As soon as she removed her boots, cooler air brushed against her skin. She lifted her skirts and eagerly rushed into the pool.

The lapping water reached her knees, cooling her down and soothing her mood. After a hot, miserable day, this was delightful and exactly what she needed. Liadain closed her eyes and realized she could stand

in this single spot all eve and be content. She reached
down, tying her skirts in a knot above her thighs.
Cupping a handful of water, she splashed it all over her
face. As soon as she bent down for another, the naked
legs that greeted her were not her own.

"The water feels good."

She stepped back, her mouth wide open.

MacGregor stood before her as bare as the day he
was born. In one swift movement, he plunged his head
under the water and then stood, flipping his hair back.

Liadain wiped the spray from her face.

Droplets of water glistened on his broad chest. He
raised his hands to ring his hair, his muscles rippling
with every movement.

She could not keep her eyes from wandering—
lower. MacGregor was so very wet. She had seen
naked men before while tending the wounds of the
injured, and she had obviously gazed upon Robert a
time or two, but never had she been witness to male
anatomy so…*endowed*. No wonder the women flocked
to him.

As if he sensed her smoldering thoughts, he cast a
roguish grin. Did he have to look upon her with that
knowing gaze?

She bent down and cupped another handful
of water, refusing to let the man observe how he
affected her.

"What is the matter, healer? Ye seem to be unable
to meet my eyes."

"Mayhap I could if ye were wearing even a single
piece of clothing," she murmured, splashing another
handful of cold water onto her face.

"But I donna have to don clothing. I am now your husband. In fact, why donna ye remove your gown?"

Standing to her full height, she placed her hands on her hips and glanced up at him. "How verra passionate," she said dryly.

A soft chuckle answered her. "I donna have to woo ye. We are already wed."

Holding her hand to the cut on her throat, Liadain spoke quietly. "I donna think I would want ye to woo me."

Tender eyes met her gaze. "I ne'er meant to hurt ye." He raised her chin with his fingers. "I was in my cups, and I didnae know my dagger...my apologies." Pausing, he waited for her response.

"'Tis the second time ye've held that bloody dagger to my throat. I meant what I said. There willnae be a third."

He nodded and his smile was somewhat remorseful. "Ye have my word. Now get out of these clothes," he said, tugging on her sleeve.

She gaped at him. "Ye *cannae* treat me this way and then be so callous as to expect me to remove my cloth—"

His lips crashed down upon hers in a brutal, punishing kiss, making her senses spin. But before she even had a chance to respond, MacGregor pulled away and simply raised his brow in an arrogant manner.

Her temper flared. She would demand respect. With all of her might, she shoved his massive chest with a heavy thump. His eyes widened as he fell backward into the water—flat on his arse. He wiped the droplets from his eyes and a muscle ticked at his jaw.

Liadain pointed her finger at him. "Ye may be my rogue of a husband in name, but I willnae allow ye to treat me as one of your common whores."

"If ye would have let me finish instead of spewing with your tongue, I only meant for ye to bathe," he said defensively. "Are your clothes nae hot? I only kissed ye to halt your words. Ye donna have to worry about me *consummating* our marriage. Ye have already been consummated."

Thirteen

LIADAIN SAT AND WATCHED THE GLOWING EMBERS OF their fire fade into its molten depths. What a day this had been, and not exactly as she had expected. She wrapped her arms tighter around her knees, placing her chin on top. With a deep, resigned sigh, she closed her eyes. MacGregor's words still stung.

Robert had been the first man to ever pay her any heed. Granted, she had been young and perhaps a bit inexperienced, but that did not give MacGregor the right to judge her for sins of the past. One would think he, of all men, would recognize that fact. She did not even believe a count could be tallied for the endless number of women the rogue had bedded.

Lifting her head, she cast him a glance. He slept with his back toward her, without a care in the world, and his gentle rhythmic breathing fired her ire even more. While his spiteful words continued to repeat in her mind, her husband was obviously unaffected by their prior exchange.

"We ride in a few short hours. 'Tis best that ye rest and close your eyes, healer."

Liadain jumped at the sound of his deep voice. With exaggerated movements, she turned her back to him, lying upon her woolen blanket with annoyance.

When sunlight drifted into her eyes, she squinted, not looking forward to the start of another long day. She should have made more of an effort to sleep. Her body and mind protested and were fatigued.

"The horses have been watered and the embers are out. Are ye going to rise soon, or will ye sleep all day?" MacGregor stood with his arms folded over his chest, casting a look of disapproval upon her. "Didnae I tell ye to sleep? Ye appear as though ye were up all night."

What an astute observation—one she wasn't about to openly agree with. She pulled herself to her feet and folded her blanket. "Pray excuse me but a moment," she murmured as she moved into the trees.

"Watch out for the snakes," he called after her.

She stopped suddenly and stiffened. "Ye are truly a beast." A very male chuckle responded from several feet behind her.

When she returned from seeing to her personal needs, the man stood head to head with her horse. Silently, his lips moved. Her husband appeared to actually be conversing with the animal. Upon her approach, he stepped away from her mount.

At a last-moment attempt to gain peace between them, she reached out and touched his arm. "Might I have a word with ye?"

He shrugged.

She fingered the straps on her bundle. "We cannae continue on this destructive path. I know ye didnae want to take me to wife, but we nay longer have a choice. King James willed it and 'tis done."

Not wanting to provoke him into another argument, she closed her eyes and continued to speak in a soft, even tone. "I want ye to know that I thought I loved Robert. I truly did." A hushed stillness enveloped them and she did not dare glance into his judging eyes. "Robert promised we would be wed, and aye, I gave him my innocence with the understanding that he was to be my husband. I willnae apologize and ye have nay right to lash out at me with such harshness. I am sorrowful that as your wife I am nae chaste, but I am nay whore. Robert is the only man I ever…"

Meeting his gaze, she stood to her full height. "I cannae change the past, nay matter how much I wish upon it. I was naught to Archie and Robert. I donna want to be the same to ye. I donna think I was mistaken when ye and I were once able to speak without hurtful words between us. I only wish ye would somehow find it within yourself to treat me with respect. Nay matter your feelings toward me, I am still your wife."

⌘

"Ye are right. I didnae want this." Declan smiled tenderly. "But…I have nay right to treat or speak to ye as such. My apologies. My words were spoken in anger. I know ye also didnae seek this marriage." He lifted the healer onto her mount before she had a chance to protest.

When he pondered his actions and words of last eve, he was not proud. He had been aware of that fact as soon as the scathing remarks left his mouth.

When her eyes had welled with tears, his heart had sunk. At that moment, he wanted nothing more than to embrace his wife and retract his hostile words, but it was too late.

His brothers were right. Sometimes he was an idiot, never considering the consequences of his actions. His mother would not have tolerated such treatment of a woman, and he silently prayed she was not looking down upon him now. Though he certainly made more than his share of mistakes, disparaging lasses was not among them. He knew he had been wrong and that irked him.

They rode for some time, and when Declan realized the only sound between them was coming from their mounts' hoofbeats, he knew he needed to make more of an effort. Well, any attempt would be better than his actions the day before.

"What is it, healer? I can see the worried expression upon your brow."

"Do ye think Rosalia's mother and Lord Dunnehl will travel to Glenorchy?"

"I donna know, but it troubles me. Lady Armstrong willingly beds the man who killed her husband."

"Surely ye donna think they…"

"Naught would surprise me. According to Rosalia, her mother would do anything for coin and status. The woman watched her husband die at the hand of Dunnehl, lass. Tell me, what woman would stand by and do naught, and then take her leave freely with such a man? The two are a perfect match. Their greed will be their undoing."

She nodded. "Aye, I believe that. Ye see the lengths

Archie attempted for such power, which ultimately led to his untimely demise."

"Your brother became careless—killing a clansman to fire Ciaran's ire and break the king's command." Declan did not intend for his tone to sound so harsh. He cast a sideways glance and smiled. "My father always said to ne'er let your anger guide ye without thought."

She returned his smile. "A wise man."

He nodded. "Aye, the wisest."

"What became of your father?"

"A few years after my mother's passing, he fell ill with the ague. He didnae suffer long."

"And what of your mother? How did she handle three lads under her roof?"

"She was a verra compassionate soul," he said, fond memories flooding him with emotion.

"My apologies if ye donna want to speak of your mother."

"And what of your clan?" he asked.

"'Tisnae much to tell. My mother died when I was verra young. I can barely remember her. And Father ne'er seemed to mind her absence. Then again, he and Archie paid me nay heed."

He smiled with compassion. "My brothers and I are verra close. Being by yourself must have been difficult for ye."

She shook her head. "Nay. They left me to my own devices and I was thankful. I took to healing. I grew herbs and plants, and was able to aid the sick. I enjoyed that verra much. If Archie and my father had been watchful over me, I ne'er would have been able to move about so freely or to do what I wanted."

"Aye, but it sounds lonely."

"At times, but I was able to assist the villagers and they became my second kin. It was my privilege to be able to offer remedies for their ailments. I take pleasure in aiding the less fortunate."

Of course she did. Declan had known there was something special about the healer the moment she agreed to help his clan. She was...kind. Everything he was not.

⁂

Finally, at least they were able to speak civil words between them. Perhaps this marriage would not be as dreadful as Liadain had initially thought. She needed to keep the conversation moving in the right direction.

"Will we be traveling to Glenorchy first or to Castle Campbell?" she asked as she wiped the sweat from the back of her neck.

"Glenorchy. I must speak with Ciaran."

"Of course," she murmured, trying to keep the concern out of her voice.

Liadain could not help but wonder what Laird MacGregor would think of her now. Would he hold her accountable for his brother's shackles? How would he feel about having a Campbell for a sister-by-marriage? One thing was for certain: Ciaran MacGregor had despised Archie. She hoped that gaining a portion of the Campbell lands would lighten Laird MacGregor's opinion of her. Her worries must have shown upon her face because she felt her husband's stare.

"Are ye *nervous*?" he asked.

She returned a sheepish smile. "A wee bit."

"Ye have naught to fear. 'Tisnae as if ye donna know my clan."

"I donna think having another Campbell underfoot would be exactly welcoming," she replied dryly.

"Ye worry for naught, healer. Rosalia and Aisling care for ye."

Shifting in the saddle, she cleared her throat. "'Tisnae Rosalia and Aisling I worry about."

He studied her thoughtfully for a moment. "Donna let Ciaran and Aiden frighten ye. Ye saved their women. They wouldnae hold Archie's treachery against ye."

"I hope your words ring true and they donna think I share the same tainted blood." She paused. "And what of ye?"

"Me?" MacGregor asked with surprise. "I told ye before. The bloody Campbell was your brother. Ye donna even remotely resemble him."

"Thank ye. I think."

"God's teeth, 'tis hot," he grunted, pulling at his tunic." His features glistened with sweat and his hair was damp.

"Aye, at least ye wear a kilt and receive a bit of air. My traveling dress isnae as forgiving. I am starting to think I should listen to Rosalia. Women should be permitted to don trews and tunics. The same as men."

He threw back his head with laughter. "Already Rosalia influences ye. I know Ciaran permits her to don trews when they ride, but Aisling doesnae yet wear them. I donna think Aiden would want her traipsing around the bailey wearing a man's trews—especially his own."

MacGregor had a rich, masculine laugh, and the gentle sparring between them was comforting. She grew tired of wanting to kill her husband at every turn.

As they rode along the dry, dusty path, the heat bore down upon them with no mercy. If she wasn't paying attention, she wouldn't have noticed that her husband had changed direction.

"Why donna we continue north?" she finally asked, wiping the sweat from her brow.

"We only travel a wee distance and then will resume our course." He did not meet her eyes and his expression became carefully guarded.

Who was she to argue? Liadain hoped they would not be going too far out of the way, wanting to curtail anything that would possibly delay the journey home to the cooler temperatures of the Highlands. They had continued for about a mile when she smiled at the sight before her.

The clustered trees suddenly cleared and opened up to an inviting loch—a wonderfully cool, refreshing loch. Mossy, green grass surrounded the pool in a welcoming embrace. A rocky peninsula jetted out from the shore, and small, white waves lapped against the stones. Her spirits instantly lifted.

"I thought we could swim for a bit and it would help to stay the heat."

"Bless ye, MacGregor." Sliding from her mount, she steadied her wobbly legs.

He took the reins and tethered the horses to a

nearby tree. Not wasting any time, he lifted his strong arms and removed his tunic. He slid out of his boots, and then with one quick movement of his wrist, his kilt fell to the ground.

Turning, he nodded in her direction. "Healer, we havenae got all day. If ye're going to cool off, best ye do it now."

With a sudden spring in his step, MacGregor bolted to where the water was waist deep and then dove in headfirst. He came up a moment later, sweeping his hair away from his face. Water sprayed in all directions and tiny droplets glistened on his tanned body, casting him in a deliciously enticing glow.

Wiping his eyes, he glanced back to the shore. "Healer! Quit standing there with your mouth open and join me."

Liadain masked the heat that stole into her cheeks by looking down and freeing her sweaty feet from her boots. She instantly sighed. Hefting her skirts, she waded into the water and let the coolness soothe her. "This feels delightful." She closed her eyes in sheer bliss.

"Come in and cool off. If ye arenae…er, comfortable removing your clothing, take off your dress and remain in your shift." MacGregor cupped water in his hands and splashed it on his face.

Granted, the man was now her husband and she certainly had received an eyeful of him. But she was not jumping at the chance to display her body so bare before his gaze. "Nay, I am fine where I stand."

He rubbed water up and down his brawny arms. "Healer," he said in a knowing tone. "Ye donna have to be so stubborn. The heat has nay mercy this day. If ye donna remove your dress, I will come and do it for ye." He gave her a rakish gaze, his eyes holding another meaning entirely.

She had the feeling he would stay true to his word. Nodding in consent, she walked back into the grass and turned away from him. Reaching down, she fumbled for the bottom of her dress.

"Do ye need my assistance?" he asked with a masculine laugh.

"Nay."

She lifted the gown over her head, while making certain that her shift kept covering the most important parts of her body. As she turned to the loch, her husband's naked arse rose in the air as he dove deeper into the cooling depths of the water. She made her way to the edge and needed all of her strength not to laugh at the sight.

Springing his head up, he wiped the water from his face. He took one look at her and shook his head. With long, purposeful strides, he headed toward her. "God's teeth, healer, we havenae got all day."

Instinctively, she tried to retreat, but the man reached out and grabbed her wrist. With one swift movement, he bent over and scooped her up in his arms.

"What are ye doing?" she squealed as she twisted and arched her body, fighting to get free.

His grip tightened around her. He walked back into the water, stopping when he was about waist deep. She could feel something beneath her bottom that made the rogue so self-confident. His eyes darkened and one corner of his mouth turned upward. MacGregor lowered his head, his lips parted, and looked as though he was about to kiss her.

She leaned her head forward and closed her eyes. The shock of his actions hit her full force as she was engulfed by rushing water. It took her a moment to register that the dastardly man had actually dropped her in the loch. Pulling herself to her feet, she wiped her eyes. A deep chuckle greeted her.

"Ye cannae say that I didnae warn ye," he jested.

"Ye are a beast!"

Liadain pulled back her arms and splashed him repeatedly, refusing to stop until the man yielded. To her dismay, he ducked his head, grabbing her around the waist. He hefted her up over his broad shoulder and threw her backward. She quickly found herself again in the same predicament. She stood, pushing her sopping tresses out of her eyes.

She approached him and smiled innocently. "Do ye know what I love about the water?"

"What?" MacGregor responded in an obviously humoring tone.

With stealthy moves of her own, she made a swift undercut with her leg and swept her husband from his feet. "Ye are much lighter."

He disappeared under the water, his expression priceless. When he did not immediately emerge, an uneasy feeling settled in the pit of her stomach. Too much time had passed. She kicked the soft bottom of the loch with her feet, searching with her hands underneath the water in front of her.

Without warning, he sprang up behind her with a boisterous battle cry that made her scream at the top of her lungs. He hauled her from her feet and lifted her above his head, tossing her once again into the cooling depths of the loch.

She pushed her soggy pieces of hair out of her eyes for a third time. "Ye are verra humorous."

He gave her a smile that remained on his extremely handsome face. "I thought as much. Are ye ready to take your leave?"

Bending her knees, she dipped herself deeper into the water. "Nay. This feels delightful. Must we?" She could not stay the whine that escaped her voice. She did not want to play the part of the weaker sex, but the temperature away from the loch was insufferable.

The amused look suddenly left his eyes and he closed the gap between them. Liadain stood and he fingered a loose tendril of hair on her cheek. Tenderly, he traced the line of her cheekbone and jaw. When his fingers brushed her collarbone and lingered against the cut on her throat, she covered his hand with her own.

"'Tis time I made ye my wife in truth," MacGregor said with quiet emphasis.

She stared wordlessly, as though his words released her from some type of inner torment. His hands explored the hollows of her back, the warmth of his arms so male, so bracing. He brushed a gentle kiss across her forehead, and then his glance slid slowly to her shift and his mouth softened.

Her thoughts were jumbled.

"What are ye doing?" she asked. His change in behavior was confusing.

His gaze roved as he lazily appraised her. "Ye are verra beautiful, lass."

"MacGregor, your emotions range from one end to the other. Ye are either verra kind to me or verra cruel. Why donna ye make up your mind and let me know when—"

His mouth covered hers hungrily, his kiss hard and searching. Her last words were smothered by his lips, and his touch was becoming more persuasive than she cared to admit. Raising his mouth from hers, he gazed into her eyes.

Without looking away, she backed out of his grasp. Lifting his fingers, he gently brushed her cheek, the touch of his hand almost unbearable in its tenderness.

"What do ye want from me?" Liadain whispered. When his eyes sent her a private message, she quickly added, "Besides the obvious."

"Cannae we reach a truce?" He rubbed his hands gently up and down her arms.

"Isnae that what I have been asking of ye all along? Why now?" Mixed feelings surged through her.

"Mayhap I acknowledge the fact that I cannae change King James's…There is nay need to look to the past. We are each other's future. What is done 'tis already done."

Her heart jolted, her pulse pounded, and her body suddenly ached for his touch. The idea sent her spirits soaring. MacGregor wanted peace between them—a chance to start anew. Her feet seemed to be drifting along on a cloud. That could have been due to the fact that they were standing in water, but frankly, she didn't care. All that mattered was this moment.

Her husband cradled her, weightless, in his arms,

and she buried her face against the corded muscles of his chest. She had no desire to back out of his embrace. She was aware of where his warm flesh touched her, feeling the occasional jolt of his thigh brushing up against her. Her body tingled from the contact.

As he carried her from the loch, his breath was uneven upon her cheek. Lifting her head, she gazed into his eyes. He pressed his lips to hers, caressing her mouth, and she quivered at the sweet tenderness. The dreamy familiarity of the moment left her weak but wanting more.

He gently lowered her onto his plaid and pulled her shift over her head. When his roughened hand slid across her silken belly and down to the swell of her hips, she could barely contain herself.

"Ye are verra bonny, lass." He took her mouth with a savage force and his lips brought smoldering heat to hers. His hand outlined the circle of her breast, and she surged at the tenderness of his touch.

He lowered his head, his tongue tantalizing her hardened nipples. Instinctively, her body arched toward him.

He was surprisingly, touchingly restrained. He began to slip his hands up her arms ever so slowly, while she caressed the strong tendons in the back of his neck. Aroused now, she drew closer to him. He rubbed the bare skin of her shoulders and kissed the hollow of her neck.

She gasped as he lowered his body against hers, the evidence of his desire rubbing against her belly. Moving his hands below her, he gripped her thighs, lifting her gently to straddle him. It was flesh against flesh, man against woman. His tormented groan was a heady invitation.

Slowly, his hands skimmed her body and she trailed tickling fingers up and down his strong arms. Passion pounded her blood, and she could sense the barely controlled power that coiled in his body.

Her desire for him overrode any sense of thought or reason. She needed him. She needed this. *Now*. At that moment she knew she would yield to the searing need that had been building from the first time their eyes met.

She slid down his shaft and gasped in sweet agony. She took him fully, his expert touch sending her to even higher levels of ecstasy. Together they found a rhythm that bound their bodies as one.

The pleasure was pure and explosive, the feel of his rough skin against hers exalting. Her eager response matched his. The involuntary tremors of arousal began and her senses spun.

She could not control her outcry of delight as he threw back his head and sought his own release.

For once in her life, she was filled with an amazing sense of completeness. They were as one—man and wife—forever bonded.

Giving her a brotherly peck on the cheek, MacGregor patted her on the top of the head and rolled to his feet. "Come, healer. We donna have all day."

Fourteen

LIADAIN CLOSED HER EYES AND PRAYED FOR PATIENCE. To be truthful, it was more of an attempt to keep her feet from trailing after MacGregor and throttling his massive frame. Why must his behavior range from hot to cold in a matter of seconds?

Pulling herself to her feet, she grabbed her balled-up shift and donned her dress quickly. Her deep, calming breaths did not work the way she had hoped. She seethed with anger and humiliation, furious at her vulnerability toward her new husband.

When she could no longer rein in her temper, she thundered toward the infuriating man with fire in her blood. Unfortunately, it was not the same heat that had warmed her body only moments before. She flashed him a look of disdain, but the lively twinkle in his eyes incensed her even more.

"What is the matter with ye?" she bellowed, slapping his arm.

He lowered his head and gave her a rakish gaze. "I donna believe anything was the matter with me. Ye seemed to enjoy yourself."

She huffed. "'Tisnae what I meant and ye know it. After what we shared, why would ye pat me upon the head and then say to me that we 'havenae got all day' as if naught had happened between us?"

"I didnae just pat ye upon the head. I kissed ye," MacGregor said defensively.

"On the cheek, as a brother!"

"Is that your problem?" He wedged her tight against his naked form and lowered his mouth to hers.

She was both excited and aggravated, the kiss sending the pit of her stomach into a wild swirl. Her thoughts were becoming jumbled, her husband's lips sending a shiver through her. She knew she was trying to make a point, but the rogue's ministrations were so utterly distracting. If she did not know better, she would have sworn he did this on purpose.

He raised his mouth from hers, his eyes flashing with amusement. "Ye see? There is naught wrong with me. The taste of ye still lingers on my lips, and yet ye clearly want me to pleasure ye again."

Liadain laughed to cover her annoyance. "Donna flatter yourself, ye rogue." She found herself inexplicably dissatisfied, not from the act itself, but from MacGregor's behavior. How can one man make one woman's blood boil from passion and then anger within a matter of seconds?

When he chuckled in response, something within her snapped. Completely aggravated, she shoved the solid wall of her husband's chest and he fell backward—flat on his naked arse.

"I am your *wife*, ye beastly man. I didnae expect

flowery words of love, but you cannae dismiss me as though I am one of your whores."

Somewhere in the middle of her rant, MacGregor sprang to his feet. His features tightened and he reached behind himself, rubbing his arse. Without warning, he whipped around and raced into the loch, repeatedly plunging himself under the water.

When he finally stood, he snarled at her. "Why did ye push me in *deanntag?*" *Stinging nettles.*

Her mouth dropped open. "I didnae know they were there. My apologies. I didnae see them."

He thundered out of the loch and she involuntarily jumped. She would not have been surprised if her husband attempted to throttle her. He grabbed his kilt and turned. "Ye want me to acknowledge ye are my wife, but lest ye forget, I am your husband…"

Trying unsuccessfully to mask the guilty expression upon her features, Liadain paled. "I am so sorry."

❧

Declan grabbed his mount and muttered under his breath. The woman was completely daft. Against his better judgment, he'd given her a good tupping, admitting the lass was his wife in truth. But was that good enough for the stubborn wench? She threw his arse in *deanntag!* Must the bloody Campbells always be a thorn in his side—well, in this case, his…never mind.

They rode in blissful silence for several hours and he welcomed the quietness. The woman had apologized so many times that he wished she'd hold her tongue. Even though a part of him enjoyed her groveling, her expressions of regret were starting to grate on his nerves. He gathered by the fifth declaration that she had not deliberately pushed him into the dreaded plant, but the fact remained that his arse still stung. And he swore the woolen material of his kilt only made it worse. He reached around and gently tugged the fabric away from his skin.

"Donna scratch," she called from behind him. "Do ye want me to take a look?"

"I think ye have done more than enough, *healer*."

She mumbled something under her breath and he could have sworn it was not too kind.

Without warning, pounding hooves rounded the bend as five men rode toward them at breakneck speed. Declan stiffened, placing his hand on the hilt of his sword.

"Stay by my side and donna move."

A portly man with a scruffy beard that grazed his rounded middle stopped before them. The man's clothes were tattered, and he had several layers of dust and grime upon his face. His mount pranced impatiently, unhappy from the restraint.

Declan held his breath. The man reeked and was in desperate need of a bath. Upon further inspection, all the men were unwashed and filthy. The man eyed him with a curious look as the others encircled them, glancing to their leader for direction.

With a toothless grin, the disheveled man gave Declan a nod. "Give me your purse." Pausing, the man then gave the healer a raking gaze. "Or your woman. Or mayhap both."

There was a heavy silence.

"Aye, I will have the woman. Her mouth looks

soft," said another one of the men, grabbing his cock and positioning his mount closer to the healer.

"Mayhap the English cur is deaf," spoke another man in a taunting tone.

"And mayhap he is only trying to figure out which one of ye to kill first," said Declan, his tone harsh.

The leader let out a hearty chuckle. "Ye arenae English. I see now ye don a kilt."

Clearly, the leader was not the brightest of the bunch. Declan's eyes narrowed. "I am nae English."

"Dè an t-ainm a th' ort?" What is your name?

"MacGregor."

The leader's eyes lit up in surprise and his men glanced around with uncertainty. "As in the man who killed the Campbell?"

"We are of the same blood," he said without inflection in his voice. He unsheathed his sword and rested his weapon casually over his lap. The men measured him for a moment, weighing their options.

"And the woman?" One of the men licked his lips, and his eyes undressed the healer from head to toe.

Declan did not dare glance in her direction, refusing to give these men any opportunity to see weakness. But something within him stirred at the sight of the man's raking gaze upon the healer. The thought of that man—*any* man—touching the lass made his blood start to boil. He would need to ponder that revelation later because, as of this moment, he needed all of his might to rein in his temper.

"She is a MacGregor," he simply stated.

The leader gave a brief nod to his men and made a dismissive gesture. "Come, lads. There are other spoils to be had." One corner of the man's lips turned upward as he turned back to Declan. "MacGregor." When their leader kicked his mount into a gallop, the other men followed suit, their foul stench lingering behind.

Declan twisted around in the saddle. "Come, healer, I donna want to be around if they change their minds and return." He sheathed his sword and moved his mount back onto the path.

"Aye, we were surely outnumbered," she spoke softly.

"*Outnumbered?* I could have ended their sorrowful lives where they stood. I speak of their stench. 'Tis enough to make a grown man cry."

Her gentle laugh rippled through the air.

"I was going to set up camp nearby, but we need to place more distance between us and them. We will ride until the sun sets." When she nodded in agreement, he was proud of her. Most women would have cowered and fallen apart before such repulsive men, but not her. It should not come as a surprise. He was discovering that his new wife was not like most women.

❧

When Liadain managed to convince MacGregor that the vagrants had long since passed and were probably preying upon some other weary travelers, he finally agreed to stop.

She sat before the open fire with her legs folded under her, studying her husband intently. The man was a mystery. When the brigands had surrounded them, he had remained strong and composed, confident in his every move, his every word. Her heart had lurched madly when he claimed her as his own. Well, she was his, but hearing him say it was comforting nonetheless.

The light from their fire cast him in a radiant glow. He grabbed another piece of wood and bent over, adjusting the embers. She recalled the passion of being held against her husband's strong body. Attempting to keep the memory pure and unsullied, she tried to forget how easily the man had dismissed her.

MacGregor pulled himself to his feet and stretched his back. Must his every movement remind her of his attractiveness? When he reached down to adjust the back of his kilt again, she had had enough.

Her guilt got the best of her. "Enough, MacGregor, 'tis enough. Let me see it."

He placed his hands over his heart in an exaggerated gesture and turned up his smile a notch. "I am now your husband. I am nay man-whore. I didnae expect flowery words of love. Howbeit I hoped ye would have at least asked me nicely to see it."

Rolling her eyes, Liadain brought herself to her feet. "Ye are verra humorous," she said dryly. She approached her husband and reached out and touched his arm. "*Deanntag* should only sting for a bit, but most men donna place their entire bare behind in contact with it."

He chuckled in response. "I think ye mean to say that most men donna have their entire bare arse thrown into it."

"Mayhap," she replied sheepishly. "Just let me take a look." When her husband's kilt fell to the ground and his eyes clung to hers, analyzing her response, she slapped him playfully in the chest. "Cease, ye rogue." She could not help laughing aloud to herself.

One corner of his mouth was pulled into a tight smile. "All right, healer. Have yourself a look," he said, facing forward in all his Highland glory.

She grabbed his brawny arm and twisted him around. "Turn aroun—" Her words stopped in mid-sentence. Even in the dim light of the fire, she could see that his firm buttocks were reddened with an angry rash.

"Well?"

"Ye have a rash. Does it itch or burn?"

"Both."

"Umm…I need to…er, what I mean to say is—"

"For god's sake, healer, just touch it already."

She rubbed her fingers gently over his tight buttocks and felt small, raised bumps brushing against her hand. Damn. It was worse than she had thought. "Sit down and hand me the water," she ordered. MacGregor lowered himself to the ground and draped his kilt loosely over his lap. He handed her the flask, and she turned and walked away from him.

"What are ye doing?" he asked with a puzzled look.

"I am making mud." Liadain dropped to her knees and dumped a healthy portion of water into the dirt.

"For my arse?"

She nodded. "Aye, for your arse."

"And mud will stop the burning?"

"Ye place the mud on the infected areas and let it dry. Once it dries, ye brush it off and it should pull out any remaining nettles. It should also help with the rash." She continued to stir the dirt until it formed a thick and pasty mud. "There. That should do it."

He stood, once again dropped his kilt, and walked over to the mud mixture. He bent to scoop up a handful and rubbed a portion onto his buttocks, missing the rash entirely.

"Ye missed the bottom part of the rash. Move lower." She shook her finger at the spot. "There. There."

"Healer, I cannae see it. Ye will have to apply it," he said impatiently. He stood there as naked as the day he was born. Well, although he did not look like a newborn bairn, he was bare. He looked vulnerable.

Liadain grabbed the remaining mud from his hands. "Verra well. Turn back around."

She knelt to the ground so his naked bottom was at eye level. At what point in her life did fate decide she needed to be here at this particular moment? Fate was surely laughing at her expense. As she delicately applied the mud to the lowest possible part of his infected area, another thought came to mind. What if other *parts* were having a similar reaction as well?

Swallowing hard, she stood. She was a healer. She could handle anything—well, almost anything. "I am finished, but I have to ask this of ye. Did the *deanntag* reach other areas of ye as well?"

MacGregor turned around and cast a roguish grin. "Ye mean my co—"

"I mean your other parts," she said through clenched teeth.

"Aye. My bollocks."

"Verra well," she growled. She grabbed some more mud and knelt before him. "I give ye fair warning…"

She lifted her hand to her husband's bollocks and was just about to apply the mud when he mumbled, "A wee bit to the right."

Liadain rose in one fluid motion. With a quick swipe

of her hands, she rubbed the mud all over MacGregor's arrogant visage. *"Se do bheatha."* *You are welcome.*

Fifteen

England, Eve of the State Opening of Parliament

As Thomas Percy glanced out at Parliament House, the golden hues of dusk brushed the horizon. Percy sighed and rubbed his brow. He had waited for more than a fortnight for this moment. And now it was finally here. How ironic it was to see such a beautiful sight on the eve of a day that would be filled with tragedy and despair. A new dawn would bring hope, and if luck was on their side, a new reign of prosperity. He would not fail.

He had a perfect view of Parliament House. Hiding in a corner alcove, his bow secured at his side, he would lie in wait until he was able to make his move. He had contemplated every possible consequence of his mission and knew one thing for certain: he would not waver.

Catesby, Fawkes, and that devilish Dunnehl had reviewed the plan so many times that Percy knew it like the back of his hand. He was not exactly thrilled to be working with Dunnehl, but the man paid well and they certainly shared the same cause. If their efforts could not remove King James from the throne and replace him with Lady Arbella Stuart, there was no other option.

The king would die.

Lady Arbella Stuart's great-great-grandfather had been King Henry VII of England; therefore, she had been the natural candidate for succession to the English crown after her cousin, Queen Elizabeth. But at the last moment, the queen's secretaries of state had swayed from their rightful path and decided to confer the crown upon James VI of Scotland, whose mother was Mary, Queen of Scots. Lady Arbella had been born in England, whereas King James was born in Scotland. That fact alone should have barred him from succeeding.

Their liege had certainly made a mess of things. They had prayed for governmental change, but one bad decision after another had led to discord and resentment among his vassals. His Majesty had opportunity to change the future, but instead, he had kept Queen Elizabeth's Privy Councillors in office. Between widespread taxation and the same failed oversight, the country was falling apart. Not to mention the repression of Catholics being the biggest travesty of all. England needed strong supporters to take a stand and regain control. Her survival depended upon it.

A shadowy figure moved against the darkened wall of Parliament House. If Percy had not been glancing at that particular spot at that single moment, he would have missed it. Fawkes slipped in a side door. Damn, the man was good. Percy would give him that.

He closed his eyes, resting his head against the cool stone. On the morrow, there would be no more king and no more Parliament. With the government destroyed, the country would have no choice. England would be forced to start anew. Lady Stuart would be on the throne one way or another.

Percy awoke later with a start, disoriented. He shook his head to clear the cobwebs, and it took him a few moments to gain his bearings. Muffled noises echoed from below. It did not take him long to register the sounds of the night guard making rounds. It must be nearly midnight. Darkness enveloped him, the only glow of light coming from Parliament House. He remained frozen in his nook, the urge to take a piss overwhelming. Willing away the thought, he did not even attempt to stand, not wanting to chance being spotted.

His heart jumped when shouts rang out and additional guards ran through the same side door that Fawkes'had used earlier. Damn. Percy did not even have time to blink before a handful of guards exited the building with someone in tow.

Fawkes.

Fawkes's capture did not come as a surprise. Catesby and Dunnehl had certainly planned for everything—even Fawkes and Percy's apprehension. Fawkes was dependable, and once given an order, the man would follow it without question. That was one of the reasons he had been chosen. Percy had no doubt that Fawkes would stick to their plan.

As the men had discussed, Fawkes would admit he had acted alone and confess that the thirty-six barrels of gunpowder he guarded were for the sole purpose of blowing Parliament straight to hell. Fawkes was the perfect soldier—and the perfect distraction. The daft fools would never think that a more devious assassination plot was underway.

By the time they realized that their beloved King James was dead, it would be too late. Percy felt privileged to complete the mission on his own. Besides, Percy and Fawkes were both prepared to die for their cause. They had nothing to lose.

Sitting high on his perch, Percy continued to listen to the uproar below for hours. Once the commotion diminished and the time was right, he crawled into position. It should not be too much longer. Dutifully studying his line of sight, he found the perfect angle.

❦

King James was furious. What fool would go to such lengths as to attempt to blow up the whole body of state? The soldier would be executed—after the man was tortured and revealed any other information. The king would make certain that the daft man had acted alone, and if he had not, the others would meet the same dire fate.

Riding to Parliament House atop his snow-white mount, the king was encircled by his most trusted guards. Addressing these sessions of Parliament was by no means an easy feat, and he went through his speech over and over again in his mind. He had to find a way to control the nonconforming English Catholics. They were nothing but a thorn in his side. Then there was the small matter of trying to convince Parliament to support money subsidies as well.

The king let out a deep sigh as they approached the walls that would imprison him for the remainder of the day. Hopefully, this session would prove more promising than the last. He was lifting his leg to dismount when a shooting pain ripped through his upper body.

Bound by sharp, stabbing agony, he fell to the ground with a heavy thump. An arrow protruded from his chest. Lifting his hand, he saw that his fingers were covered with blood.

Shouts rang out from all around him. It was complete and utter chaos. The king struggled to remain conscious, his breath shallow. It was so difficult to breathe. Someone may have spoken to him, but his mind became cluttered from all of the commotion.

"The arrow is through his back. We will have to pull it out."

"He'll bleed to death."

"The arrow came from the rooftop! Over there! Over there!"

"His Majesty was encircled by guards. No one could have made that shot from there."

A bitter voice cut through the madness like a splash of cold water. "No one but MacGregor…"

Something in the king's mind clicked as he thought back on MacGregor's demeanor when he was forced to wed the Campbell's sister. "Bring. Me. MacGregor."

Sixteen

Glenorchy

EVERY STEP HER MOUNT TOOK MADE LIADAIN'S HEART heavy with dread. Her thoughts pounded her brain like wave after crashing wave. What she believed Laird MacGregor would think of her no longer mattered. She was about to find out, and this bitter torture would finally come to an end.

Laird MacGregor's home stood impressively before her on an island surrounded by green, grassy moss. It was smaller than Castle Campbell, but it was an elegant castle with a stone barbican with round turrets and square towers. The clean breeze of the loch teased her senses, and the water mirrored the deeper color of the sky. It was quite lovely.

They rode single file over the *cabhsair* that extended over the water to the island. They traveled under a huge portcullis and then reached the courtyard. An elderly man greeted them. With a full head of gray hair, the man stood tall, proud. His eyes held the silent wisdom of the ages.

"'Tis good to see ye, Niall," said her husband. The man grabbed the reins as MacGregor slid from his mount.

"*Ciamar a tha sibh?*" Niall asked with a warm smile. *How are you?*

"*Tha gu math. Tapadh leibh.*" *I am fine. Thank you.* "'Tis good to be home."

MacGregor patted his horse on the rump and then approached Liadain. He had extended his hand to assist her when he was abruptly attacked from behind. "What the hell?" A huge beast jumped onto her husband's back, pushing him flat against her mount.

"Magaidh!" called Rosalia in a scolding tone. Her dusky rose dress hugged her full-figured frame, and her chestnut hair had grown since the last time Liadain had seen her. "Come!" she ordered unsuccessfully.

Twisting around, MacGregor pushed the dog away and smiled at Rosalia. "I see his lairdship didnae have the bollocks to take ye to Glengarry after all," he said with a trace of laughter in his voice.

"Och, nay. I took her to Glengarry. 'Tis where we spoke our vows, Brother." Laird MacGregor came toward him with an unreadable expression on his face.

The man looked very formidable, his chest broader than her husband's. The laird was certainly handsome in a rugged sense, but not quite as bonny as her new husband. Well, not too many men or women were blessed with a prettier face. Though there was no denying that the men hailed from the same clan.

Her husband smirked in response. "And I thought ye would be somewhere…*lairding*. I see naught has changed."

As quickly as the remark was thrown, Laird

MacGregor's lips broke into a smile. "'Tis good to see ye, Declan." They embraced in a manly hug and each slapped the other on the back.

Laird MacGregor's eyes narrowed when he spotted Liadain, and she became increasingly uneasy under his scrutiny. As he stepped toward her, she drew in a sharp breath. To her surprise, he reached up and lifted her from her mount. "Thank ye for your words to King James. I know it must have been difficult to speak against the bloody...er, your brother. Ye have my thanks."

She managed to smile and wondered if he would feel the same when he found out she was wed to his brother. When he looked as though he would question her further, her husband interceded.

"There is much to explain. Let us drink some ale and I will tell ye all about it."

Laird MacGregor nodded and turned, slapping her husband on the shoulder. "Aye, let us seek Aiden."

The men left her standing there without as much as a backward glance. How typical of the past three weeks. Liadain wondered if her husband would always be so difficult to comprehend and jumped when a hand touched her own.

"Liadain, 'tis so good to see ye again. I thank ye for all ye have done." Rosalia smiled warmly.

"It was naught, my lady."

"My *lady?* After all we have been through, ye donna need to 'my lady' me."

"How do ye fare?" asked Liadain. Her brother had not often taken others against their will and held them in the bowels of hell.

Archie had been an idiot for thinking Ciaran MacGregor would blindly storm Castle Campbell and start another clan war against the king's orders. It was difficult to stay the memory of her brother holding Aisling and Rosalia captive in the dungeon. His treatment of them had been repulsive—no food, no water, left to sit in the muck for hours. When Archie had ordered the death of Aisling's bairn, Liadain knew she had to intervene. Enough was more than enough.

To her surprise, Rosalia simply glowed now. "Ciaran and I wed, and I couldnae be more joyful. Come inside. Ye must be weary from your journey."

The interior of the great hall was quite large. A staircase swept down, and lovely tapestries hung on the wall. A beautiful painted-glass window was displayed at the top of the staircase, and colored prisms danced against the wall. There were two fireplaces in the hall, each adorned with wooden carvings of animals and fir trees. Long wooden tables and benches graced the floor, and a raised dais boasted several intricately carved chairs.

"'Tis true, then. The rogue has returned from court."

As Liadain glanced up, Aisling walked down the staircase. Her long reddish curls complemented her ivory skin.

"My lady, 'tis wonderful to see ye again," said Liadain, reaching out and taking the hands of her sister-by-marriage.

She was aware that Aisling's petite frame and graceful appearance were not to be underestimated. Aiden's wife definitely held fire when crossed, making the fiercest of men run for cover—mainly her husband.

Aisling glanced briefly to Rosalia, and then turned back to Liadain and smiled warmly. "Ye were calling me by my given name before, Liadain. We arenae so formal here. After what we shared…please." Aisling gestured for them to sit.

Two young maids whispered and giggled as they passed through the hall, and Rosalia nodded toward the women. "They already hear of the rogue's return. So what of ye, Liadain? Where do ye travel?"

She looked away and could not meet their questioning eyes. She immediately stiffened. Having spent so much time worrying about Laird MacGregor and his brother, she had never given much thought to the MacGregor women. What would they think? When she tried to speak, her voice wavered.

Aisling reached out and touched her arm. "Liadain? What has happened?"

⁂

"*Wife*?" Aiden chuckled, and Ciaran threw back his head and roared with laughter.

Clenching his teeth, Declan ground out, "I donna know what ye both find so humorous. Did ye nae hear me when I said that Castle Campbell is mine?" He knew he sounded abrupt, but their reaction was not as he had expected.

A silent message passed between his older brothers. "We heard ye, Brother. It only comes as a wee bit of a shock that His Majesty ordered ye to wed," said Ciaran with an amused expression.

"A bloody Campbell," Declan reminded them, running his hand through his hair. How he wanted to wipe that smug look from Ciaran's face. "I won the tournament fairly, and she wasnae part of the prize. Cranborne—"

"Ye know she is naught like her brother. Aiden and I are joyful for your union. 'Tis best this happened to ye, nay matter how it came to be."

"What?" Surely he did not hear them correctly. He was shackled—to a bloody Campbell. A female. The enemy. Were his brothers in their cups? How in the hell could they be joyful about such a union?

"Ye heard my words. I think your anger is misplaced. The Campbell's lands are my own. Castle Campbell is yours, and it comes with a bride. What more could ye ask for? I couldnae have planned it better myself," said Ciaran with a wry grin.

Aiden patted Declan on the shoulder. Thankfully, his brother removed his hand quickly for it was about to be broken. "Declan, ye have yourself a bonny wife and certainly have bedded more than enough women to satisfy your wenching ways. Give it time. Ye may find that marriage even agrees with ye. Look at Aisling and me, and Rosalia and Ciaran."

"Aye," he spat. "Both women hold your bollocks in the palms of their hands. 'Tis something I clearly envy."

"Nay matter what ye think, 'tis done. Ye have a home and a wife—responsibility. I trust ye to see to both," said Ciaran, his voice ringing with command.

Declan shook his head in disgust. "Of course, Your Majesty. Ye know my purpose in life is to do your bidding," he said, holding his hand over his heart. Ciaran was about to speak when Declan added, "Lest I forget...Rosalia's mother was at court with Dunnehl."

Stirring uneasily in his chair, Ciaran sat back and there was a heavy silence. "Tell me—everything."

"Lady Armstrong approached Liadain. Liadain spoke to her freely and didnae know of Rosalia's past until I told her as much," said Declan.

"Damn." Rolling his neck to the side, Ciaran sighed. "Her mother knows she is here at Glenorchy?"

Declan shrugged. "She knows she *was* here. So does Dunnehl."

Pinching the bridge of his nose, Ciaran grunted. "Was that all?"

"I trust the healer to have told me everything."

"See, Brother? Already ye are trusting your wife," said Aiden, patting him again on the shoulder.

Declan glared at him.

"I donna want ye to mention any of this to Rosalia. She will only be distraught, and I willnae have it. Her mother and Dunnehl have done enough damage," ordered Ciaran.

Declan nodded. He would never do anything to cause Rosalia more grief. The poor lass had been through too much. "Do ye think Dunnehl or her mother will come?"

"It doesnae matter. She is now my wife. She is mine," Ciaran said sternly. "Nae a single word of this to anyone. Why donna ye see your wife settled? We will ride to Castle Campbell on the morrow. Our men will be relieved that they nay longer hold the castle for the king, but for our own. Most of the Campbells took their leave when your wife went to court, unsure of the king's judgment."

After Ciaran's dismissal, Declan took a leisurely walk to the bailey. Damn. There went his hope for a secret escape. Castle Campbell. He would need to think of another name.

"Declan!" called Rosalia while the massive dog nipped at her skirts.

"Who is that wily beast?"

"'Tis Magaidh. James brought her with him from Mangerton."

"James?"

Rosalia reached down and scratched the dog behind the ears. She did not need to bend too far. "Aye, James Montgomery." She cast her eyes downward and spoke in a soft tone. "He was the captain of my father's guard, my friend. He is as a brother to me."

Something in his mind clicked. "Ciaran spoke of Montgomery. The man helped ye escape Dunnehl's cohorts. As I recall, my brother didnae take too kindly to your familiarity with Montgomery."

She laughed. "Aye, they donna exactly see eye to eye."

Declan rubbed his chin. "Hmm…then I would think to befriend this man."

"He is hunting now but will return this eve. Ye two would probably get along. Donna get along too well, lest Ciaran thinks ye are plotting against him," she jested.

"Any man that doesnae see Ciaran as a god is my friend," he murmured with a heavy dose of sarcasm.

"Declan…"

He waved her off. "Enough of Ciaran." He lifted

her from her feet and swung her around. "I hear congratulations are in order. I now have another bonny sister-by-marriage."

She giggled when he placed her back on her feet. "Aye, I love your brother with all my heart."

"I saw it in your eyes from the first time we met."

Her face flushed. "I hear congratulations are in order for ye as well. Liadain is so kind. I wish ye both much happiness." She smiled. "Will ye be staying for a while?"

"Ciaran, Aiden, and I will travel to Castle Campbell on the morrow."

"With so much haste? I was hoping ye would remain for a bit," she said in a disappointed tone.

Declan grabbed her shoulders and glanced down into her bonny eyes. "My dearest Rosalia. Ye are now a married lass and shouldnae be dallying with the likes of me. I am truly flattered, but ye must move on with your life. What would my brother say?"

His new sister-by-marriage slapped him in the chest. "Cease, ye rogue. Lest ye forget, ye are married as well. One would think ye would nay longer speak as such. I see some habits are difficult to break. Besides, I can assure ye as a new bride that I wouldnae take too kindly to your wenching words."

"I may have spoken the vows and I may be shackled for the rest of my days, but I willnae mind my words. They are my own and I willnae change them—or me," he quickly added. "Being wed doesnae mean I am dead."

"Nae unless your new bonny bride kills ye," Rosalia muttered. Peeking around him, she smiled at Liadain in greeting. "Did Aisling get ye all settled then?"

The healer nodded. "Aye." She raised her brow at Declan. "I didnae know if ye wanted me to unpack your belongings. I wasnae sure when we would be traveling to Castle Campbell."

"We leave on the morrow."

Seventeen

Rosalia sat to Liadain's left and MacGregor to the right. If Rosalia had not been conversing with her during the evening meal, Liadain would have been eating alone. MacGregor had barely uttered a word to her since their arrival at Glenorchy.

She straightened her spine, resolved to hide her issues. "Are ye joyful to be home, Husband?" She reached for her tankard, thinking that perhaps if she called him something other than "MacGregor," it would improve his darkened temperament.

He raised his brow, then glanced back to his meal. She had almost given up hope that he would respond when he finally opened his mouth. "'Tis good to be home...*healer.*"

He should've kept it shut.

She placed a piece of bread in her mouth before scathing words decided to escape it. Killing the arrogant beast in the great hall amidst a room full of MacGregors would not be in her best interest.

Her husband cleared his throat and captured her eyes. "My apologies that my mood has been so..."

"Foul?"

"I wasnae exactly thinking of that particular word, but aye." He nodded reluctantly.

"Then cease. 'Tis verra annoying," she said tersely.

He chuckled. "Are ye always so forthcoming?"

"We are wed. There is nay need for games."

As though she had struck him, MacGregor stiffened. "Thank ye for reminding me. How could I forget?" he muttered loud enough for her to hear.

His words left her with an inexplicable emptiness. Liadain settled back, disappointed. The rogue did not want to be shackled, and he clearly let her know it at every turn.

❧

Declan had never thought the word "husband" would ever escape her lips. Why must the healer constantly remind him of the weight he carried? Deep in his gut he knew that he needed to make this work, but damn. Every time he brought himself closer to accepting that fact, he lost control. His freedom was being stripped from him far too early.

He gulped another mouthful of ale. What he needed was a distraction. He glanced around the great hall and spotted Aire and Mary. The women were huddled against the far wall, their smoldering gazes reminding him of a sorely missed past. With their long auburn tresses and full hips, the lasses were indeed the perfect pair to ease his troubles.

Mary whispered something to Aire and ambled toward him with swaying hips. She looked like a cat on the prowl. She bent over and gave him a perfect view of her ample bosom as she picked up a tray and raised her brow. "Welcome home," she said with a sultry glance.

Declan gave her an amused look. "Thank ye. 'Tis good to be home."

When Mary hesitated a bit too long and her eyes held another meaning entirely, the healer cleared her throat. Casting Mary a haughty glance, his wife spoke in a clipped tone. "I am Lady Liadain MacGregor. The man ye are so blatantly offering yourself to is my husband."

Mary's eyes held his a moment longer, and then she turned and bowed her head. "My apologies, my lady," she murmured, turning on her heel.

He reached around the back of the healer's chair and leaned in close. Lowering his voice, he whispered in her ear. "Jealous?"

"Nay. I willnae be disrespected so openly."

Removing his arm from the back of the chair, he shifted in his seat. He felt an odd twinge of disappointment that his wife was not envious of another woman. He was studying her profile intently when Rosalia called out, startling him.

"There ye are," she said, speaking like a mother scolding her son.

"I know I am late. Pray tell me ye saved me something to eat, Rosalia." A man came toward them with an arrogant swagger and a build similar to Ciaran's. His ash-blond hair was tied at the nape of his neck and he carried a bow. He stepped onto the dais and walked around the table. Reaching Rosalia, the man bent over and kissed her on the cheek.

Ciaran cleared his throat as the man deliberately

ignored him, reached out, and stole a piece of meat from Rosalia's hand, tossing it straight into his mouth. When Ciaran's face hardened and his jaw started to tick, Declan chuckled. He liked this man already.

He pulled himself to his feet and approached the man. "I assume ye are Montgomery."

Raising his brow, Montgomery stood to his full height and studied Declan for a moment. "And ye must be the rog—"

Rosalia reached up and slapped Montgomery's arm. "James," she said in a scolding tone.

Montgomery extended his hand and Declan shook it. "I have heard much about ye as well," said Declan, peering around the man's shoulder and casting a glance at Ciaran.

His lairdship returned a blank stare, but Declan knew the true meaning behind Ciaran's look. Declan would definitely befriend this man. Being too occupied with firing his brother's ire, Declan failed to notice that Montgomery had stepped around him. When he heard Rosalia groan, he whipped his head around.

His newfound friend had lifted the healer's hand, brushing a brief kiss on the top of it. "I have ne'er seen a bonnier lass," Montgomery said smoothly.

The healer giggled and something within Declan stirred at the sound of her giddiness. He did not remember his wife ever laughing that way with him. He had never denied her beauty. The problem was everything else that came with it.

"Your tresses are as black as a starless night." Montgomery continued with his flowery words.

"James, this is…" Rosalia interjected.

"My wife," said Declan with more conviction in his voice than he had intended.

Montgomery wisely released the healer's hand and cast a roguish grin much like Declan's own. "Then let me congratulate ye. Your wife is simply exquisite. Ye are a verra lucky man."

Declan smirked. "Luck has naught to do with it."

～⁂～

Liadain could not make her excuses soon enough. Men were raking on her nerves—well, one man in particular. She sought the solace of the garden and sat on a bench as a flowery scent tickled her nose.

One more night and she would be home. It would be in her best interest to resume her daily activities and keep herself occupied. Of course her healing plants would need tending, and there would always be someone in the village who suffered an ailment. Pondering her marital arrangements, she was curious whether she would keep her own bedchamber or if MacGregor would accept Archie's. Her husband's thoughts were so difficult to discern that anything was possible.

MacGregor had not been close with her since their time together at the loch. She tried not to take it personally, but her mind constantly burned with the memory. She often recalled the warmth of his touch, shivering with vivid recollection. She didn't remember Robert rousing her passion to that degree.

As rapidly as the pictures came back into her mind, she stayed them. The heat she so openly welcomed turned cold. MacGregor did not love her. He did not want her. He barely acknowledged her existence.

Liadain was not sure how much time had passed, but since the sun had set some time ago, she surmised that she had better take her leave while she could still see. Deliberately avoiding all the MacGregors, she circled along the outer wall of the bailey undetected. She'd had years to perfect the art of masking her presence. Lifting her skirts, she tiptoed up the steps. When she reached the hall to her chamber, she made a mad dash.

She rushed inside her bedchamber and leaned back against the wooden door. She stripped her gown, donned her nightrail, and climbed into bed. Liadain could barely contain her excitement, knowing she would be able to crawl into her own bed on the morrow. She pulled up the blankets with a deep, contented sigh and closed her eyes.

She swore she had just fallen into a blissful slumber when she awoke with a start. The light from the single candle had almost dissipated. She could barely make out MacGregor fumbling his way at the foot of the bed. She rolled over, trying desperately to ignore him.

The bed shook and MacGregor cursed.

Unfortunately, she was now fully awake. "What are ye doing?" she asked, sitting up and blowing the tresses from her eyes.

"My apologies that I woke ye."

"Ye moved the entire bed and ye didnae answer my question. What are ye doing?" She pulled up her knees and rested her chin on top.

"I'm searching for my sack."

Liadain gave a quick nod to her right. "'Tis over there on the floor. 'Tis late. What do ye want with it now?"

He lifted his bundle and started to walk toward the door. "I will sleep below stairs."

"With your whores?" The words were blurted out before she even realized they had left her lips. She was empty and drained, but that was no excuse. This argument would be entirely her fault.

He stopped dead in his tracks. "What?"

Her husband's vexation was evident, and her annoyance increased when she found that her hands were shaking. The last thing she wanted was to start another argument, but when she did not immediately respond, MacGregor dropped the bag to the floor. He stood to his full, imposing height and she became aware that this might not bode well for her.

"What did ye say?" he asked with a silken thread of warning.

Biting her lip, Liadain looked away.

"Healer!"

She flinched at his tone. "It was naught," she said quietly. She watched him out of the corner of her eye as he sat down beside her on the edge of the bed.

"Do ye honestly believe that I would bed another woman?"

She turned her head away. How did he expect her to answer such a question? His actions this eve did not reinforce a favorable opinion of him.

Curses fell from his mouth. "Ye donna have to answer. Ye just did." A chill hung on his words.

Liadain glared at him with burning, reproachful eyes, and her mood veered sharply to anger. "What am I supposed to think? Ye donna speak to me. Ye barely look at me. Ye blame me for this marriage and constantly remind me of that fact at every turn. Ye clearly donna want me. So tell me, MacGregor, how am I to believe ye will stay true to your vows?" Her accusing voice stabbed the air.

He chuckled nastily. "If I have to answer that question, then ye donna know me at all. Ye insult me and my honor."

She shot him a cold look. "Insult ye? Ye have done naught but insult me ever since we met. I may be a Campbell, half-Campbell," she clarified. "But I am naught like my brother. I donna want to play the games of men and yet I always find myself in the middle of their plots. Praise the saints," she said, throwing her hands up in the air in exasperation. "I didnae ask for this either, but I at least try. We are bonded and bound by God. There is nay undoing what has already been done. I know ye didnae want this, but must I hear it at every turn? If we donna stand together, we will surely fall apart. Is that what ye want?"

He stared, wordlessly.

"Ye were kinder to me before we wed. I thought we may have even been friends. Granted, your views have changed since then, but they donna have to. I am still me. If ye want the kind of marriage where I am to be seen and nae heard, that is clearly your choice, but nae one I would make. I have seen the kindness within ye and I wish to have it back. This man who has nay concern for anyone but himself isnae the same man I have come to know. If ye decide to bed other women, I—"

MacGregor brushed a gentle kiss across her forehead. "Shh...I willnae bed another. I am a man of my word and I stay true to my vows. I donna want anger between us. Let me just hold ye." He lay down beside her and pulled her close, her bottom nestling into his groin.

Liadain drew a deep breath. What did this mean? She had no idea, but she was determined not to reveal her joy at seeing him like this. Her fingernails gently stroked her husband's forearm as he held her snugly against him. She was fully aware of where his warm flesh touched her. The gentle snort in her ear made her chuckle. The infamous rogue had fallen asleep.

∽

Sunlight glimmered upon her eyes and she brushed her hair away from her face. Liadain reached over and patted the bed. It did not take her long to realize she was alone. The empty bed left her with an inexplicable feeling of emptiness, but MacGregor probably wanted to get an early start to Castle Campbell. And more importantly, she would be home at last.

She threw the blankets from the bed. Home was waiting for her, calling her. She donned her day dress and repacked her sack, thankful that this would be the last time she'd need to. Not wanting to keep her husband waiting, she hefted her burden out the door and dropped it to the floor. When she glanced down the hall and no one was there to assist her, she decided to carry the bag herself.

She dragged the bundle down the steps. When she finally made it to the bottom, she decided to let the heavy load sit. Someone would be along shortly and could secure it to her mount. She walked into the great hall with a lighter spring in her step.

Rosalia was playing with the giant dog. "Good morn."

"Give me Ciaran's tunic, ye beastly dog," said Rosalia through clenched teeth, pulling the cloth from the dog's jaws. She glanced up and smiled. "Liadain, I hope ye slept well."

She nodded. "Have ye seen my husband?"

"Aye. He didnae tell ye?" Rosalia gazed at her questioningly. "He took his leave this morn to Castle Campbell."

Eighteen

DECLAN BREATHED DEEPLY, THE MORNING AIR FRESH and crisp. He needed all the help he could get to clear the cobwebs in his head. With Ciaran and Aiden by his side, he galloped to Castle Campbell to inspect his new home.

When he had awoken at dawn to soft, warm flesh snuggled against him, he had thought he was dreaming, that an angel as pure as the heavens was sent from above to capture him in her embrace. It took him a moment to recognize that the temptress in his bed was undoubtedly his own wife. They had conversed when he woke her. Well, the healer talked; he merely listened. A sharp pang of guilt stabbed at him. As of late, he could admit he was downright bitter at times.

When the lass had suspected that he would bed Mary and Aire, he had needed all his strength to keep from strangling his wife. Granted, his mind may have wondered about the wenches in his own private musings, but he would have never bedded them. God's teeth! He was wed. He was not an idiot. He had spoken his vows, and his mother would've castrated him had he not obeyed them.

As they advanced to Castle Campbell, he saw that his new home was even more desolate than he remembered leaving it. Ciaran was right. Although some of the villagers remained, most of the Campbell clan had dispersed when his brother ended the bloody Campbell's life. How fitting that the waste removal had already been completed.

When the Campbell's men surrendered, Ciaran had given them a choice. Wait for King James's verdict on their laird's treachery or take their leave peacefully. Fortunately, most of them chose the latter.

The men thundered through the gates. Who would have thought that a MacGregor would now own the home of King James's right-hand man? The bloody Campbell was probably rolling over in his grave. A smile played over Declan's lips as he glanced at the tower house that dominated the courtyard.

"I see the look upon your face, Brother. Ye should be proud. This is a formidable castle," Ciaran said as he dismounted.

"'Tis a wee bit bigger than Glenorchy, but ye probably need something as big as this to fit your swelled head," countered Aiden, tying off his mount.

Declan shrugged. "Mayhap, but the space should make it easier to avoid my wife."

Aiden chuckled. "Good point. I may pay ye a visit more often to escape Aisling's ire."

Giving Aiden a slap on the shoulder, Declan cast him a knowing glance. "And ye know Aisling always has a way of finding ye. Ye cannae hide even though ye try."

"There is that."

"Ye should probably think upon a stable master. Ye will need to find someone knowledgeable to care for the mounts. Mayhap someone who remains from the village. Come. Let us view your new home, Brother," said Ciaran with pride.

Declan was eager to explore. They walked into the great hall, which boasted a vaulted ceiling. Finely woven tapestries were displayed on the gray stone walls, and fine wooden furnishings graced the hall in abundance. There were four floors of accommodation. The storage cellar, kitchens, great hall, and solar were on the first floor and chambers on the two upper floors. Since the men were already too familiar with the dungeon, they deliberately did not seek it out. With all the fine furnishings, this was obviously the home of a man who'd been in favor with King James.

And now it was his.

"Are ye speechless, Brother?" Ciaran regarded him with amusement.

"I donna think I have ever witnessed such an occurrence," jested Aiden, a flash of humor crossing his features.

For the first time that Declan could remember, he was friendly, smiling, and relaxed with his older brothers. "I am truly in awe."

His brothers laughed. "Before ye and Liadain take up residence here, ye need to seek men at arms," directed Ciaran. "I will speak among my men and find ye a captain for your guard."

"I will require some MacGregor men, but there is nay need to appoint the captain of my guard," said Declan.

Ciaran hesitated, measuring him for a moment. "Why? Ye need to have—"

"I have already found him."

An uncertainty crept into Ciaran's expression. "Who?"

Declan observed him, analyzing his reaction. He loved to unnerve his lairding brother. Wishing he could freeze this particular moment in time, he paused. "Montgomery." Ciaran's eyes widened for a brief moment. If Declan had not been watching, he would have missed it.

"Damn," spat Ciaran. Aiden chuckled until Ciaran's eyes darkened in warning. Declan knew that glare all too well. "Why, Brother? Why would ye appoint Montgomery as the captain of your guard?" He threw up his hands in the air in exasperation.

"How quickly ye forget that Montgomery was the captain of Armstrong's guard. The man protected Rosalia and has more than enough skill to fill the title. And besides, he has nay place to call home," said Declan defensively.

Aiden chuckled again and Ciaran snarled at him. "Why must I take in all of the strays? 'Tis bad enough I get strapped with Magaidh drooling in my boots and ripping my tunics to shreds, but now I will have Montgomery constantly nipping at my wife's heels. The man was just about to take his leave."

"Aye, 'tis why I offered him the title. And Montgomery does seem to have a sweet fondness for your wife." In an exaggerated attempt, Declan winked at Ciaran.

"I think Montgomery overplays his attentiveness to my wife only to fire my ire."

Declan waved him off. "Ye worry too much, Brother. He cares for Rosalia as a sister."

"I watched as he attempted to dally with your new wife as well. I am surprised ye didnae flatten him in the middle of the great hall."

Turning his head away slightly, Declan knew his face had reddened. He did not think his thoughts were so openly known. He would need to be more careful, more guarded.

Aiden clapped his hands once. "What say ye? Should we take our leave and return to Glenorchy now?"

"Ye both can take your leave. There is something I wish to do before I return. I should be back around the time ye sup."

Ciaran raised his brow. "Are ye sure? We can stay until ye are ready."

"Nay. I will join ye later."

❧

Fury almost choked Liadain and curses fell from her mouth. She found herself wandering aimlessly and ended up at the stables, where she poured out her grief to her horse. At least the mare was a sympathetic listener.

She wasn't sure how much time had passed, but as soon as she headed back toward the keep, Rosalia and Aisling sought her out.

"Is everything all right?" Rosalia asked, giving Liadain a warm smile. "Ye seemed somewhat distraught this morn."

"If that rogue is causing ye grief, ye let me know and I will deal with him. I have had plenty of practice keeping Aiden on a straight path," Aisling offered, placing her hands on her hips.

"Ye both are verra kind, but I assure ye I am well."

Aisling and Rosalia exchanged glances and then grabbed Liadain's arms. The women pulled her along through the courtyard and headed toward the gardens. When they reached the same bench Liadain had occupied the night before, the women flanked her and made her sit. Aisling and Rosalia sat down on each side of her, and an unsettling feeling settled in the pit of her stomach.

"We are sisters-by-marriage. If we donna stick together, the men will surely make us daft. We depend upon one another and naught ye speak travels beyond our ears," Aisling said reassuringly. "When Aiden and I first wed, we were in love. Let me tell ye, it was a long, tedious journey to get there, and believe me when I say that it wasnae an easy feat. After Lady MacGregor passed, I was the only woman in attendance—with three daft men under the same roof. That was indeed painful."

Rosalia touched Liadain's shoulder. "When Ciaran brought me to Glenorchy, we had many troubles. If it wasnae for Aisling's counsel, I donna know what I would have done."

Aisling patted Liadain's thigh. "We know Declan is—well, Declan. We have all tried to help him, but if someone doesnae want your assistance, ye cannae make them take it. We are here for ye if ye want to talk about things. Or scream in frustration. We do understand and want ye to know that ye arenae alone."

There was a heavy silence.

Liadain had never needed anyone but herself. Now she had two women offering her support. She was not sure how to respond. She smiled sheepishly, thinking to be honest. "I am honored that ye offer me comfort, but I truly donna understand why."

Aisling's brows shot up in surprise. "We are kin."

She gasped. "Kin? Why would ye consider me as such? My brother held ye both and—"

"Ye saved us," Aisling simply stated.

"But I am a Campbell." She bit her lip and glanced down at her hands.

Rosalia rubbed her back in a soothing gesture. "Ye are wrong. Ye are a MacGregor and we are kin. We care for our own."

Caught unaware by their affection and support, Liadain merely smiled. "I donna know what to say to that. Ye honor me."

Aisling waved her off. "Cease. Now tell us what is on your mind. We cannae read it."

As soon as Liadain opened her mouth, words flew out like a raging river. She wasn't sure of half the things she said.

"Men are fools," spat Aisling. "They donna know what they want until ye tell them. Besides, ye are a verra bonny lass and ye know one thing for certain. Declan enjoys women overmuch. He will eventually soften toward ye. Ye think now that he has all the power." She giggled, shaking her head. "Ye hold more than ye think."

"I donna know about that. He said we were taking our leave for Castle Campbell yester eve and I had hoped to start anew. Yet, here I am and he isnae," Liadain spoke with disappointment.

"Liadain, he traveled first with Ciaran and Aiden to inspect the castle. I donna think he would take his new wife into a home that has nay servants. Ye donna even have a cook," explained Rosalia, giving her a sympathetic smile.

"I suppose ye are right."

Aisling stood and straightened her skirts. "Ye know what I think? Ye need a distraction." Aisling glanced at Rosalia and winked. "I think we need to create something, a surprise, for your new husband when ye do take your leave."

It took Rosalia a moment to understand Aisling's hidden meaning, but when she did, Rosalia flew to her feet. "Ye are right. Let us travel to the village and seek Cylan."

"Cylan?" asked Liadain, raising her brow. She stood and adjusted her skirts, not sure if she should be cautious or excited.

"Aye. Trust in us," said Rosalia.

Nineteen

"Ye lasses wouldnae be venturing outside the castle gates alone now, would ye?" Montgomery leaned against a wooden post in the stable with his brawny arms folded over his broad chest. His boldly handsome face smiled warmly down at Liadain, and with his kilt low over his lean hips, the man was almost as smooth as MacGregor.

Rosalia waved him off. "James, we arenae alone. There are three of us. We only head to the village. Leave off."

"Without an escort."

"Aye, without an escort," Rosalia mocked him.

"Och, nay ye donna. The MacGregor wouldnae like it."

Rosalia huffed. "We have something to attend to that doesnae require a man's escort. We willnae be away long."

"And that is exactly why I will come along. When ye have something to attend to, it usually involves mischief. Wait for me to saddle my horse, Rosalia," Montgomery ordered, giving Rosalia a glare that would surely make a grown man tremble.

Rosalia rolled her eyes. "Make haste, ye daft man." She turned to Aisling. "Ye know he will chaperone us whether we allow it or nae. We might as well just allow it. Mayhap he will be less annoying that way."

"I doubt it," countered Aisling.

⌘

Declan was grateful his brothers had taken their leave. It gave him the chance to roam the halls of the castle, exploring in peace and quiet. He was truly blessed to have such a home. He had attempted to memorize every nook when he turned a corner and noticed a large wooden door.

The heavy door creaked on its hinges. He stepped inside and saw that books graced the shelves along the wall. Placing the tip of his finger on one of the spines, he tilted it, briefly studying the title. *De Magnete* by William Gilbert. Scientific work was not his strong suit. Declan gave the book all of the attention it deserved and quickly pushed it back onto the shelf.

The Campbell library held quite a collection of reading material. He was curious if the healer spent any time in here. Perhaps she had her own selection of books about healing. With one last glance around, he walked out and shut the door.

As he moved about his new home aimlessly, he found himself heading toward the family rooms. He searched for the healer's chamber, believing it was somewhere down the hall. He opened and closed several doors and did not stop until he found what he sought. Declan perceived it was his wife's room the moment he crossed the threshold.

A small wooden desk was placed before a stone fireplace. When he spotted an open book upon the desk, he walked over and casually fingered the pages. It was a journal—the healer's own personal thoughts. He could not resist a peek inside, but he should have tried harder to thwart his curiosity. Willow bark, sage, yarrow, devil's something or other. Clearly the healer needed more excitement in her life—although, if he ever had an ailment, she would be the first to know.

Declan placed the journal back approximately where he had found it. A bed with tall corner posts graced the far wall with a bedside table to one side. Herbs and plants, some familiar, some not so much, were scattered upon the shelf. He shook his head and wondered if she had any other interests. That was the moment when the idea struck him. He would make his wife a peace offering.

He closed her door and made his way out into the bailey. Granted, he had no stable master, but there should still be supplies somewhere. Declan searched the stables, and it did not take him long to realize nothing remained.

Damn.

"May I help ye, sir?"

A young lad, approximately ten years old, stood about as tall as Declan's waist a short way off. The boy's head was capped by a mass of bronze-gold hair. Although the lad was dressed in tattered, dirty clothing, he stood proudly. When the lines deepened along the young boy's brows and under his brown eyes, Declan walked over and knelt down beside him.

"And ye are?" asked Declan softly.

"John. Mother says I shouldnae speak to men I donna know." The boy smiled sheepishly.

"Your mother sounds like a wise woman. I assure ye, I mean ye nay harm." He returned the boy's smile, giving him a pat on the shoulder.

"Mother says men may voice that as well. How do I know ye speak the truth?" John asked, folding his small arms over his chest. The boy swallowed hard, lifted his chin, and boldly met Declan's gaze. If John's hair was long enough to toss over his shoulder, this would surely be the younger male version of his wife.

"Ye are a wise young lad to question someone ye donna know, but I assure ye, I am here by King James's order. I am the new master of the castle. My name is MacGregor."

"MacGregor? The MacGregor killed the Campbell. His Majesty would ne'er give ye the castle. Ye speak with the devil's tongue. I am going to tell Mother about this. She will come and ye will wish she hadnae. Ye better run, sir."

Declan put the matter aside with sudden good humor. "John, why donna we both take our leave and seek your mother? Tell me, where can I find her?"

Taken aback, the boy glanced up, obviously weighing his options. Cautiously, he stepped away from Declan. "I suppose it would be all right for me to take ye to Mother. Come with me."

Declan followed the boy, who consistently gazed back at him over his shoulder. Though he understood the lad's behavior, it unnerved him that John believed he would do him harm. As they circled the castle, they came to a small, crumbling building detached from what Declan remembered as being the kitchens. A woman emerged, her hair pulled into a tight, unflattering bun. She wiped her hands on her apron and her eyes widened.

"John! Come here at once," she called, her voice trembling with concern.

Declan raised both of his hands. "I mean ye nay harm."

John ran to her side and the woman held her son in a protective embrace. "What do ye want?" As he slowly approached, she shooed her son inside.

"I mean ye nay harm," he repeated, stopping a short distance in front of her.

"So ye have said. State your purpose," she replied.

"Per His Majesty's orders, I am the new master of Castle Campbell. I am Declan MacGregor." When there was an uncomfortable moment of silence, he continued. "Could ye tell me your name?"

Pursing her lips in thought, the woman finally answered. "I am Anna. I believe ye already met my son, John."

"Aye, he is a good lad. Do ye live here?" asked Declan, nodding to the building behind her.

"Aye, I was the cook for the Earl of Argyll. When he was killed, my son and I had nay other home or kin. Will ye be expecting us to take our leave then?" Anna asked with uncertainty.

Declan broke into an easy smile. "My wife will be arriving soon and I find myself in desperate need of staff, primarily a cook. Ye and your son are welcome to stay for as long as ye wish. Unless, of course, ye are a dreadful cook or ye donna want to cook for a

MacGregor," he added. "Besides, I believe ye already know my wife. She would probably welcome some faces that are familiar."

"And who is your wife, m'laird?" Anna asked hesitantly.

"The earl's sister."

Anna's smile broadened in approval. "I assure ye nay one has ever taken their leave from the table hungry, m'laird. It would be a pleasure to have her return. Liad—…er, Lady Campbell was sorely missed."

"Lady MacGregor," Declan clarified.

"Of course, my apologies. If there is anything ye require, please ask."

"Why do ye nae live in the servants' quarters in the castle?"

Reaching up, Anna fixed a piece of hair that was already securely fastened. "Umm…The Campbell didnae want my son about. He didnae favor children, m'laird."

Declan studied the building, which was small and in desperate need of repair. A strong wind or rain would surely collapse the roof. "Ye and your son will move into the castle at once. If ye need assistance with your belongings, let me know."

Her eyes lit up in surprise. "Thank ye, m'laird."

"There is something I would ask of ye. Do ye know where there are any supplies for building?"

"Depending upon what ye seek, there is a cart in the woods with a few wooden planks. I am nae sure what else is there." She walked toward him and gestured into the trees.

"Thank ye, Anna. I am fixing to make something for my wife. Do you know her well?"

"Well enough, m'laird. Lady Camp—…er, MacGregor often tended to the garden and dallied in the kitchens upon occasion. She said it soothed her soul."

"I am sure it did. Did ye find it difficult with the blood—…er, the Campbell?"

Anna shifted her weight, looking uncomfortable. "I cannae speak for everyone, but the Campbell wasnae a kind man. John and I tried to remain out of sight. I believe Lady MacGregor attempted the same, but it didnae always work out that way."

That revelation did not astonish him. Declan had figured as much and gathered that the bloody earl never really concerned himself with anything that did not impact him. Declan turned and gave Anna a winning smile. "I hope to change that. I am naught like the Campbell."

Her features became far more animated. "I already know that. Come. Let us see what we can find for your lady wife," Anna said, walking toward the cart in the trees. "John!" she called over her shoulder.

When the lad darted out of the door, Declan chuckled, remembering the countless times he and his brothers spied upon their father. He smiled at the memory of innocence lost. "Ye know, John. I could use a strong lad like ye to help me."

The boy became instantly wide awake and glanced up at him, his infectious grin setting the tone. "I will make ye proud, m'laird."

Twenty

"Ye are fitting me for what?" Liadain gasped.

Aisling rolled her eyes. "Declan will love it."

Liadain's voice raised an octave. "He isnae the one who has to wear it." She took a deep breath, but it did not soothe her nerves the way she had hoped. If she could have made herself disappear, she would have. As casually as she could manage, she asked, "Why even wear anything at all?"

Aisling and Cylan exchanged a silent glance with a hidden meaning. "Ye arenae thinking upon this the right way. Such a gown is meant to entice your husband, to give a promise of what is to come," said Aisling with a grin.

"Praise the saints. This wasnae what I had in mind when ye said we were traveling to meet Cylan in the village. And this is by nay means a gown," said Liadain in exasperation. Cylan held up the thin fabric to her frame but she promptly ignored the seamstress. "Ye cannae be serious. MacGregor and I are already wed. What is the point?"

Aisling tapped Liadain's arm with her finger. "The point is to capture your husband's attention."

"And what if I donna want his attention?" Liadain asked with an air of indifference.

"Every woman wants to keep her husband's interest, and if ye think upon it, ye will realize I speak the truth," said Aisling.

"Truth or nae, ye donna have to worry upon that. I am sure MacGregor doesnae have an interest in me, Aisling. The man can barely look at me without snarling like an angry boar."

Aisling shook her head in disagreement. "Surely ye cannae be so daft as to think that Declan has nay interest in ye. Why do ye think ye rile him so?"

Rosalia giggled. "Declan doesnae know what he wants. He ne'er did. Ye need to tell him or show him. And whatever ye do, donna make him guess. For a start, why donna ye call him by his given name? He is your husband."

Liadain shrugged her shoulders. "He calls me 'healer' and I call him 'MacGregor.' 'Tis the way of it."

"Aye, he is a MacGregor—and a stubborn one at that. Yet Rosalia is right. Why donna ye start by calling him Declan?" asked Aisling.

"I understand what ye are both trying to do, I *think*, but the man simply doesnae want to be shackled. In fact, I verra recently called him 'husband' and he corrected me, his feelings perfectly clear. He doesnae want this and I cannae force it upon him."

"Ye are going about this the wrong way," Aisling said. "The secret is to make Declan realize that he wants ye. He does, but he's too stubborn to admit it. He will in time, but I suggest ye make it on your own terms. I donna think even the gods would know how long it would take the rogue to recognize something on his own accord. He is a man. Make him see."

Liadain did not need Aisling to remind her. She was painfully aware of MacGregor's masculinity. Her husband's maleness was not the problem. It was everything else that came with that.

"Ye are aware if I don this...*gown*, I may only further provoke my husband's anger."

Rosalia and Aisling laughed at the same time, and Rosalia nudged Liadain. "Ye will provoke Declan all right, but nae his ire."

Aisling reached out and touched her hand. "Do ye want to make this marriage work? Will ye do anything to see it so?"

There was a heavy silence before Liadain could convince herself to speak the truth. "I want my husband to be able to gaze upon me without spite." She paused and then relented. "All right, I will do as ye suggest."

Aisling glanced at Rosalia and Cylan. "And I think we all agree that Declan will not look upon ye the same way again."

The women cast scheming grins and Liadain prayed the plan would not fail. Since her previous attempts at peace had not worked, she was perfectly willing to try something new. She was not asking for miracles, but it would be nice if MacGregor was not scowling at her all of the time. As the women took their leave from Cylan's, Montgomery was pacing.

"What took ye so long?" he snapped.

Rosalia tapped him playfully on the chest. "If ye must know, my monthly courses arrived and I had to—"

Montgomery shook his head, waving his hands in the air in front of him. "Cease. I donna want to know."

When Liadain cast a puzzled look at Rosalia, the woman raised her brow and returned a smile. Leaning in close, Aisling whispered in Liadain's ear. "Rosalia taught me that as well. The words ne'er fail to get said reaction. Ye must admit, 'tis somewhat humorous seeing men discomfited upon occasion."

Liadain tried to suppress a giggle as Aisling circled around to grab her mount. In an apparent attempt to escape Rosalia's open declaration of womanly burdens, Montgomery walked hastily toward Liadain.

"'Tis good to see a smile upon your face."

She was not about to tell the man that her joyful expression was at his own expense. Who would have thought that mentioning monthly courses would make a grown man into a bumbling fool? Liadain placed her newfound knowledge in her mental arsenal. She could learn a lot from these women. When she cast her eyes downward, mainly to keep from laughing aloud, Montgomery gently touched her shoulder.

"My apologies. I didnae mean to make ye uncomfortable."

"Ye didnae make me uncomfortable."

He dropped his arm and bobbed his head as if he did not believe her. "Did your husband tell ye then?"

She raised her hand and smoothed her tresses in a nervous gesture. "Tell me what?"

"He asked me to be the captain of his guard. I will be escorting ye to Castle Campbell."

Wonderful. Now she would have two rogues under the same roof. Her husband had become surprisingly protective when Montgomery approached her in the great hall. Why would he ask the same man to be the captain of his guard? Men and their games.

Liadain looked up at Montgomery with an effort. "Nay, he didnae. Congratulations. Ye must be verra proud."

He shrugged his shoulders. "Surprised mayhap."

"I trust my husband made the proper decision."

"I was the captain of Armstrong's guard for years. Rest assured, ye are safe in my hands, my lady."

She returned a warm smile. "'Tis verra good to know I have so many brawny men watching over me. I have the utmost faith in your abilities."

"James."

"Pardon?"

Montgomery's eyes lit up like summer lightning. "James. *Is mise* James. I would have ye speak it upon your rose lips and grace me with such a gift."

She was momentarily speechless. "My husband—"

"Has naught to do with ye calling me by my given name. I am afraid I must insist, my lady." He winked when he caught her eye.

"Praise the saints. Would ye cease pestering Liadain and get onto your mount?" Rosalia bit out.

"Pray excuse me but a moment." Montgomery turned on his heel and approached Rosalia. He patted her horse on the flank and then cast a wooing smile at Rosalia. "I see being wed to the MacGregor hasnae stayed your tongue, wench. Mayhap I should have a word with your new husband about your insolence."

Rosalia nodded briefly. "And mayhap I should have a word with Ciaran about ye, ye beastly man. My husband only waits for ye to mess things up so he can toss ye out of Glenorchy with naught but the clothes upon your scrawny back. 'Tis bad enough Ciaran wants to run ye through. Donna display your open affections to his brother's wife, ye daft fool."

Liadain untied her mount and feigned an interest in the thickness of the reins. For the second time, she suddenly wanted to disappear.

"I am the captain of his guard, Rosalia. I would ne'er dally with his wife," Montgomery said as if he stated the obvious.

"Aye, and that almost sounded convincing. Like the time when Lord Humphries threatened to cut off your manhood for bedding his wi—"

Montgomery held up his hands. "Enough. Ye made your point. Let me get my horse."

"Donna fret over them," said Aisling. She positioned her horse beside Liadain and smiled. "Rosalia and James are constantly at each other's throats. Ciaran would love to remove him from Glenorchy. In truth, there is naught he wants more, but I know Rosalia would ne'er permit it."

Liadain raised her brow. "What do ye mean?"

"Rosalia and James are as siblings. He had known her since they were bairns. The two of them are inseparable. James is her family as well as her friend. Granted, it makes for a dangerous combination and an unhappy husband, but Ciaran loves Rosalia. In truth, he would allow Montgomery to stay if only to see a smile upon her face."

"'Tis quite obvious in the way he gazes upon her with such love." Liadain could not help but wonder if she would ever be blessed with such a gift.

❧

"Hold it right there and donna move. That is it, John." Declan pounded the nail and swore when he moved the board.

John laughed. "I didnae move. It was ye, sir."

Grunting, Declan shoved the wood back into place. He drove in the nail once again, and this time the board held right where he wanted it.

"Ye did it! Do ye think it strong enough to hold her plants?"

Declan chuckled and attempted to wiggle the board, which did not budge. "Aye, it will hold." Taking a step back, he studied his handiwork. He ran his hand over the wood and thought the shelf was not too bad for something he had basically just thrown together. With the last shelf in place, the healer should have enough space to organize her plants and add a few more if she so desired.

"Now we must move the plants and herbs. Do ye still want to help?" Declan asked John.

"Aye, but there is something I donna understand." John's forehead furrowed.

"And what is that?"

"Why would ye move your lady's plants in here when she already has a chamber of her own?" John asked, casting a puzzled look.

"She is my wife now and this is the lady of the castle's chamber. That is why."

John's eyes came up and studied Declan's face. "But she already has a room. Donna ye think she will be upset when she enters her chamber and finds naught is there?"

He reached out and placed his hand upon John's shoulder, trying to stay the smile that played on his lips. "She willnae be distraught. She is the lady of the castle now. This is where she belongs. Besides, we are only moving her belongings in here. We arenae throwing things out. Do ye understand?"

John shrugged. "Do ye think we can eat first?"

A lad after his own heart. "Of course. Let us find your mother."

When they entered the kitchens, Anna was preparing the evening meal. She wiped her hands on her apron, then glanced up and smiled. "Pray tell me my son hasnae been underfoot," said Anna.

Declan rubbed the top of John's head. "Nay. He has been my helper. All the shelves are up in my wife's chamber for her plants and herbs. I donna know what I would have done without his assistance."

John stood tall and puffed out his thin frame. "I did help him, Mother."

A warm smile lit Anna's features. "Ye are a good lad, John, and ye make me verra proud. Now take your leave and wash up."

"Ye didnae have to do that, but my son enjoys the male companionship." As John walked off, Anna pulled out a loaf of warm bread and placed it on the table.

"He is a good lad," Declan said.

"Thank ye for spending time with him."

Declan pulled out the bench tucked under the rough table and sat down. "Anna, what of John's father?"

She glanced uneasily over her shoulder, then poured mulled wine into a tankard. She handed him the mug and turned away from him before she spoke again. "His father is dead. We donna speak of him."

"My apologies for your loss. John has nay other men in his life?"

"Only a few who still remain from the village," said Anna, smiling sadly as if deep in thought. "When the Campbell was here, John was attached to some of the men. But after the earl died and most of the men took their leave, my son had only me."

John bolted into the kitchens. "All done, Mother." He flew into the seat next to Declan. "After we sup, I am to help the master move his lady's plants into her new chamber. He said that she willnae be upset when we move her belongings since we arenae throwing anything out. His lady must move into a new room because she is now the lady of the castle."

Anna giggled. "That is right, John. His lady wife must stay in a new chamber."

Declan sat contentedly and listened to the conversation flow between mother and son. He wondered if the gods would ever grace him with such a gift one day. He had never thought of bairns—basically because he was not the most favorable of men. It was Ciaran's responsibility to see to an heir of succession anyway.

Declan mentally shook away the cobwebs when he heard Anna ask the question again. "My apologies. Nay, I willnae be returning to Glenorchy."

Twenty-One

LIADAIN BROKE HER FAST AFTER A RESTLESS NIGHT OF tossing and turning in her empty bed. What Rosalia and Aisling had said made sense at the time. MacGregor was probably seeing to the staff. Of course her husband would not be avoiding her. That would be ridiculous. But she could not stay the slight feeling of abandonment that plagued her.

"Ciaran? I thought Declan was to return to sup last eve. What do ye think happened?" Rosalia whispered.

"I donna know. He said he had something to attend to before he returned to Glenorchy. Aiden and I will travel to Castle Campbell after we break our fast."

"Mayhap we can come along," Rosalia suggested, gesturing slightly toward Liadain.

"I donna see why ye cannae." Ciaran leaned forward at the table and cleared his throat. "Liadain, would ye want to travel to Castle Campbell this morn?"

"Aye. Should I pack or keep my belongings here?" She was not sure of anything anymore.

"'Tis best ye stay at Glenorchy until Declan sees to the staff. He has already assigned Montgomery as the captain of his guard, and I have a handful of MacGregor men who will serve him," said Ciaran.

"Ye will be back at Castle Campbell before ye know it," said Rosalia, giving her a reassuring pat on the arm.

Aisling leaned back in her chair. "I willnae be able to accompany ye. Teàrlach doesnae feel well this morn."

"What ails him? Do ye want me to take a look?" Liadain offered.

"Nay," Aisling waved her off. "My son isnae warm. He keeps relieving himself and 'tis something that needs to run its course."

"If it continues for more than one day, let me know and I will gladly see to him."

Aisling nodded her thanks. "'Tis good to have a healer in the clan who can care for more than battle wounds or brotherly injuries," she jested, poking her husband in the chest with her finger.

"Wife, ye know we only throw punches when they are deserved." Aiden looked down the table to Ciaran for obvious intervention. "Ye could help me out, Brother."

Ciaran went back to his meal. "Ye are on your own with that one."

"What is that about?" asked Liadain, leaning in close to Rosalia.

Rosalia spoke softly. "They are brothers under the same roof. Donna be surprised when the occasional fist is thrown. 'Tis why they require us women to balance out their wild ways."

Montgomery approached the dais and gave Ciaran a small nod. "MacGregor, if ye are taking my lady to Castle Campbell, I will accompany ye. 'Tis my responsibility to see her safe."

Ciaran cocked his head and was about to speak when Rosalia elbowed her husband in the side. "Ye are the captain of Declan's guard, James. Of course ye should accompany us." When Montgomery gave Ciaran a smug look, Liadain thought she might get a firsthand look at flying fists.

Montgomery positioned himself before Liadain at the last possible moment. "My lady, I will accompany ye to Castle Campbell after ye break your fast."

"Thank ye," she murmured, discomfited.

"James. *Is mise* James, remember?" He raised his brow and waited for her to respond.

"Aye, thank ye…James," she said quietly.

"And must I remind ye again of a certain lady wife?" asked Rosalia. Her coolness was evidence that she was not amused. Montgomery turned toward Rosalia and winked, and Ciaran's entire body turned to stone. "Ignore him, Husband. He only behaves that way because he knows it irritates ye."

"I only count the days until he willnae be underfoot. Let him plague my brother. They deserve each other," said Ciaran.

❧

Declan dreamt of her. Raven tresses encircled him, ivory skin warm to the touch. She was laughing, and his heart sang with delight. He was so blissfully happy, fully alive. He could not remember a time when he had felt so at peace, and he exhaled a long sigh of contentment.

He looked her over wantonly and she stared at him

with longing, as if she had waited for this moment for so long. No obstacles stood before them. She was not the Campbell's sister and he was not the third son of the MacGregor. Their souls were bound together as one—man and woman. Husband and wife.

Lightly, he fingered a loose tendril of hair upon his wife's cheek. Mockingly coy, she ran her finger along his jaw. He had placed his hand on her shoulder in a possessive gesture and the healer reached out, catching his hand in hers. Her skin was silky smooth and his breathing hitched at her gentle and overwhelming beauty.

His wife lowered his hand to her taut belly, linking her fingers with his and holding them in place. "There is something I have been meaning to tell ye, Husband." The healer's eyes sparkled as though she was playing a game. If he was not careful, he would fall into their molten depths.

"And what is that?" His tone was patient.

A secretive smile softened his wife's lips. "I am with child."

A single tear swept down his cheek. He would raise his child with all the love and compassion his own parents had bestowed on him. He was choked with emotion and his next words sounded foreign upon his lips. "Liadain, I love ye with all my heart."

"Declan," his wife whispered, her voice sounding far away.

He struggled to hear her. "Liadain," he called out.

"Declan! Would ye get out of bed, ye daft fool?"

Something jolted him awake, and he thought briefly it was a firm shove from his pestering brother. He opened his eyes and quickly closed them, caught up in the tender memories that slowly faded from his thoughts.

"Please tell me I am dreaming." Declan opened one eye. "Nay, ye are still here. What are ye doing here, Ciaran? Donna ye have your own household to torment?"

Ciaran walked around the bed, studying Declan's chamber. "Ye were to return to Glenorchy last eve."

Declan sat up and ran his hand through his hair. "I told ye. I had something to attend to. It was too late. Besides, ye arenae our mother. I donna need to offer an excuse, and I damn well donna need another of your lectures."

"Cease. The women are below stairs, as well as Montgomery."

Declan threw the blankets from the bed. He walked over to the chair and picked up his kilt. "I found myself a cook. She made the bloody Campbell's meals."

Ciaran's eyes widened in surprise. "Ye donna think she will poison ye?"

"Nay, she despised the bloody Campbell as much as we did. I will speak to the healer to confirm the same." His tunic had fallen to the floor. He placed his foot under the fabric, tossed it into the air, and caught it with this hand.

"Ye mean to say, your *wife*?" asked Ciaran with a look of disapproval.

"Aye, they are one and the same."

"Declan, we had this conversation before."

He raised his hand to cease Ciaran's tongue. "Aye, and I have nay desire to hear it again."

"Aye, but ye will. Liadain has proven herself. She is

your wife. Ye will treat her with respect, Brother. She isnae one of your whores."

Closing the distance between them, Declan stood within a hairbreadth of his brother. "Donna lecture me on how to treat my wife. Unlike ye, I am verra aware of how to treat and pleasure a woman. Mayhap ye should keep your attention on your own wife and leave me in peace."

To his surprise, Ciaran took a step back. Perhaps his brother was tired of having the same argument. "I will meet ye below stairs," said Ciaran. When Ciaran walked out the door with his arrogant swagger, Declan shook his head. He held such similarities with his brother, and yet they were different in so many ways.

Declan dressed, then proceeded to the great hall. It was a contrast to the vast emptiness of what he had encountered the day before. Montgomery stood with a handful of MacGregor men, while Ciaran and Rosalia were seated at the table and his lady wife…was nowhere to be seen.

Montgomery approached him with long, purposeful strides. "MacGregor, the men are assembled. With your command, I shall take them into the bailey for training."

"Aye, I shall speak with them later." He watched his men depart the great hall. His men. His guard. His life was truly changing for the better.

He moved over to the bench and smiled at Rosalia. "Sister," he said, giving her a nod in greeting. He sat beside her and faced Ciaran from across the table. "I must thank ye for the men."

Ciaran sat still, his eyes narrow. "Use them wisely, Brother, lest I take away what I have given."

An unwelcome tension fell between them and Rosalia cleared her throat. "Mayhap I should see to Liadain." She pulled herself to her feet as John bolted through the great hall like a whirlwind.

"I told ye I didnae mean it!" John screamed playfully.

The healer chased after John, her hair tousled and her cheeks flushed. "John, ye will pay for that!" She pretended to step to the right and then moved with lightning speed to the left, capturing John and pulling him close.

The lad screeched with laughter as the healer tickled his sides. "Cease, please!"

She continued to poke him as he wiggled within her hold. "Do ye yield? I will only cease if ye do. I donna believe I heard a yield. What say ye?" the healer asked.

"I yield! I yield!"

For a brief moment, Declan simply watched her with John. She was happy, content. She had not graced him with a smile for so long that he had almost forgotten the heartfelt beauty that she was. She was magnificent, almost glowing.

As soon as the healer released John, the lad made a mad dash out of the great hall. Ignoring the others, Declan spoke only to his wife. "What was that about?"

The healer sat down beside him. "John thought to poke some fun and dropped a worm down the front of my dress."

Ciaran chuckled and Rosalia giggled.

Declan merely raised his brow. "Did ye get it out?"

"I donna need assistance if that is what ye are asking." She picked an imaginary piece of dirt from her dress and then turned her head away from him.

"At least it wasnae a snake," he said jestingly. When the healer turned her head and pursed her lips, he decided to change the subject. "Ye know Anna and John, then?"

"Aye, they lived with us for many years. Anna cooked for my brother and John has always been about."

"Ye donna think she will poison us?" he asked half seriously.

"Anna? If she didnae attempt to kill my brother while he was alive, she can be trusted. Besides, John is a wonderful lad when he isnae stirring up mischief."

Declan had pretty much confirmed the same.

"'Tis great, Liadain," Rosalia said. "Now ye have your guard and your cook. Ye should be able to stay at Castle Campbell."

"Aye, mayhap a man in the village will tend to the stables," offered Ciaran.

"When they hear my lady wife has returned and Anna cooks, I donna think we will have trouble finding someone."

❧

It was good to be home. Liadain could barely contain her excitement and could not rest in the great hall any longer. She needed to move. "Rosalia, do ye want to come with me to the gardens? I am nae sure anything lives, but I am curious to see if there is anything worth saving."

She had taken a step away when MacGregor reached out to stay her. "If John gives ye any trouble, ye let me know and I will have words with him," he said sternly. A devilish look came into his eyes and a flash of humor crossed his face.

She giggled at her husband's attempt to make her laugh. "Aye, as long as they are worms and nae snakes, I think we are fine." When she turned, his hand smacked her playfully on the bottom. She whipped her head around, but he had started to converse with Ciaran, pretending not to notice her reaction.

"He missed ye," Rosalia whispered as they ambled to the gardens.

"Donna be ridiculous."

"Why else would he smack your bottom and jest with ye?" Rosalia asked.

"'Tis a beautiful day."

"I know what ye are doing. Ye are clearly changing the subject."

"Aye, I am." A strong flowery scent blew through the air and Rosalia froze in mid-step. "What is wrong?" asked Liadain with concern.

Rosalia became suddenly pale, reaching for her stomach. She ran to the wall, bent over, and heaved, losing her contents.

Liadain was immediately by her side. "What is wrong?"

Rosalia gulped hard as tears streamed down her cheeks. "I donna know. Please donna speak of this to Ciaran. I donna want him to be concerned. I have been feeling poorly for well over a fortnight." Her face was pale and pinched, and she brushed the tresses from her eyes.

"For over a fortnight?" Liadain's voice unintentionally went up a notch. "Tell me. What do ye feel?" she asked, reaching out and rubbing Rosalia's back.

"I have bouts of sickness almost every day."

"Hmm…Do ye notice 'tis at a certain time of the day?"

"Nay, it happens all day."

"Is it when ye eat?"

"Nay, 'tis constant. It can be right after I eat or when I smell something. I donna know what causes it." Rosalia took a deep breath, holding her stomach.

"When was the last time ye had your monthly courses?"

Her eyes widened. "My monthly courses? I donna know. I have ne'er had them regular. I may miss several months and then it comes, and sometimes it doesnae."

"Do ye notice your stomach increasing?"

"Thank ye for pointing that out, Liadain. Ye sound like my mother. Ciaran is more kind and doesnae mention as much."

"I am nae referring…" Liadain thought to rephrase the question. "Do ye notice your breasts are swollen?"

"They appear the same to me, but they do ache at times. I donna know. What does all of this have to do with my monthly courses?" Rosalia placed her hand high upon the wall, turning her head to the side. She stretched her back and positioned her face so that it was hidden by her arm. A loud sigh escaped her.

"My lady, I think ye are with child," said Liadain. Rosalia's entire body went rigid and Liadain could not see the expression on Rosalia's face.

"I am nae with child," Rosalia said as if the answer were obvious.

"How do ye know?"

She paused. "I know. It cannae be…I am barren."

"*Barren?* How do ye know this to be true? Even if ye donna have your monthly courses timely, that doesnae mean ye are unable to carry a child. Rosalia, ye have all of the symptoms of a woman with child. Who told ye this?"

"My mother."

Twenty-Two

DECLAN STOOD IN THE BAILEY AND REVELED IN THE JOY of a silent moment. He had spoken with his men, then left them in Montgomery's care. Anna had recommended a man in the village to tend the stables. And Ciaran had gone. All in a good day.

"Will we be staying here this eve or returning to Glenorchy?" asked the healer, walking up beside him.

"Ye look weary. Why donna we stay?"

"I donna have my sack or nightrail. Mayhap we should return and then come back on the morrow," she said softly, giving him a tender, tired smile.

Declan swung her into the circle of his arms. "Ye donna need a nightrail and ye willnae have the need to sleep this eve."

She clamped her mouth shut, evidently stunned by his bluntness. "Ye are acting strangely, MacGregor."

"Why? Because I want to be with my wife?" Her eyebrows shot up in surprise and he chuckled at the shaken expression on her face. "What is the matter?"

She wiggled out of his grasp. "I donna know. I think 'tis the first time ye ever referred to me as your wife. I am clearly at a loss. To what do I owe the honor?"

"I am nae always an arse."

"Ye caught me by surprise. It may take some getting used to. Ye should try nae being an arse more often." She leaned in, teasing him. "Ye know? Ye might find ye even like it."

Declan pulled his wife close and held her in a tender embrace. "Please accept my apologies. I know I am nae an easy man to understand."

"At least ye speak in truth."

Her body molded to him like a second skin. She was so warm and soft, comforting. Perhaps this was meant to be—here, now. Maybe it was about damn time he accepted his fate.

"I will try," he spoke softly.

"'Tis all I ever asked of ye."

He was about to kiss her when she backed out of his embrace and the moment was clearly lost. He would need to make certain there was another. "We almost have enough staff to remain. Why donna we spend one more eve at Glenorchy and then return on the morrow with your belongings?"

"That sounds wonderful," she said with a tired smile.

"I am sure it will be good for ye to be under your own roof again."

"It will be. Although, I will have to start my plants anew. The garden was a mess and someone even removed the herbs from my chamber."

Declan contemplated whether to tell her about the changes in her new chamber and then decided against it. There was plenty of time to start anew. "I met with

Montgomery earlier, and there is something I must ask of ye."

An uncertainty crept into her expression. "Aye?"

"I know there are hidden passageways within the castle. 'Tis how ye managed to bring Aisling to safety. I know at least one of them travels to the dungeon. I need ye to show me all of them."

Relief passed over her features. "I donna mind. I will show ye anything ye ask."

"Really?" he asked with a roguish grin.

His wife slapped him with an answering grin. "Cease. Ye have already seen that."

Declan shrugged. "It doesnae mean I donna want to see it again."

Her eyes lowered to the ground. "If ye want to take a walk, I will show ye the passages."

❧

Liadain walked with her husband around the outer wall of the castle, remembering the last time she had been there. Just around this very corner was where he had placed his dagger to her throat. She never would have believed that this handsome Highland rogue would become her mate. For all of the torture the man put her through, he was not going to get off that easily by offering a simple apology for his dreadful behavior. With a devilish grin, Liadain decided to have some fun of her own.

"And here is where ye sprang out of the brush and placed your dagger to my throat the first time." She pointed to the stone wall. "And there is where ye threw me into the wall and threatened to slit my throat." She spoke as if she were merely reciting ingredients for a recipe. She knew it irritated her husband, but frankly, he deserved it for all of the aggravation he had caused her. She jumped when he grabbed her arm and spun her around.

"And here is where I will kiss my bonny wife." MacGregor's mouth covered hers hungrily and he whispered in between breaths, "If I ever hold a dagger to your bonny neck again, ye have leave to pummel me." He pulled back and gazed into her eyes. "I speak the truth."

Liadain had a burning desire, an aching need, for another kiss. Her husband needed to stop…talking. "Donna worry. As I told ye before, there willnae be a third. Kiss me, MacGregor." She did not need to ask her husband twice, her last words smothered on her lips.

His tongue plunged into her mouth, and her knees weakened. It was a kiss for her tired soul to melt into. He began to slip his hands up her arms, ever so slowly, while she caressed the back of his neck.

He pressed her even closer and she could feel his desire hardening against her belly. Blood surged from her fingertips to her toes with a giddy sense of pleasure. It had been too long since she'd felt this way. An undeniable magnetism was growing between them, and she wanted so much more of him—here, now. She no longer cared about the past. This day, this moment was her only concern.

He pulled back and placed his forehead to hers. "Ye are my wife. I should be with ye properly—in a bed," he said, his breath uneven upon her cheek. As she was about to protest, he added, "Besides, my men watch from above on the wall."

Liadain shuddered in humiliation. She discreetly twisted her head around and glanced above. "I donna see anyone."

"They are there," he simply stated.

She did not doubt her husband's word and she tried desperately to calm her racing heart. She straightened her day dress and he draped his arm over her shoulders, squeezing her affectionately. As he took a deep breath, she was joyful to see that the man was just as affected as she was.

"Come, show me the passages."

Escorting MacGregor through the darkened passageway from the dungeon into the interior of the castle, Liadain placed her hands on both sides of the cool stone wall. The lower temperatures of the cavern felt good to her feverish body.

"MacGregor, ye are sure ye donna want me to light a candle?"

"Nay, I must know my way around if there is nay light. I count the steps and touch the walls. Where does this tunnel take us?"

"This is the main passage and it branches off ahead to the bedchambers, Archie's study, and the great hall. There is another tunnel to the stables."

"Lead me to the study. I am at your mercy."

She giggled. "Take my hand." She fumbled behind her and grabbed MacGregor's rough hand, placing it on the wall beside her. She covered her fingers with his and guided him until he felt the partition. "This way leads to Archie's study and the bedchambers. If ye go straight, it leads to the great hall."

"Lead on, healer."

"I ne'er thought I would see the day when a Campbell led a MacGregor through the secret tunnels."

A warm laugh answered her. "Ye? Who would have thought a MacGregor would own Castle Campbell? How could your brother be the right hand of the king and yet be so daft?"

"I have asked myself the same. I ne'er understood Archie. He was a man who held so much—yet had only a wee bit, if that, of honor."

Liadain heard a shuffle and then he bumped into her back and curses fell from his mouth. She was not even sure they were words she had heard before.

"Keep your feet up, husband."

"How many times did it take ye to walk these walls without light before ye didnae stumble?"

"I have had my whole life to figure it out. I started by counting steps and then learned to feel for the openings."

"I am joyful ye did, else my sisters-by-marriage would still be rotting in the dungeon."

"I am stopping now," she said, even though the dolt still bumped into her. She turned around and extended her arm until she touched him. "Give me your hand."

"Healer, that isnae my hand. I told ye I would take ye properly—in a bed."

Liadain was thankful for the darkness. "Donna flatter yourself. Ye know I cannae see. Just give me your hand," she said through clenched teeth. The palm of MacGregor's hand encircled her breast. "*That* isnae my hand."

"Donna flatter yourself. Ye know I cannae see," he repeated in the same mocking tone.

She removed her husband's hand from her breast and placed his palm back on the stone. "If ye rub down the wall, ye should be able to grasp the—"

"I have it." MacGregor pushed on the latch and a narrow beam of light sprang through tiny cracks in the wall. He pushed open the door and walked straight into Archie's study. "This may prove convenient."

"Archie thought as much." She followed her husband in and noticed that not much had changed. She turned around and closed the stone door, which was designed to easily slide into place. The door was a perfect match to the wall. If one did not know what to look for, the entrance certainly would never be spotted. Archie had been downright clever at times.

MacGregor studied the fireplace and the decorative pieces that were throughout the room. Fine woven tapestries from Spain and Italy graced the walls.

He sat down in the chair behind the massive wooden desk. "Mmm…this is what it felt like to be the right hand of the King." He rubbed his open hand across the grain of the wood. "He didnae want for anything. Everything is of verra fine quality."

She shrugged. "I suppose. I was ne'er interested in such trivial treasures."

"Trivial treasures?"

"When he died, do ye think it mattered that he had so much of value?"

MacGregor opened the drawers to the desk. "Empty."

"Did ye honestly think otherwise? I am sure naught remains. I donna believe Archie would have kept anything of importance in the desk drawers anyway. He may have been daft with his plotting to gain more lands, but my brother was wise in matters of the state. Viscount Cranborne said as much when he would meet with Archie."

"Do ye know where he would have kept such things—papers of importance or other trivial treasures mayhap?"

She cast her eyes downward. "Nay, I donna know."

"Healer. If ye know—"

"I would tell ye. I honestly donna know. Archie ne'er involved me in matters of substance. As long as he didnae see me, he didnae bother. And I made sure he saw me as little as possible."

"I have seen enough this day. Are ye ready to take your leave to Glenorchy?"

Liadain smiled politely, even though she did not believe for a single moment that this would be the last time they stayed at the laird's castle. With Rosalia's current condition, Liadain should stay close or at least be on hand in case the woman needed her.

❧

Riding to Glenorchy, Declan reflected on the day's events—well, more so on his bonny wife. His light-hearted temptress was hard to resist, and he found her smile was somewhat contagious. He glanced over to see her raven curls lifted by the wind. She was exceptionally beautiful.

"What did I do now?" the healer asked.

He regarded his wife with curiosity. "What? Ye didnae do anything."

"Ye gaze upon me and I see ye are clearly thinking of something. Tell me—nay, let me guess. Ye are wondering whether to trust me. Ye hold some doubt in the back of your stubborn MacGregor mind that I know where Archie stored his precious papers. As I told ye before, and I will continue to say the same, I donna know. I avoided his study like the plague."

His eyes widened in surprise. "How do ye know what I am thinking?"

"There has been enough trouble between us already. The last we need are lies and deceit to add to the mix. I have ne'er spoken untruths to ye and I ne'er will. I speak in truth, but of course that is for ye to decide."

"If ye speak in truth, then tell me…Would ye have permitted me to take ye right there by the wall?"

Her cheeks turned to crimson and she shied her head. "What kind of question is that to ask your wife?"

"Remember, healer, ye donna speak untruths," he said.

"Nae with your men watching us from above," she said as though her response was obvious.

"And if there were nay men upon the wall?"

She grunted. "Why would ye even ask me such a question? Ye are despicable, MacGregor."

"I know. I will have your response."

There was a heavy moment of silence.

"What do ye think?" she asked with a heavy dose of sarcasm.

Declan smiled with complete male satisfaction. "I think I just received my answer."

Twenty-Three

LIADAIN SAT QUIETLY AT THE EVENING MEAL AND CAST stealthy glances at her husband. MacGregor was actually making an effort to keep the peace between them.

His leg brushed against her thigh and her body immediately tingled from the contact. Must his every move remind her of his sensual presence? When her husband reached for a piece of bread, his muscles strained against the fabric of his tunic. She was behaving like some giddy lass. No man should rattle a woman like that—ever.

"Ye havenae stopped smiling since Liadain and Declan returned, Husband," said Rosalia, nudging Ciaran's shoulder.

Liadain could not hear Ciaran's full response, but she managed to make out something about a vow to his father. That was odd. Ciaran's father had passed away some time ago.

"While we were away, Cylan came from the village," said Rosalia, giving Liadain a knowing look. She took a drink from her tankard, studying Liadain over the rim. When she could only manage a nod,

Rosalia leaned in close. "I took the liberty of placing the package in your chamber."

"Thank ye," she whispered back.

"Since ye and Declan arenae battling, does it mean ye have found peace between ye?" asked Rosalia with concern.

"I hope as much. 'Tis all I ever wanted."

"He loves ye and he is a stubborn MacGregor. It was only a matter of time before he admitted the truth. I am joyful to see it."

"Rosalia, I wouldnae exactly speak of love. We have merely reached a truce. I didnae expect a miracle."

Rosalia raised her brow as if to disagree and then promptly changed the subject. "After the meal, may I speak with ye alone?"

"Of course."

A warm body melted into hers, the touch familiar. "After the meal, I want to show ye something," said MacGregor as he winked at her, his eyes holding a secret meaning.

"I have already seen it, MacGregor," Liadain said dryly.

He chuckled in response. "Ye know, Wife, your jesting does make me laugh."

She leaned in close, tapping him playfully in the chest. "Ye know, Husband, I find it humorous that ye *think* I jest." Her husband raised his tankard and gave her a mock salute. "After I speak with Rosalia, ye can show me whatever 'tis ye need to show me."

"Ye are sitting right next to her. Why cannae ye speak now?"

Liadain was not exactly thrilled with the idea of

deceiving her husband, but Rosalia's situation was none of his concern. A sudden memory of Rosalia's cleverness came to mind and she stilled her expression. Not very adept at telling untruths, she recognized she would have to be convincing.

She placed her lips next to MacGregor's ear and whispered, "My monthly courses have arrived and I—"

He pulled away and held up his hand. "Healer, ye donna need to speak upon it. That was clearly much more than I wanted to know."

She had to turn her head away from him or a laugh would have surely escaped her. Were men truly that daft? God's teeth! They slayed men on the battlefield without so much as a second thought, but mention birthing or monthly courses and they fled like frightened rabbits.

Cowards.

When the meal was finished, Rosalia led Liadain out of the great hall. They walked casually to the stable. "I thank ye for nae mentioning this to Ciaran or Declan. I thought upon more of what ye spoke, but I am nae convinced 'tis true. I could nae bleed for several months and still be without child."

Liadain held open the stable door and gestured Rosalia through. "I understand it may seem that way, but 'tis verra possible ye are with child. Ye have all the symptoms. Do ye remember when last ye bled?"

"Three months past. I have been losing my contents for well over a fortnight and my breasts ache from about the same time."

A horse whinnied and Liadain approached the black beast, raising her hand to pat him upon his thick neck. "Please donna think my next words are meant to be harmful. It isnae my intention. When someone is with child, she may notice that her midriff somewhat thickens."

"I truly donna know," Rosalia said, exasperated. She placed her hands over her stomach protectively and briefly closed her eyes. "I pray the gods bless me will such a gift. To be able to give Ciaran a son would be worth all of the pain I had to endure as an Armstrong."

Liadain's mind immediately turned to Lady Armstrong and Lord Dunnehl. Would the man who had killed Rosalia's father show up on her doorstep? Rosalia was happy and content at Glenorchy. If the beastly pair decided to pay her a visit…Liadain would feel like she was no better than Archie. She would ruin everything. Yet, she didn't want to mention her encounter with the couple to Rosalia in case she worried for nothing. There was no clear answer and Liadain prayed the fates would show her kindness—or mercy.

But for now, Rosalia was safe with Ciaran forever by her side. Her sister-by-marriage was starting anew. Perhaps one day Liadain might find herself, and her home as well.

❧

"I missed ye, Declan."

Declan whipped his head around as the blond woman fingered her bodice. Her firm, high breasts were hard to miss, and her full, red mouth left very little to the imagination. What was her name? He could not remember.

He had lost count of how many women he had

bedded. The healer had been kind enough to warn him that at some point in his sorry life, his past would come back and bite him in the arse. Hell. It might have been easier if he asked himself which women he had not bedded.

"I search for my wife," he said, mumbling the only words that came to mind.

The woman giggled. "Your *wife?* I cannae believe Declan MacGregor has settled himself with a wife. Well, she can join us if ye would like."

"I donna think 'tis something she would enjoy over-much," he said dryly. "I am a man true to my vows."

"Donna be so dramatic. Why donna we take our leave to the stables?" She cocked her head to one side.

The woman's eyes glowed with desire as she moved closer and knelt before him, attempting to lift his kilt. Without thought, he slapped her hand away.

The woman's mouth dropped in astonishment.

"I donna think my wife would agree," he said between clenched teeth.

"Nay, she wouldnae."

He was startled at the sound of the healer's voice behind him, and the blond before him jumped to her feet. His wife raised her hand to his shoulder.

The woman held up her hands. "My lady, 'tis only a misunderstanding. I didnae know he spoke his vows lest I wouldnae have made such an offer."

Declan was about to speak when the healer silenced him with a glare. "Truly? It was only but a moment ago when I heard my husband decline your…*offer* and clearly state that he was wed. *Dè an t-ainm a th' ort?* What is your name?

The woman cast a helpless glance and then reluctantly spoke. "Elspeth."

His wife stood to her full height and studied the woman from head to toe. "Elspeth, if ye ever come near my husband again with such a proposal, I will have ye banished from Glenorchy."

Elspeth boldly met the healer's gaze. "Ye arenae the lady of Glenorchy."

Declan rubbed the bridge of his nose and sighed. "She is my wife. *Chan eil e gu difeir.*" *It does not matter.*

Elspeth's eyebrows flew up in surprise at Declan's defense of his wife. "My apologies." The woman huffed and turned on her heel.

The healer whipped her head around. "Husband, how many times must I continue to save ye—"

Declan pulled her into the circle of his arms and his lips came crashing down upon hers. So often scolded and lectured, he thought it refreshing to have someone actually defend him for a change. Just when he thought he had figured out his wee raven witch, she surprised him with something unexpected.

She pulled back with passion-glazed eyes. "And donna think to distract me by kissing me."

A grin lifted the corner of Declan's lips. "Is it working?"

"What?"

"'Tis what I thought. Come and let me show ye what I wanted. There is still time left." He grabbed his wife's hand, leading her away.

"Time for what?" she asked, puzzled.

"Trust me."

"Aye, 'tis what I am afraid of."

～⚬～

As Liadain's mind relived the warmth of her husband's kiss, she followed him in a helpless trance until she glanced around and did not recognize her surroundings.

"Where are ye taking me?"

"To the parapet." He led her up the stone staircase, unbolted the door, and pushed it open.

A rush of air cleared her senses. MacGregor placed his hand at her back, guiding her toward the edge. The sun had set only a few moments earlier and they both stood silently. She peered out over the glistening loch, the dark azure sky beckoning her. The wind brushed up against the soft hairs on her neck, and it was as though the air itself whispered secrets of another time, another place.

Her husband's eyes darkened with emotion, and she was enthralled by what she saw. The brawny Highlander's determination was breaking before her, his walls crumbling, his defenses weakening. The heart-rending tenderness of MacGregor's gaze was strangely flattering. She lowered her head under his scrutiny, and he lifted her chin with his finger and smiled.

"Ye are verra beautiful."

Shaken by the unexpected compliment, Liadain paused. "Thank ye."

His mouth twitched with amusement. "I would be tempted to steal another kiss, but I am afraid I wouldnae stop. When I take ye next, it will be in our bed." She was about to protest when her husband pulled her close and tapped her playfully on her bottom. "Mayhap your woman's time will be through by then."

Praise the saints. She was an idiot. For a brief moment, she had thought to speak the truth, but she could not break Rosalia's trust. Spinning untruths always made matters worse. When would she learn?

"We will be home on the morrow," she said, needing to speak the words aloud for reassurance. "Thank ye for sharing this view with me. 'Tis truly lovely."

He lifted her hand and brushed a kiss on the top, his eyes never leaving hers. "'Tis my pleasure, lass."

"Do ye bring all your women up here?" She bit her lip when she realized what she had done, the words out before she could stop them. She had to mess things up and open her mouth. Straightening her spine, she prepared for the battle to come.

MacGregor stared off into the distance, more than likely contemplating whether or not to toss her from the parapet, when a roguish grin lit up his face.

"My apologies. I deserve whatever 'tis ye have to say," she said softly.

"Must ye know, healer, ye are the only woman I thought to share the view with." He paused. "Only my wife has been here and had the privilege."

"I had nay right to—"

He placed his finger to her lips. "Shh...ye had every right. I cannae blame ye for the question—especially after ye saved me once again from my error in judgment. I donna know where they all come from. Truly."

Liadain raised her eyebrow. "If ye wouldnae have thought with your..." she said, gesturing to his manhood, "ye wouldnae be placed in these circumstances so often."

MacGregor threw up his hands in the air. "Now ye

tell me. And where were ye several years ago, healer, when I could have used your words of wisdom?"

"Ye know ye wouldnae have listened to me."

"Ye are probably right." He rubbed her cheek with the back of his hand. "Ye are chilled. Why donna we step inside? 'Tis our last eve at Glenorchy. On the morrow we will be home."

"Aye, I bet John will be waiting for ye at the gates."

"He is a good lad." He hesitated. "Do ye know of his father?"

Liadain wrapped her arms around herself. "John's father? Nay, Anna ne'er spoke of him and I ne'er pushed the issue. It was apparent she didnae want to speak of him."

"Hmm…"

Twenty-Four

DECLAN WATCHED THE HEALER SLEEP WELL INTO THE night. He watched every breath she took, even the slightest of movements, and memorized every tempting curve of her body. She was an undiscovered treasure that he had left buried for far too long and for no apparent reason except his own stupidity. His mother and father had never quarreled. Perhaps he could even find a way to finally make them proud because in a few short hours, he would make the final journey to his new home.

Not wanting to wake his slumbering wife, he left the bed before the light of day. He wandered the halls of Glenorchy aimlessly, finding himself climbing the steps to seek the solace of the parapet.

"What are ye doing here?" asked Ciaran in the shadows of the early morn.

Declan approached his brother. "I could ask ye the same."

"I couldnae sleep. I know something troubles Rosalia."

"Mayhap she regained her wit and realizes she chose the wrong brother," he said, jestingly.

"Donna start. Why are ye up and about?"

"I couldnae sleep, either."

"Mayhap Liadain has regained her wit and realizes she chose the wrong brother," Ciaran repeated in a dry tone.

"Ciaran, donna even attempt to jest. Ye will ne'er be as good as me, Brother. I have had many years of practice." He paused, running his hand through his hair. "What do ye think troubles Rosalia?"

Ciaran's expression became more serious. "I donna know. She hasnae been sleeping. She tosses and turns, and I have heard her even leave the bedchamber upon occasion in the wee hours of the morn."

"Did ye ask her?"

"Aye, but she insists there is naught amiss and changes the subject."

"Give her time. If something is troubling her, she will tell ye when she is ready."

Ciaran lifted his brow. "I suppose. Since when did ye begin to offer such sound advice?"

"Since the bonny Campbell wench made me see the error of my ways."

"That is the first time I have ever heard ye use the words 'bonny' and 'Campbell' in the same breath. Howbeit I donna care who made ye see your faults—as long as ye see."

Standing in silence, they watched the amber rays of the rising sun. A light mist floated above the lapping water of the loch.

Ciaran cleared his throat. "Do ye need anything further before ye take your leave?"

He leaned against the cool, dewy stone. "Nay, I

donna think so. Ye arenae so far away that I cannae travel to Glenorchy if I need to." And that was the moment Declan had another revelation.

He would be the first to admit that Ciaran was a pain in his bloody arse, but his brother was family, his kin. When their father passed away, his brother had stepped right in, assuming their sire's mantle without question. The last Ciaran likely needed was a reckless younger brother. Somewhat regretful of his prior ill-behavior, Declan was aware that Ciaran's actions were only those of a concerned brother.

"What is troubling ye? Having second thoughts?" Ciaran asked, puzzled.

"Nay…'tisnae easy for me to speak, but I want to thank ye for all ye have done for me."

A soft gasp escaped Ciaran. "What? I couldnae have heard your words correctly."

"Ye heard me perfectly clear. I know I wasnae an easy man to get along with, and there are some acts I regret considerably, but I cannae change the past even if I could. I hope ye can trust in me again, Ciaran, and we may be as brothers as we once were."

Ciaran slapped Declan on the shoulder. "Ye are eternally my brother, my kin. Aiden and I will always be concerned for ye. Ye were killing yourself, whether ye realized it or nae—constantly in your cups and nae to mention your wenching ways. I couldnae stand by and watch ye fall to your knees before my verra eyes. I tried to guide ye, to help ye. I cannae speak to the depths of relief I feel now that ye are starting anew with a wife and responsibilities." It was the first time Declan noticed that his brother's eyes filled with compassion, not judgment. "I only hope ye find peace in your life and within yourself."

Declan could only nod. His words caught in his throat, and he was afraid that if he opened his mouth, his eyes would water like those of some feeble-minded lass. Refusing to lose the infamous MacGregor resolve, he held back his emotions. He had only shed tears once before—upon the death of his beloved mother. He would not allow himself to do it again.

⚜

Liadain gathered her belongings and dragged her sack down the steps. The weight did not bother her. Frankly, she would have carried any weight or treaded through anything to return home. She turned at the sound of Magaidh's bark, and of course her husband walked into the great hall as soon as she reached the bottom step.

"Wife? What are ye doing?" MacGregor approached her with long, purposeful strides and then he reached for her bag. "Ye should have waited for me. I would have brought it down for ye."

Lowering her voice, she murmured, "Since ye didnae join me last eve, I wasnae sure if ye took your leave again without me."

He cast a roguish grin and then he leaned in close. "Healer, ye slept as the dead. I was next to ye the entire time and took my leave early this morn so I wouldnae wake ye. And nay, I wouldnae take my leave without ye." He stood to his full height and brushed her cheek with the back of his hand. Tenderly, his eyes melted into hers.

"My apologies, I am eager to be home."

"Why donna we break our fast and then take our leave?"

Liadain took her seat next to Rosalia in the great hall and her heart sank. Rosalia's color was a pasty white, and a beaded sweat shined upon her brow. The poor woman looked as though death were upon her.

Leaning over, Liadain whispered, "Rosalia, ye were ill again this morn?"

Tears slowly coursed down Rosalia's cheeks. "My stomach is verra unsettled."

A compassionate smile curved Liadain's mouth, and she reached out and rubbed Rosalia's back. "'Tis all right. It will pass in time. I will leave ye some herbs ye can mix with water to make a broth, and it will alleviate some of your discomfort."

When Ciaran leaned forward at the table and his eyes narrowed, Liadain promptly turned her head away from him. "Do ye have everything ye need, Husband?"

MacGregor swallowed a mouthful of food and nodded. "Aye, I spoke with Ciaran and I believe all is in order. Once we return, we will get everything underway. I would like ye to take me one more time through the passages. I need to know my way around without stumbling like a blind fool. Is there anyone else who knows of the tunnels?"

She thought for a moment. "Besides Archie and myself, I cannae think of anyone. My brother wasnae too trusting and I donna think he would have told many."

"Good. I donna want to worry that someone will sneak in and slit my throat in the night." He lifted his brow and a faint light twinkled in the depths of his eyes. "Unless of course I have to worry upon ye."

She laughed. "Ye are the only one who has been caught holding daggers at the throat of others."

"Ye have a point." He shrugged.

After Liadain broke her fast, she made certain her mount was loaded with the last of her belongings. Although she thoroughly enjoyed Rosalia's companionship, she needed time to herself. Anxious to be on her way, she had almost been able to make her escape when Ciaran approached her with a dark look of determination.

"Liadain, is Rosalia ill? What ails her? I need to know." Ciaran's eyes stopped her dead in her tracks as her thoughts raced.

She knew Laird Ciaran MacGregor was not a man to cross, having witnessed his wrath set upon Archie. But she could not betray the confidence that Rosalia had placed upon her, either. She feigned an interest in the straps of her mount.

"Did ye ask Rosalia?" A strong grip encircled her arm and Ciaran whipped her around.

"Ye will tell me what ails my wife," he said through clenched teeth.

She gasped, when her husband flanked her. "Release my wife," he said, his voice laced with a stern warning.

As if Ciaran did not realize he still held her, he dropped her arm. "I must know and ye will tell me." When she backed up, Ciaran attempted to follow.

Her husband pushed Ciaran firmly on the chest, his expression enraged. "Leave off, Brother."

Ciaran's eyes darkened dangerously. "She knows

what is wrong with Rosalia, and I will have the truth," he bellowed, pointing at Liadain.

"She doesnae know anything, Ciaran," Declan said with an edge to his voice.

A heavy silence fell.

Rosalia burst into the stables. "God's teeth! I can hear ye from across the bailey." When no one responded, Rosalia cast a puzzled look at Ciaran. "Husband?"

The fierce MacGregor laird's eyes softened. "I know something ails ye and I want to know the truth. *Now.*" He raised his hand and smoothed Rosalia's tresses. "Something is amiss and ye will tell me. 'Tis enough already. Ye make me mad with worry, Wife." His tone was not so much an order as it was a plea for her to share the truth.

Rosalia's eyes welled with tears. "I am nae certain and I say it again—I am nae certain." Reaching out, she placed her hand on the massive wall of Ciaran's chest and smiled. "'Tis a possibility—a slight possibility—I am with child."

The brawny MacGregor laird fell to his knees and wrapped his arms around Rosalia's middle, resting his head upon her stomach. He held on to his wife like she was his salvation into this world and the next. If Liadain had not witnessed it firsthand, she would not have believed it.

Her husband pulled her along behind him. "Let us leave them." When they exited the stables, MacGregor stopped. "Did ye know Rosalia was with child?"

For a long moment, she looked back at her husband with uncertainty. "She didnae want anyone to know for fear it wasnae true. I gave her my word I wouldnae—"

His expression softened. "Healer, I understand. If ye gave your word, ye gave your word."

She closed her fallen jaw at her husband's demeanor. "I thought ye would be cross with me."

"Then clearly ye donna know me as ye think ye do."

Rosalia and Ciaran walked out of the stables arm in arm. Rosalia wiped her tears and Ciaran grinned briefly with no trace of his former animosity. His smile was without malice, almost remorseful.

"Congratulations, Brother," said MacGregor, giving Ciaran a manly hug and a firm slap upon the back.

Ciaran nodded and then turned to Liadain. "Please accept my apologies."

"There is nay need for apologies. Ye were concerned for your wife. I understand your worry."

"Declan, we arenae certain I am with child. I donna want to be overly joyful and then it doesnae happen," Rosalia said softly.

He nodded. "We willnae celebrate—yet. Howbeit 'tis my hope if ye are with child that he is much like his Uncle Declan. Of course he will be a bonny lad and good with the lasses."

Rosalia coughed and Ciaran grunted. "We only pray the bairn is healthy," said Ciaran, rolling his eyes.

"What say ye, Wife? Are ye ready to travel home?" MacGregor asked, his comforting hand upon Liadain's shoulder.

The man did not need to ask her twice.

❦

Declan hefted her sack over his shoulder and climbed the steps of his new home to their chambers. He dropped the bundle and swung open the door, gesturing for his new wife to enter. He could not wait to see the expression on her face when she noticed the shelves for her healing plants and herbs. And her look was everything he had hoped for.

She gasped. "This wasnae here before. Did ye do this?"

He tossed the healer's sack upon the bed and smiled. "Aye, with some help from John. We moved your plants from your old chamber."

A thoughtful smile curved his wife's lips. "I cannae believe ye did this for me. I truly thank ye. I believed they were all dead and someone had just tossed them out. 'Tis good to know something survived the aftermath of Archie's reign."

"'Tis why I didnae make it back to Glenorchy. John and I were working and wanted this to be a surprise."

"'Tis a wonderful gift. Now I have plenty of room to add my willow bark and other plants I have gathered from court." She stood on her tiptoes and brushed a soft kiss against his cheek. "'Tis perfect. Really perfect," she said, fingering the shelves. "Ye donna mind that my chamber will have plants hanging from the walls?"

"Whatever keeps a smile upon your lovely face."

Like a gust of wind, John bolted into the room. "Ye are back! Mother told me as much. I had to see it for my own eyes," he said, panting between breaths. "Did ye see the shelves we put up?"

"I did and I truly thank ye both for the wonderful gift."

"I told ye she would love it." John elbowed Declan

in the side and then cast the healer a puzzled look. "Ye didnae mind that we moved your plants? He said that ye had to change rooms because ye are his lady and this is where ye belong now."

She looked at John, a small smile playing upon her lips. "When ye grace me with such an offering, how could I mind?"

Declan gave the boy a playful tap on the shoulder. "Let us find your mother, lad."

"I will just unpack and then join ye below stairs," Liadain said.

John looked up at Declan and smiled as soon as they closed the healer's door. "Ye were right. M'lady wasnae cross with ye for moving her belongings."

"Nay, lad." A thought suddenly popped into Declan's mind. "Wait here. I forgot something." He turned around and pushed open his wife's door.

"Healer…"

A soft gasp escaped her. "MacGregor!"

Declan could not help but point and stare. "What the hell is *that*?"

Twenty-Five

LIADAIN WHIPPED THE DELICATE GOWN BEHIND HER back as her husband stood as still as a statue. She tried to mask her guilty look by offering him a demure smile and did not fool the man for a moment.

"I repeat, what the hell was that?"

She turned away, hastily stuffing the transparent material back into her bag. "It was naught."

A firm hand touched her arm. "Nay, it was definitely something." He tugged her away from the sack and then proceeded to pull out the dreaded gown. He held up the wicked cloth, studied it intently, and then turned and held up the delicate material to her frame. His eyes darkened and Liadain could swear that he actually growled.

She pulled the devilish garment out of MacGregor's hands before the situation had a chance to become worse—not that she thought it could. But when a small voice spoke, she was aware that she should not assume anything.

John's shuffling feet entered into the chamber. "Do ye come or nae, sir?"

Her husband's eyes twinkled with liveliness. "Nae yet."

Liadain playfully slapped at her beast of a husband. "Cease. It means naught. This was only a foolish gift from Rosalia and Aisling."

"I donna think 'tis foolish at all. Mmm…I will admit that my sisters-by-marriage can at times be verra wise."

John sighed, tapping his foot. "Are ye coming?"

"Rest assured, healer, we will be discussing this later."

Wonderful—just what she had hoped for. She knew the rogue would not forget about this. He would continue to hound her until he received the answer he sought. What possible reason would she be able to divulge for having such a naughty gown in her possession if she did not intend to wear it?

She unpacked her sack for the last time and welcomed the distraction. Her new chamber was certainly much roomier than her last. Glancing to the shelves, she smiled. Perhaps the peace offering was a new beginning. With the last of her belongings put away, she wandered into the kitchens where Anna, John, and MacGregor were sitting at a small wooden table enjoying fresh baked bread.

Anna jumped up from her seat when she spotted Liadain. "My lady."

Liadain waved her off. "Please donna fuss over me." She sat down on the bench and reached for a piece of bread. "It smells delightful." She felt MacGregor's heated gaze upon her, and her heart fluttered. She was strangely flattered by his interest.

"The new master is taking me to watch his men

practice swordplay in the bailey," said John with a look of worship.

"How lovely," Liadain said. She made an error in judgment by glancing into MacGregor's sparkling eyes.

"Aye, why donna ye come with us? Mayhap I will even pick up a sword with Montgomery," he said, placing the last piece of bread into his mouth.

"Rosalia says Montgomery is quite skilled." When MacGregor raised his brow and his lips twitched with amusement, she quickly added, "With a sword."

"John, I donna want ye in the way," said Anna, giving her son a reprimanding look.

"He willnae be in the way. Will ye, John?" asked MacGregor.

The lad shook his head adamantly. "Nay, sir, I give ye my word."

"Well then. There ye have it." He rose from the bench and nodded to John. "We donna want to keep the men waiting."

Swallowing the last of her bread, Liadain brushed off her hands and stood. "Donna worry. I will watch over him."

"'Tis good to have ye home, m'lady."

It was good to be home.

The clanking sounds of metal swords rang through the bailey. The men formed a circle around Montgomery and another man. Sweat beaded on both of their foreheads, and the other man grunted when his blade was met with strong resistance.

Walking along the edge of the bailey, Liadain watched the men. She sat down on a bench near the stone wall. Once the men had ample opportunity to show off their prowess, she would make her escape to see to her plants.

⁂

Declan watched his bonny wife circle around his men and sit on the bench. She was difficult to miss with her curvy figure and full rosy lips. He could not wait to taste them—again.

John tugged on his tunic. "Well?"

"Well what?"

John let out a loud sigh. "I have been speaking with ye, and ye havenae been listening. Mother would scold ye if she were here."

He chuckled with amusement. "Ye have my undivided attention."

"Do ye think ye could teach me how to wield a sword?"

Declan shook his head and looked back at Montgomery, who had extended an arm to his fallen comrade. "I donna think your mother would approve."

"Mayhap if *ye* speak with her she would."

He ruffled John's hair and smiled. "We shall see. It might be better if Montgomery would instruct ye. I am more suited for the bow."

"Then will ye teach me the bow?" the lad asked with persistence.

John reminded him of someone he knew. When Montgomery finished toying with his man, he dismissed the remainder of the guard. Declan was pleased with his efforts.

"The men are well trained," said Declan.

"Aye, but there is always room for improvement."

Holding out a sword, Montgomery smiled. "Shall we show them how 'tis done?"

Declan nudged John out of harm's way and grabbed the sword from Montgomery. "Ye know swordplay isnae my strong skill."

"So your brother has said," Montgomery responded. "'Tis an essential, though, in close quarters."

Montgomery lunged.

His blade only nearly missed Declan's ear. With two quick steps forward, Declan hefted his sword but Montgomery effortlessly twisted out of his way and blocked his swing. He had just lifted his weapon to administer another blow when Montgomery moved swiftly to the side, elbowing him square in the back.

"Ye made your point," he grunted.

"Ye overexaggerate your movements and your body speaks where ye will strike. It gives me plenty of time to prepare a defense, but your form is good."

"Thank ye, I think."

"Strike at me. Now," Montgomery ordered.

He followed the captain of his guard's instructions, swung, and to his surprise, Montgomery fell backward to the ground with a heavy thump. When he placed the tip of his sword at Montgomery's throat, the man smiled. "Verra good. Your lady watches."

Declan's eyes widened. Montgomery had actually taken a fall to protect Declan's pride. Extending his arm, he pulled the captain of his guard to his feet and then turned around and shared a smile with his bonny wife. He definitely owed Montgomery.

The healer approached as John raced to Declan's side. "Ye did it! Montgomery yielded!" John shouted.

Declan twisted his head around as the captain of his guard gathered his swords, attempting to hold back a smile. There were not many men who did not let their pride consume them. No wonder his sister-by-marriage favored the man's friendship and Ciaran despised him.

Placing his hand upon John's shoulder, Declan smiled. "Ye need to return to your mother now. There is something to which I must attend."

❧

Liadain noticed MacGregor watched her intently. She had to admit that there was a maddening hint of arrogance about him. Her fingers suddenly ached to touch her husband as she admired his powerful set of shoulders.

"There is plenty of time for that later, healer." His voice was soothing, yet oddly disturbing. "I need ye to show me the passages once more."

"Of course," she said. Still thinking it unwise to permit him to see how much he rattled her, she spun on her heel.

Neither of them spoke as they walked along the outer barmkin wall of the castle. MacGregor did not broach the subject of her shameful gown, and she did not offer any explanation. When they reached the entrance to the tunnel, he cleared his throat.

"'Tis verra well hidden, and unless ye know of the passage, I donna think it would be compromised."

Liadain nodded. "I donna believe anyone has ever discovered this entrance—well, except mayhap ye when ye bolted from the brush and frightened me almost to my death."

He gave her a wicked smile. "Come now, healer, the only reason I startled ye was because of my bonny looks. Ye have ne'er seen a man as handsome as me. Admit it." He nudged her arm.

"I admit naught," she retorted. "Come now, rogue, and follow me through the dark." Entering the passageway, the dolt immediately bumped into her. "MacGregor, truly."

"My apologies," he uttered behind her. "Donna light a candle. I must know my way."

The tunnel was dark and damp, cooler air surrounding them. "Reach out and feel for the wall." When he did not respond, she assumed that he had. "Keep your hand on the wall and move forward carefully until ye feel the wall separate."

They shuffled their way through the corridor and when the wall bowed, she stopped. Her husband promptly stepped on her heel.

"Ye need to tell me when ye stop," he chided her.

"I realize that. Give me your hand and donna place it upon my breast." A warm chuckle answered her. She scrambled for her husband's hand. Placing his hand on the wall, she rubbed his fingers back and forth. "Do ye feel that?"

"Aye. So if I walk straight, I travel to the great hall. If I move to the left, 'tis to my study."

"Aye. Do ye want to lead and I will follow?"

MacGregor grabbed her and spun her around, changing positions. "Are ye ready?"

"Lead on." With one hand upon the wall and the other holding his tunic, Liadain shuffled her way to Archie's study.

When Declan opened the stone door, he held up his hands in delight. "It wasnae as troublesome as the first time."

She raised her brow and folded her arms over her chest. "Ye speak in truth. Ye arenae as troublesome as the first time."

He smiled and sat down in the chair behind Archie's desk. He leaned back and casually crossed his ankles, lifting them to rest on the desk. "Healer, donna jest unless ye can handle it back."

"Was that all ye wanted to see? I would like to tend to my plants. Mayhap on the morrow we can ride to the village."

He waved his hand in a dismissive gesture. "Aye, 'tis all I wanted to see—for now." When he undressed her with his eyes, his double meaning could not have been any more transparent.

Clearing her throat, she hastily looked away and walked out the door. The man was so brazen and comfortable with his every move. She despised the fact that he could see right through her.

As she reached her husband's bedchamber door, she paused and could not cease the curiosity that plagued her. Since the rogue was currently occupied in the study, she could not resist a peek.

Liadain slipped inside his bedchamber and quickly closed the door. The massive bed was just as she remembered. Approaching the stone wall beside the fireplace, she studied the portrait of her father. The painting was not in her father's likeness. It portrayed her sire with warmth and compassion, the complete opposite of everything the man had been.

As she studied the painting, nagging questions hammered at her heart. The portrait looked odd on the wall, especially when there was an empty space above the mantel. She thought her father's portrait would be the last thing her husband would want in his chamber. Having a Campbell laird staring at the man while he slept would surely give anyone nightmares. She decided to remove it.

She hefted the painting from the wall and placed it on the floor. She doubted MacGregor would even miss it.

Wonderful. A prominent empty space was now on the adjoining wall, as well as above the mantel. She tried to remember if they had another tapestry to fill the spot. As she considered her options, she noticed something sticking out of the wall where the portrait had hung.

Liadain ran her hand over the rough stone and felt a distinct indentation—similar to the entrance to the passageways. She pushed at it and the wall separated.

Squeezing through the gap, she was immediately engulfed in pitch black. She cautiously moved her way back out, thinking it best to light a candle. As she reentered the small opening, she saw it was a passageway with only enough space for her to stand. She held up the candle to the partition, and in the center of the wall was another ridge.

Liadain gave the wall a push and it creaked open. She stepped carefully into what looked like another modest chamber. As she lit another candle, the room was illuminated—a study. Maps adorned the walls and golden trinkets lined the shelves. When she spotted a dark wooden desk, she could not resist a peek inside.

She walked around the desk and opened a drawer. She pulled out a stack of notes in Archie's handwriting and flipped through them. None of it made any sense. Perhaps MacGregor could sort through them. He would certainly trust her once she disclosed her discovery. If Archie had any method to his madness, MacGregor could decipher it. She put everything back where she had found it, shoving the papers back into the drawer and closing it.

Randomly pulling out another drawer, she sighed. Letters, papers, notes. What did Archie need with all of these? Shuffling through them, she spotted a detailed map of Parliament House with what looked like lines that all led to a centralized giant 'X.' Odd, what would Archie be doing with that? Her brother had been to Parliament House many times. She was about to place the document back when a bold name jumped off the page at her.

Catesby.

She thought of her time at court. Could it possibly be the same Catesby who had befriended MacGregor? She scrolled down the page, hoping to catch his first name. Well, at least that was her intent until another name caught her attention.

Percy.

This could not be a coincidence. Liadain sat down behind the desk and continued to read. God's teeth! What had her brother been into?

According to what she read, her brother had met more than a handful of times with Catesby and Percy.

She gathered they had wanted to remove someone from his position of power, probably some English lord who tried to invade Archie's territory. She grunted. Her brother had always been overly greedy.

As she continued to read, she stirred uneasily. This could not be true. *Dunnehl. Fawkes.*

She continued to sort through her brother's notes, looking for anything that would give her an inkling of the association between the men. Pulling out the last document she could find, she slowly read the contents.

Her heart leapt into her throat.

A little less than one year ago, Archie had met with Catesby, Percy, Dunnehl, Fawkes, and... *Cranborne* to map out an assassination of someone at Parliament House.

She placed her head in her hands. "Robert, what did ye do?"

She needed to find MacGregor. Her husband would know what to do. How could Robert plot to kill someone with Elizabeth and his new bairn by his side? How long had Archie been scheming with Dunnehl? Her chest felt like it would burst, and unanswered questions knotted inside her.

Liadain hastily made her way back. As she exited the wall and pulled it closed, she glanced around the empty chamber. In her nervousness, she grabbed her father's portrait and hung it back upon the wall. With one last look around, she fled through the adjoining door, needing to pull herself together. She jumped when a male voice cut through her musings.

"Healer, where have ye been?"

Twenty-Six

MACGREGOR WAS NAKED.

His brawny chest was covered with tawny hair, and Liadain longed to touch him. Her husband relaxed on her bed with not a care in the world, his arm casually upon his raised leg, looking as though he were a gift from the gods.

He arched his eyebrows mischievously and cast an irresistibly devastating grin. "I took the liberty of placing your *gown* on the chair for ye to slip into. I will even turn my back if ye want."

"How kind of ye," she said, her mouth dry. "Although I am quite flattered by your efforts, there is a pressing matter that we need to discuss."

His expression darkened. "Healer, whatever 'tis ye need to speak with me about can wait until the morrow. This eve, ye are mine, *Wife*." His eyes were full of promises, and then he winked at her.

Something within her stirred at his open declaration of claiming her as his wife. It had been far too long. She was perfectly aware that they both desired each other. Perhaps the man was right and this was what they both needed. The letters weren't going any-where, and perhaps once she had a chance to discuss them with him, the answers would be clear. "Turn over," she ordered him, casting a playful smile.

She walked over to the chair where he'd placed the wicked gown. She hoped to hell Rosalia and Aisling knew what they were doing. At this juncture, she would try anything to capture her husband's heart.

Liadain quickly disrobed and donned the wicked attire. She ran her hands over the delicate material. What did men see in this clothing or lack thereof? "MacGregor, I cannae do it. I feel foolish."

He rolled over onto his back and sat up slowly, his expression holding a savage inner fire. "Ye donna look foolish." Desire pooled in her husband's eyes as he slipped from the bed. He approached her with admir-ing glances, and his maleness became increasingly evident with every step he took.

Slowly, he raised his hand and fingered a lock of her hair. "Ye are beautiful, Wife."

Liadain could not speak. She could only gaze into her husband's eyes. She loved this side of him—the kindness, the desire, the passion, the dropping of all his ridiculous pretenses. This was the man she had grown so fond of and who had captured her heart.

She threw herself into her husband's arms and he brought his lips down to hers. Her calm was shattered by the hunger of his kisses. His firm mouth demanded a response, one that she was more than willing to give. She was shocked at her own delight in his touch.

His lips seared a path down her neck, her shoulders.

She laced her fingers in his hair, pulling him close. His gentle touch sent currents of desire through her.

She felt the thrill of her husband's arousal, and when he moved his thigh between her legs, the glorious heat nearly caused her knees to buckle. As if he sensed her impending need, he bent down and swept her from her feet, weightless, into his arms. She placed her arms around his neck, and for a moment, he merely stood there, holding her and gazing into her eyes. There were no words to be spoken.

He carried her and gently eased her down upon the bed. He pulled back slightly and lightly ran his exploring fingers over her curves. Her skin tingled when he touched her, shivers of delight sliding sensuously up her arm.

Liadain placed her hand on his rock-hard chest and brushed the tawny hairs. His gaze slowly dropped from her eyes to her shoulders to her breasts. His hand outlined the circle of her breast.

Her gown crept up to her thighs as she moved closer to him. He pulled the fabric upward over her belly, her chest. He lowered his head and his tongue caressed her sensitive nipples, her breasts surging at the familiarity of his touch. His tongue continued to tantalize the buds, which had swollen to their fullest.

When MacGregor's strong hand seared a path down her abdomen and onto her thigh, she thought she would come undone. He explored her thighs and then moved up, his lips again teasing a taut, dusky pink nipple.

He paused to kiss her, whispering his love for each part of her body. The stroking of his fingers sent pleasure jolts through her. Completely aroused now, she drew herself closer to him.

He paused and his body moved partially to uncover hers. "I want to see all of ye."

She wiggled her way out of the delicate gown and tossed it to the floor. She moaned softly as he lay her back down. It was flesh against flesh, man against woman. Her breasts tingled against his hard chest.

"Ye are verra bonny, Wife," he said, his voice low and purposefully alluring. He took her hand and guided it to himself.

Her fingers encircled him and he moved his body against her.

When he reached between her thighs, opening her legs and then inserting his finger, she gasped in sweet agony.

"Ye are so wet for me, Wife."

Her desire for him overrode all sense of reason.

He recognized her need and entered her in a single thrust, sending a jolt of pleasure straight through her. A moan of ecstasy slipped through her lips.

The hot tide of passion raged through her. It was a raw act of possession. In one swift motion he had swept away all her doubts and fears.

Sweat beaded upon his forehead and his chest heaved. She surrendered completely to his masterful seduction, her eager response matching his. When they were roused to the peak of desire, he pulled back and gazed into her eyes. With another heavy thrust, she arched her back and couldn't control the outcry of delight and the feeling of satisfaction her husband left within her as he spilled his seed.

Liadain looked up and her heart lurched madly. When he collapsed on top of her, she could feel his heart pounding against her own. Though she was hesitant to admit it, there was an undeniable bond between them.

He rolled onto his side and draped his arm over her. She lay panting, her chest heaving. They shared a smile and both burst out laughing because his breath was as labored as hers.

"God's teeth, lass, are ye trying to kill me?"

She giggled in response. "I thought ye were trying to kill me." She ran her fingernails up and down his arm. "That was verra enjoyable, Husband."

His eyes held some unidentifiable emotion. "For me as well." He gathered her into his arms and held her snugly against him.

Liadain had never dreamed her husband's hands would be so warm, so gentle. She could no longer deny herself his touch and was astonished at the sense of fulfillment she felt. She allowed her thoughts to emerge from their hidden depths, and looking back, she knew MacGregor was kinder than he wanted anyone to know.

She lay in the drowsy warmth of her own bed with her husband, thinking of the days to come.

◦◦◦

His wife stirred in the cradle of his arms. As Declan pulled her closer, a curl tickled his nose, along with the scent of lavender. How many times had he taken her last eve? Frankly, it did not matter. Her bottom nestled into his groin and he kissed the top of her head.

He was not sure if it had been the first, second, or perhaps even the third time he sated his needs, but when his wife gazed upon him with such a look of longing, something within him stirred. It was if the healer's eyes spoke of hidden feelings she silently screamed to express. He realized he was not a perfect husband, but perhaps in time, she would grow to have a certain fondness for him.

He glanced down at her and smiled.

As if sensing his stare, she stretched and groaned. "Am I dead?" Her voice was raspy.

"I donna know, lass. Nae unless I am as well. Just to be certain, would ye want me to take ye again then?" he jested, nudging his nose into her hair.

She moaned. "MacGregor, after last eve, I donna think I can even move from this bed."

"Come now, healer, ye need to practice if ye intend to keep up with me."

Opening one eye, she smirked. "I couldnae keep up with ye if I tried."

"Ye didnae have any trouble last eve," he said silkily.

She slapped him in the arm and then rested her head on the top of his chest. Her fingernails lightly brushed and tickled his skin. "I enjoyed last eve with ye, Husband."

He rubbed his hand over her back. "I am joyful to hear it."

"MacGregor, do ye trust me?"

"Aye." Declan did not hesitate and was not exactly sure why he answered as quickly as he did, but it was the truth. "Why do ye ask?"

His bonny wife rested her chin on his chest, met his

eyes, and cast a weary smile. "Last eve, I entered your chamber while ye were in the study." When his eyes narrowed, she continued. "I was curious if ye changed Archie's room."

"Wife, ye can enter my chamber any time ye wish."

"I saw the portrait of my father and—"

"MacGregor!" someone bellowed in the hall, followed by an incessant pounding upon the bed-chamber door.

Declan grunted through clenched teeth, especially for being interrupted after giving instructions he was not to be disturbed. "God's teeth, Montgomery! Ye better have a damn good reason for—"

"A messenger comes from Glenorchy," Montgomery paused. "'Tis Rosalia." His words were laced with worry.

Without warning, the healer sprang from the bed and ran to the chair. Hastily, she donned her chemise and started to dress. The moment was clearly lost.

Declan climbed out of bed and grabbed his kilt from the floor. "I know I will only be in your way, but I will accompany ye to Glenorchy."

Montgomery knocked again and Declan partially opened the door. If the captain of his guard noticed his lack of clothing, the man did not indicate it. "My wife is dressing."

He nodded. "MacGregor, might I accompany Lady MacGregor to Glenorchy?"

When the healer's dress bunched up in the back, she turned around and gestured for Declan's assistance. As he stepped toward his wife, she began to speak as a warrior on the battlefield, spewing orders.

"There is nay need for ye to come along if Montgomery will escort me. Rosalia has been having bouts of sickness. If she bleeds, there will be more of a concern and I will be longer. I will send a messenger if I willnae be home. In the meantime, why donna ye spend some time getting to know your new home?"

He straightened her gown. "I would like to walk around the castle and get to know the grounds. And I havenae yet tried to use the false door in the stable. Ye're sure ye donna mind?"

She smiled as if she already knew the answer. "I wouldnae have suggested it otherwise. Have a care in the tunnels. I donna want to come home and find I have to search for ye."

He kissed her hand and then walked back to the door. "Ye can accompany my wife, but take another man with ye."

Montgomery's eyes were filled with gratitude and concern. "Ye have my thanks. I will ready the mounts and meet Lady MacGregor below stairs."

Declan closed the door and his wife approached him. He brushed the back of his hand to her cheek in a gentle gesture. "I will wait for ye to return home, Wife." He pulled her into the circle of his arms and then placed a gentle kiss to her forehead.

She nodded in response and then whipped her head up with a concentrated look upon her features. "MacGregor, 'tis important when I return that we discuss what I attempted to speak with ye about last eve."

"Ye mean before I distracted ye?"

"Aye, I must make haste." Standing on her tiptoes, his wife kissed his cheek. "I will be back soon,

Husband." She grabbed her healing supplies and tossed them into her sack. Casting one last glimpse at him, she smiled and hastily walked out the door.

⁌

Liadain breathed a sigh of relief when they finally arrived at Glenorchy.

Rosalia was bent over on a bench, her face concealed by her hands. Liadain dismounted. As she approached, Rosalia looked up and tears swept down her cheeks.

"I am such a daft fool," she cried.

Liadain knelt down and rubbed Rosalia's arm. Even though she felt Montgomery's gaze burning into her back, at least the man had the decency to remain quiet. "Ye arenae a daft fool. What ails ye?" she asked with sympathy.

Wiping her tears, Rosalia gulped. "My apologies. Ciaran left this morn with Aiden, Aisling, and my nephew to go to the village. I was alone and I was so frightened. I couldnae keep my stomach from retching and I could barely stand. It usually passes, but when I couldnae get it to cease, I sent a messenger to Castle Campbell. I thought I was losing my bairn. My apologies that ye came for naught."

"'Tis the first time ye are with child. If ye donna know what to expect, it can be a troubling," Liadain soothed. "The last thing ye need is to fret over us making the journey. Ye are my sister-by-marriage. Ye are kin. I am sure ye would do the same."

Rosalia smiled sheepishly. "Since ye came all this way, ye might as well stay for the noon meal. Ciaran should be returning in a few hours."

We would love to stay," said Liadain, tapping Rosalia's leg.

Pulling herself to her feet, Rosalia locked arms with Liadain, guiding her toward the great hall with Montgomery in tow. Lowering her voice, Rosalia whispered, "I cannae apologize enough. Declan and Ciaran will more than likely want to throttle me when they find out."

"My husband understands, and your husband loves ye. They will be relieved ye are well," said Liadain reassuringly. "Donna think upon it too much. Women have been giving birth since the beginning of time. Ye willnae harm the babe. The sickness that plagues ye is the bairn's way of telling ye he or she is fine. I agree 'tis verra inconvenient, but 'tis a good sign."

Rosalia giggled in response. "Then he must be one verra healthy babe."

As soon as they walked into the great hall, Montgomery reached out and grabbed Rosalia's arm. "Might I have a word with ye?"

Montgomery huddled with Rosalia, and the last thing Liadain wanted to do was sit after the tedious journey. She had just reached out to pet Magaidh when a shout rang out behind her.

Twenty-Seven

DECLAN COULD NOT DENY THE EVIDENCE ANY LONGER. His wee bonny wife was consuming his every waking moment. He found himself daydreaming of her and her long raven tresses. The more he had come to know her, the more he was aware of the fact that she was nothing like the bloody Campbell. She was kind and good-hearted, someone he was proud to call his wife. He could not wait until she returned from Glenorchy—perhaps they could even repeat their extended bout of lovemaking.

With a lighter spring in his step, he ambled out into the bailey, where he was halted by a loud commotion. All he managed to make out was a bellowing command to open his gates.

John ran toward him. "'Tis the king's men. They carry His Majesty's banner."

Declan could not stay the sense of foreboding that washed over him. Damn. He knew it was too good to be true. He had won Castle Campbell fairly and wed the healer, everything King James had commanded. He prayed his liege was not taking back his word.

Why else would His Majesty's guard be pounding at Declan's gates? This had to be some cruel jest. Typical—as soon as he started to make sense of his life, everything was going to be pulled out from under him. Perhaps he was overreacting. After all, he had done nothing wrong. No sense dwelling upon it. There was only one way to find out their purpose.

"Open the gates," Declan ordered his men. Turning to John, he placed his hand upon the boy's shoulder. "Seek your mother and stay with her." He gave the lad a brief nod of dismissal and John ran off.

What the hell was this? Roughly a score and a half of men galloped into the bailey. A few carried the king's flag, a red cross on a white background. Uncertainty increased with every moment. When prancing hooves encircled him, he knew this could not bode well. The bailey was full of mounted, armed men. Whichever way this would turn, his people were sorely outnumbered.

"Make way, make way," said a portly Englishman, pushing his mount through the crowd.

As the horses parted, Declan made a deliberate attempt not to stiffen, but a chill ran down his spine as soon as he spotted Lord Dunnehl. Perhaps it was simply his own uneasiness, but the arse certainly took his bloody time adjusting his seat in the saddle. When Dunnehl's lips twisted into a cynical smile, Declan knew one thing for certain. The man thoroughly enjoyed this—whatever this might be.

A man of the royal guard came forward. "Declan MacGregor, you are hereby charged with treason against the Crown. In accordance with the laws granted by His Majesty, the King of Great Britain, I order you to stand trial for your crimes. Seize him."

Two men flanked Declan, and his gaze narrowed at the guard who was clearly in charge. At the same time, the remaining handful of MacGregor men unsheathed their swords, waiting for Declan's command.

"I havenae committed any crimes against the Crown. 'Tis ridiculous. I demand to see King James," said Declan.

Dunnehl smirked and threw up his hands in the air in an overdramatic movement. "Demand? You demand to see the king you attempted to kill at Parliament House? You have some bollocks, I dare say. There is plenty of time for that later. And lucky for you, King James is residing at his northern estate near my home in Northumberland. Confess your crimes and mercy may be awarded upon your soul. Perhaps your death will even be quick. Regardless, I would not worry, MacGregor. King James wants an audience with you, too."

When Declan caught a sudden movement out of the corner of his eye, he turned. John bolted out into the bailey and Anna clutched a kitchen knife in her hand, chasing her son.

"John! Ye come here at once!" she ordered, gesturing for her son to come back.

"John! Donna ye interfere. Stay with your mother!" ordered Declan.

Blatantly ignoring them both, John rushed one of the men who restrained Declan and kicked his shin. "Let him go! Let him go!" When John's kick had no impact on the guard, John bent his head forward and sank his teeth into the man's hand, hard.

The guard yelped in pain.

Without warning, the brute smacked John to the ground, the sound of the crack driving a nail right through Declan's heart. When the lad sat up, blood dripped from the corner of his lip and he swayed, disoriented.

Anna ran to her son's side and fell to her knees. She dropped the knife and cradled John to her bosom.

At the same time, curses fell from Declan's mouth and his fist automatically came into contact with a face. Spinning around, he kneed another man in the groin. Someone grabbed him from behind and attempted to restrain him.

"He is only a lad," Declan bit out. He refused to submit without a fight, and it took four men to subdue him. It came as no surprise when the MacGregor men were also relieved of their weapons and restrained.

"Lord Dunnehl, control your men. You are not to intercede," ordered the guard in command.

"Enough of this foolishness. Seize the Highlander and leave the whelp to lick his wounds. Bring the Highland woman. Perhaps her Highland tongue will soften around my English cock," spat Dunnehl.

Springing to his feet, John fearlessly charged at Dunnehl. "Ye willnae touch my mother!"

Only when the sun reflected from the blade did Declan realize that John wielded the knife. He screamed upon deaf ears as Anna ran after John. Instinctively, one of Dunnehl's men unsheathed his sword. This had gone too far. He needed to stop this madness.

"Nay! Donna ye touch them!" Declan bellowed with reckless anger. He fought to release the iron grip of the men that held him and his furious glare swung to the leader of the guards, but it was too late.

Anna pushed John out of the way and then glanced down. She gasped, panting in fear. A sword was slowly pulled from Anna's gut, blood pooling into her hands. The light was snuffed out of her eyes and then she collapsed to the ground.

"Mother! Mother! I will kill ye! Ye English cur! I will kill ye!" John dropped to his knees and held his blood-soaked mother tenderly in his arms, rocking her gently back and forth. "Mother, please donna leave me. Mother," he sobbed.

Declan's anger became a scalding fury and he was breathless with rage. He swung his head back and a man's nose crunched under the forceful blow. He could not remember all of what happened next, but John's cries would forever be imbedded in his mind. He would personally kill the smug English cur who sat so mightily above them.

With a firm knock on the head, Declan fell to the ground. He lifted his eyes to Dunnehl and spoke through clenched teeth. *"Mo mhallachd ort! An diobhail toirt leis thu!" My curse on you! The devil take you!*

Dunnehl chuckled. "I know not what you speak, Highland barbarian. Save it for His Majesty." Casting John one last glance, Dunnehl spoke without remorse. "You will be all right, my dear boy. I was raised without my mother and I turned out just fine." He gave his man a nod and smiled. "Leave MacGregor's men with the whelp to bury his mother. They are no match for the king's guard. Bind MacGregor and put him on a horse. We need to make haste. His Majesty waits for his traitorous head."

⌘

Liadain jumped at the uproar. Twisting around, she watched in shock as Ciaran and Aiden assisted John into the great hall. He was covered in blood and dirt, and she barely recognized the boy. She gasped and ran to his side.

"John! Where are ye hurt?" She frantically searched the boy's body for any sign of injury and was taken aback when he had no external wounds. A glazed look of despair was spread over his features, his expression one of mute wretchedness.

A chill silence surrounded them.

"John," she repeated. When the boy did not respond, Liadain knelt down beside him and turned him to face her. "Look at me. Whose blood is this?"

"He arrived at the gates when we were returning from the village and hasnae spoken a single word," said Ciaran with concern.

Her stomach knotted. Searching for a plausible explanation, she began to question him. "Where were ye? Did this happen at Castle Campbell? Where is your mother?"

John gulped hard, tears slipping down his filthy, bloodstained cheeks. "Dead."

Uncertainty made Liadain's voice harsh and demanding. "What do ye mean? What happened?" A large hand encircled her arm and Ciaran pulled her to her feet.

Effortlessly, Ciaran scooped up John's tired and

ragged body. "We can discuss this further in my study." Practically stepping on Ciaran's heels, Liadain followed him with Montgomery and Aiden. Ciaran placed John onto a chair, and the lad looked helpless and lost.

Kneeling beside him, Ciaran placed his hand on the boy's shoulder. "John, ye are a verra brave lad and were wise for coming here. Ye are safe now. Howbeit ye need to tell us what happened. Do ye understand? 'Tis verra important that ye do."

John nodded but couldn't speak through his tears. He wiped his eyes, then tried to speak again. "The king's men came to Castle Campbell and demanded to see the master. They took him."

"What do ye mean they took him?" blurted out Liadain.

Ciaran shook his head at her when she spoke. When John started to sob again, Ciaran squeezed his shoulder. "It will be all right, lad, but ye need to tell us all."

"They said he committed crimes against the Crown. I tried to help him, but I couldnae. They wanted to take my mother and she…He pulled out his sword and…" John could not finish. He didn't have to. Tears streamed down his filthy cheeks, and there was a heavy moment of silence.

"'Tis all right, lad. Where are Declan's men?"

"They are at Castle Campbell. The king's men left them there to bury my mother and they only took him. There was over a score of them. When the English bastards took their leave, I ran to the stable and took a horse. I rode here with much haste. He and m'lady have been naught but good to me and Mother."

"Did they speak of what crimes Declan committed?" asked Ciaran.

"The king's man didnae really speak upon it. There was some fanciful lord who did most of the talking. The lord said the master attempted to murder King James."

"Murder the king? Tis absolutely ridiculous," said Liadain.

"John, I want ye to think verra hard. Did they say where they were taking him?" asked Ciaran with a concentrated look upon his features.

"I heard them say the king was staying at one of his northern estates. The lord, I think his name was Dunnehl, said it was near his home in Northumberland."

"Dunnehl?" everyone said at the same time.

John cast a nervous glance. "Aye, I think that was his name," he answered cautiously.

A muscle ticked in Ciaran's jaw. "Did they speak of anything else, lad? Anything at all? Speak what ye remember even if ye think 'tisnae important. Did they mayhap mention how, when, or where Declan attempted to kill the king?"

John was deep in thought when his face suddenly lit up. "Aye, I remember. I donna think he mentioned how or when, but he said where. Parliament House."

Ciaran stood and patted the boy on the shoulder. "Ye did verra well, lad. Donna worry. We will get him back. Aiden, take John out and have someone clean him up," he ordered. Sitting down behind his wooden desk, Ciaran sighed. "Ye will stay at Glenorchy, Liadain. We will travel to Northumberland and fetch my brother."

"Nay," countered Liadain. "We ride to Castle Campbell."

~~~~~

Declan was breathless with rage. He swallowed, trying not to reveal his fury, and smirked when he remembered all of the countless times he chose to ignore his father's never-ending advice. Why was it at this particular juncture in his life that he found his sire's life lessons slipping through his thoughts? As if his father's words were able to hold his emotions in check, he silently repeated one of his father's lectures.

"If ye let your anger guide ye, it will do ye nay good."

True. Perhaps even get him killed before he had an audience with King James.

"A well thought plan is always best."

Declan had to admit, that one was by no means an easy feat. He would need to give this further thought.

Riding the last few hours in silence did not help relieve his anger; the urge to drive a stake through Dunnehl's black heart was overwhelming. Knowing he would only fuel the fire if he showed any signs of weakness, he kept his eyes straight ahead and spoke not a single word. He let his mind race with torturous thoughts, realizing how many ways there were to kill a man. And he mentally took pleasure in them all.

English cur.

Once he met with the king, he would be able to clear the air and his name. The whole situation was complete and utter chaos. Who would even believe such an absurd accusation that he attempted to kill his liege? Anyone who knew him was completely aware that he never made it a point to concern himself with politics.

He and the healer had traveled from court directly to Glenorchy. How could he have been involved in a plot to kill the king? But until he could speak directly with His Majesty, he would keep his mouth shut and his eyes forward. And then he would make Dunnehl pay for what he'd done.

Twenty-Eight

LIADAIN'S BLOOD BOILED. HER HUSBAND HAD BEEN forcefully taken to stand trial for crimes he had not committed. If she had not discovered Archie's secret study, MacGregor surely would have been convicted of an unspeakable act against the Crown. She pulled her drifting thoughts together and now the pieces fit so clearly—Catesby, Percy, and Fawkes latching on to MacGregor not long after they arrived at court. How many times had the men sung the praises of her husband's skill with a bow? And it was all a ploy. Of course there was no question about Dunnehl's hand in this. And she could not help wondering whether the tournament and her marriage were part of the plan as well.

The only question that still hammered away at her was the extent of Robert's entanglement in this mess. The man had been elevated to Viscount Cranborne. He had Elizabeth and his bairn. Why would he be scheming with such unsavory men?

Ciaran and Aiden had only needed a short time to gather their men and supplies before leaving for Castle Campbell. She cast a worried glance at John, whose head was bowed. The lad had barely spoken since they rushed from Glenorchy.

Ciaran rode up beside her. "We waste precious time. Could ye enlighten us with your urgency in traveling to Castle Campbell?"

"I discovered something in the castle that will help clear my husband's name. We need to get—"

"Mother!" John pushed his mount forward, dashing to the mound of dirt the MacGregor men encircled. The boy dismounted and knelt before the fresh grave. He gulped hard, tears flowing down his cheeks.

Ciaran cleared his throat. "Healer, I feel for the lad, but we need to make haste."

"I need only a moment."

Sliding from her mount, she clamped her lips shut and held back a sob. The boy was alone and had no one. When she tried to speak, her voice broke miserably. "John, there are nay words I can offer ye to make this right. Your mother was a verra wonderful and kind woman. Howbeit I promise ye that ye arenae alone. Ye still have me."

After a moment, John rose and turned to face her. "I loved my mother and she didnae deserve this, but I am nae alone. I still have ye, Aunt."

Liadain's mouth dropped open. "*Aunt*? Ye are Archie's son?" she whispered. She was not as shocked as she should have been when the words left her lips. The way Anna always dodged questions regarding John's father, perhaps in some way she had always known.

He nodded. "Mother and the earl would often spar with each other, and sometimes I heard their words.

Aye, I was his bastard son. 'Tis why he didnae want me under his roof or underfoot."

She embraced him. "John, ye will ne'er be alone. Rest assured, my husband and I want ye about. Ye are kin. My family. *Our* family. We shall speak later," she said.

She gave the boy a quick kiss on the top of his head and smiled. For a brief moment, she was blissfully happy. She actually had a nephew, kin. Archie had been a fool for denying his son.

But right now they needed to save her husband.

Liadain kicked her horse into a strong gallop, the men following closely upon her heels. They entered the bailey and quickly dismounted.

Approaching Ciaran, she spoke cautiously. "I donna think it wise to show everyone what I need to show ye." She hesitated, waiting for his response.

"Water the horses. We will be taking our leave shortly," Ciaran ordered Calum and Seumas. "Aiden, come with us."

As they climbed the stone steps to the bedchambers, she explained her discovery. "So when I moved the portrait, I found the latch and it opened into another room. I found Archie's secret study."

Ciaran's eyebrows shot up in surprise. When they reached MacGregor's chamber, the men followed her in. She was hefting the portrait when Ciaran reached out and grabbed it. He lowered the painting to the floor, and when he turned, Liadain pointed to the latch.

"Could ye light the candle by the bed?" Liadain asked Aiden.

When the wall cracked, she pushed it open. Ciaran

followed her in as she held up the light to the partition and searched for the other indentation. She gave it a firm push, and the wall creaked open. Stepping into Archie's study, she turned and sought another candle. She lit the wick and illuminated Archie's madness.

Ciaran and Aiden examined the maps on the walls and the golden trinkets that lined the shelves. Ciaran gestured Liadain over to the desk.

"What did ye find that will clear my brother's name?"

She pulled open a drawer and removed the stack of notes in Archie's handwriting. "Naught I read made any sense—until now. My brother kept records of every meeting, every conversation."

She separated out the detailed map of Parliament House and handed it to Ciaran. As he studied it, she continued. "I couldnae understand what Archie would be doing with that map. He had been there many times. Then I found this." Ciaran handed Aiden the map and reached for the other paper Liadain held out.

"Archie kept a detailed log of names, dates, and conversations. According to what I read, he met more than a handful of times with Catesby, Percy, and Fawkes. I gathered the men had wanted to remove someone from their position of power, but I could not fit the pieces together. The three men were at court and befriended my husband there. I donna believe in coincidence."

"I donna think 'tis enough here to clear my brother," said Ciaran, discouraged.

Once Liadain handed him the last paper, she watched his expression change as realization sunk in. "Dunnehl. So Campbell plotted with Catesby, Percy,

Dunnehl, and this man named Fawkes to remove someone from power, and it just so happened they would end this man's life at Parliament House. I agree. I donna believe in coincidence." Ciaran folded the documents carefully. "Was there anything else?"

She was not quite willing to share the last piece of information. *Yet.* She could not open the drawer that implicated Robert in this madness. Yet, she would not let her husband die.

"Nay, there wasnae anything else."

Aiden and Ciaran exchanged a silent glance and abruptly walked out of the study. Liadain blew out the candles and closed the walls behind them. She was not able to keep up with the men's long strides and had just walked out into the bailey when the last horse was galloping through the gate. Rushing to her mount, she was immediately halted by an iron grip.

"I donna think so, m'lady."

"An diobhail toirt leis thu!" Liadain spat at Montgomery. *The devil take you!*

"Lest ye forget, m'lady, I grew up with Rosalia. Naught ye say will shock me."

He pulled her hand away from her saddle. "I understand the reason ye want to travel with them, but 'tis nay place for a woman. 'Tis a man's business and ye will only be in the way. Mayhap even slow them down. Laird MacGregor will see to his brother. Ye need to have faith in him. In the meantime, I was instructed to see to your safety, m'lady. We can either remain here or I will escort ye back to Glenorchy where ye can stay with the women. What say ye?"

Anger lit up her eyes as she stared at this Highland

brute. "Stay with the *women*? Are ye completely daft? How am I to stand by while there are men out there who want to kill my husband for a crime he didnae commit? And ye ask me if I want to stay with the *women*?" she repeated.

The beast actually had the nerve to smirk. "Ye are under my care, my watch. Now we can either do this the simple way or the hard way. The choice is up to ye."

Liadain growled. She was tired of these brutish Highlanders thinking women had no inkling of sense whatsoever. She did not become MacGregor's wife or the sister of Archibald Campbell, the seventh Earl of Argyll, without gaining a few knowledgeable scars herself. Perhaps if the men listened to their women even half the time they would not find themselves in such predicaments.

As she reached again for the saddle, she was lifted from her feet and hefted over the Montgomery's shoulder. "Let me down!" She kicked and wiggled, and his firm grip only tightened.

"Donna say I didnae warn ye, lass."

Upside down, she spotted the MacGregor men returning from Anna's grave. "Help me!" she screamed. The men hesitated, then purposefully ignored her. All of a sudden, they looked extremely occupied—every last one of them.

She felt a chuckle beneath her. "Captain of the guard, remember?"

"Stop. Please," she implored. He placed her back on her feet, and she brushed her hair out of her eyes with as much dignity as she could muster.

"Do we have an understanding?" Montgomery asked.

She nodded. "I donna want to travel to Glenorchy. I want to remain here. This is our home."

"Verra well. I will see to the men. And in case ye were thinking of doing something rash, my men are instructed to stop ye," he said in a warning tone.

Liadain's mind was racing and she knew what she had to do. "I will see to the meal."

❧

"Would ye like more?" Liadain asked Montgomery politely. She scooped another heaping helping of porridge into his bowl and he smiled his thanks. Since there were only a handful of men remaining, she sat with Montgomery and John in the kitchens. No need for formality, and besides, it worked more to her advantage.

"John?"

"I donna think I can eat," he whispered, playing with his food.

She hesitated and then stood up from the table. "Here. Let me freshen it up for ye. 'Tis probably cold by now." She took John's bowl and walked over to the pot and scooped him another helping. When she returned to her seat on the bench, she tried not to stare at Montgomery. She had to admit, it was quite difficult.

While John tarried with his meal, Montgomery's features began to tighten and he shifted his weight on the bench.

"John, 'tis been a verra long and exhausting day. If ye arenae going to eat, why donna ye wash up and seek your bed? The rest will do ye good." He nodded in agreement as he finally took a small bite of food.

Montgomery slowed down his pace, wiping the sweat from his brow.

It should not be long now. The man should be starting to feel the effects of the Auld Wife's Huid she had covertly slipped into his oats. That would teach the brute to toss her over his shoulder like some light skirt. In the meantime, she would continue to try not to smirk.

Stay with the women, my arse.

Liadain adamantly refused to sit and wait in the hope that her husband might or might not return to her. Ciaran carried the papers for King James. If all else failed, she would guard the one of most importance. She would only play her hand after the last card was dealt, as a last resort.

Montgomery's stomach rumbled and he abruptly stood. "Pray excuse me, m'lady." He turned on his heel with his bottom cheeks clenched, taking awkward baby steps toward the great hall. When his hand reached down to cup his backside, she could not suppress a smile.

"John, if I am nae here when ye awaken on the morrow, travel to Glenorchy and I will seek ye there." She stood and John's tired eyes looked back at her. She kissed him on the top of his head. "Rest good this eve and I will see ye soon, Nephew." He nodded and then she snuck out the kitchen door.

Liadain walked a few yards back into the woods. Unraveling the reins, she silently led her waiting mount through the trees. Praise the saints for the false door in the stable. Contrary to what Montgomery thought, she was not some daft female. She had easily led her horse through the tunnel and into the woods undetected. No one knew these lands better than she did. She would take the long way around the castle, not efficient, but at least she would not be captured by her husband's own men. She had a mission and would see it through.

❧

Dunnehl emerged from his fancy tent, stretching his back and rubbing his hands over his generous midsection—no doubt with a belly full of food. If the situation were not so dire, Declan would surely laugh. The English cur had no idea how to travel lightly. It took two men to set up his sleeping quarters. Declan would not have surprised if Dunnehl had someone to wipe his English arse.

While being held captive, Declan came to the realization that there was quite a significant difference between the pompous English lords and the rugged Highland lairds. Give Ciaran a blanket, the stars, and a handful of supplies and he would last a sennight. He did not think Dunnehl would last without the luxury of his shelter for one eve. These English lords were nothing but a bunch of fanciful peacocks.

Declan sat on the damp ground, his hands tied behind his back. If he could get free of his bindings, he would punch the smirk right off Dunnehl's face. He shifted his weight, uncomfortable. Damn. His leg was starting to cramp. Rolling his neck, he briefly closed his eyes. When someone fiddled with his bindings from behind, his eyes flew open only to find Dunnehl standing before him with his hands placed upon his generous waist.

"What are you doing?" asked Dunnehl, raising his brow.

"Untying him. He cannot eat with his hands tied," said the guard.

"And how is that our problem, my dear boy? He is nothing more than a Highland dog. Let him eat like one. If he's hungry, he'll eventually eat."

The guard rose to his feet and then tossed a chunk of bread on the ground in front of Declan.

Dunnehl smiled. "Highland *barbarian*."

Twenty-Nine

LIADAIN TRAVELED AS FAR AS SHE COULD, FINALLY slowing her mount when she could no longer hold the darkness at bay. Regrettably, there was no moon to guide her and she would be forced to stop. At least Ciaran and his men would need to make camp as well. Besides, on the morrow she would need to spend all her energy on catching up with them.

She slipped from her horse and walked along the outer edge of the path until she found a small clearing. She tied off her mount on a sturdy tree. Fumbling through her sack, she grabbed a blanket and then flattened it upon the damp grass. She let out a long sigh as she settled down for what she knew would be a prolonged eve of restlessness.

Her makeshift bed was uncomfortable, but the hard ground did not bother her. To be truthful, she was more concerned with what her husband must be feeling. Was he outraged? Scared? Were his captors hurting him? She had to have faith that she and the men would arrive in time and this nightmare would abruptly come to an end.

Once King James read the papers written in Archie's own hand, His Majesty would have no choice but to free her husband. She was a healer and did not wish death on anyone, but she sorely prayed that when the king found out the truth, he would take Dunnehl's vile head. How could one man disrupt so many lives?

Liadain closed her eyes and a cool breeze brushed against her cheek. If she and MacGregor made it through this latest predicament and the rocky start of their marriage, they could survive anything as long as they were together.

He had never made any promises of love, but his kindness was all she had ever asked for. And when he called her "wife," she felt truly at peace. Her heart swelled with something she could not quite place her finger on.

Hugging her arms to her chest, she closed her eyes if only for a moment.

In the dream, the crowd chanted as two guards escorted MacGregor to King James. His Majesty's royal robes flowed behind him, billowing in the wind. The man stood with an air of regal grace and authority. The king gestured for MacGregor to kneel before him, and the guards forcefully threw her husband to his knees at His Majesty's feet. Her husband's open tunic displayed his broad chest as his hands were tied behind his back. His tawny hair was plaited into two war braids but disheveled. His breathing was labored. He knew he was going to die.

"I awarded you Castle Campbell. I gave you a wife. You attempted to kill me," the king said, his voice deep.

A lady's laugh wafted through the air, sounding

foreign to Liadain's ears. As she turned, she saw Lady Armstrong leaning against the stone wall with Lord Dunnehl pressed against her side. Dunnehl fingered Lady Armstrong's tresses, and the evil woman brought up her hand to stay her giggles, clearly relishing the moment.

Liadain's anger became a scalding fury. *"Mo chreach! Cha tugadh an donas an car asaibh!" The devil could not get the best of you!*

"Healer," called MacGregor in a troubled voice. "Donna have pity upon my soul. I couldnae bear it." He lowered his head and waited.

What was he waiting for? The guard handed the king a sword—a very big broadsword. This could not be happening. She refused to believe it. Her husband was innocent. Where was Ciaran with the papers? Why was MacGregor as still as a statue? He should not accept this fate.

With one swift movement, King James raised the blade.

Liadain could only think to whisper the words, "Power of eye be yours. Power of the elements be yours. Power of my heart's desire."

A loud clattering noise jolted Liadain awake. She sat up, rubbed her eyes, and then froze. An enormous red stag stood no more than a few yards away, rubbing its massive antlers on a tree stump. At first glance, the animal must have had nearly sixteen very sharp points on the top of his head. The creature was an impressive sight.

The deer cast a quick glance at Liadain's mount and then lowered its head, paying the horse no heed. She could not believe it was already morn. The sun started to peek through the trees and an early chill hung in the air. Slowly, she stood up and stepped from her blanket.

When a twig snapped behind her, the deer shot off into the forest. She approached her horse and opened her sack, replacing the blanket. When she turned around, she nearly jumped out of her skin.

The man stood very tall and brooding, his eyes flashing with outrage. "I am *verra* angry, Lady MacGregor."

❧

Declan was pulled to his feet and pushed to his mount. He was tired, hungry and, frankly, fed up. If one more man had an overwhelming need to pull him, kick him, or refer to him as a dog, the coolness he tried so carefully to display would quickly become a raging fire.

Hell. By the time Dunnehl folded his blasted tent, it would already be on the morrow. Declan wanted to make haste. The faster he could have his audience with King James, the better. His patience was wearing thin. He wanted to straighten out this whole bloody mess and get back to his life.

His wife had probably returned from Glenorchy by now, and he could only imagine what she must be thinking. The only saving grace was the fact that she was safe with Ciaran and Montgomery. Declan was not sure what he would have done, had Dunnehl attempted to harm her.

When his mount finally started to move, Declan needed all of his might to keep from screaming in frustration. At the rate they were traveling, the winter solstice would soon be upon them. A guard coughed beside him—the same man who had attempted to free Declan's bindings last eve.

Curious if the man would converse with him, Declan spoke jestingly. "Does King James's guard always travel with so much haste?"

The man kept his eyes forward, and for a moment Declan did not think the man would respond. "Only because we travel with Lord Dunnehl are we delayed."

"Aye, it makes sense. The man cannae even wipe his own arse without assistance," said Declan. The guard chuckled but covered it quickly with a cough. It did not come as a surprise—even Dunnehl's own Englishmen could not stand him. "Do ye know why we travel to His Majesty?"

The guard's expression was a mask of stone. "You tried to kill him," he said blandly.

"Aye, so I have heard. At Parliament House. Did anyone see me there?" When the guard shrugged his shoulders, Declan added, "Do ye know how I tried to kill him?"

The man kept his eyes straight ahead and did not respond.

"What difference does it make if ye speak with me? I will be awarded an audience with the king and still be judged."

"You shot him from atop one of the Parliament buildings with an arrow." There was a distinct hardening of the guard's eyes and his tongue was heavy with sarcasm. "No one could have made that shot but you. His Majesty lives. You failed."

There was a heavy moment of silence.

"I donna suppose it would make any difference if I told ye I was innocent."

The guard grunted. "That is what the guilty say."

❧

"Now, Montgomery," said Liadain in a calming voice, nervously holding up her hand and backing away from him.

Montgomery closed the distance between them, his look menacing. "Donna *Montgomery* me." He reached out and encircled her arm. "We are returning at once. This is nay game, Lady MacGregor. These are verra dangerous men. Ye saw what happened to Anna. That could have been ye. That could *still* be ye if ye continue down this path."

Liadain shrugged off his hold and her eyes narrowed. "Donna speak to me like I am some daft female. I know the dangers," she spat.

Realizing it was not in her best interest to infuriate the captain of her husband's guard even further, she attempted a more subtle approach. "Montg…er, James, my husband will certainly value your loyalty to him, but I have to reach Ciaran. 'Tis of most importance that I do."

"Lady MacGregor," he said in a patronizing tone. "If I have to throw your wily arse over my shoulder again, I will do it. Donna tempt me. Now get on your mount. We are returning to Castle Campbell."

She folded her arms over her chest in a defiant stance and flipped her hair over her shoulder. "Now listen to me, ye Highland brute. I am the wife of the man ye serve. I am the sister of Archibald Campbell, seventh Earl of Argyll."

He threw back his head and roared with laughter.

"Ye think throwing titles at me will change my mind, lass?" he asked. "I donna care if ye are the bloody Queen of England."

"Please, I cannae return without my husband." Tears of frustration welled in her eyes.

"I told ye. Laird MacGregor and his brother will see to your husband. 'Tis nay place for a woman even if ye are Argyll's sister."

"Would ye please trust me in this?"

"Trust is earned," he said sternly.

There was a heavy moment of silence.

Liadain let out a heavy sigh. "Ciaran has letters written in my brother's hand. They should be enough to free my husband, but 'tis nay guarantee." Reluctantly, she proceeded. "I have another paper that will secure my husband's freedom."

He raised a brow. "Then why didnae ye give it to Laird MacGregor before he took his leave?"

"Because it will destroy the life of another man and I am only willing to hand it over if all else fails." She studied Montgomery intently and then placed her hand on his forearm. "What if this was Rosalia? Would ye let anyone stop ye?"

"'Tisnae the same and ye cannae pretend otherwise. This matter is completely different."

A warning voice whispered in her head to tread carefully. "Then what if it were ye? Would Rosalia turn around because some burly Highlander stood in her way, or would she do anything within her grasp to free your name?"

His features clouded with uneasiness and he hesitated. "I donna like it."

"I didnae ask ye to. Please. I love him. I cannae take such a risk with his life."

For some reason, she was not as surprised by the revelation as she thought she would be. Ever since MacGregor had been taken, she had felt an extraordinary void that she could not explain. Her fear for him overrode all sense of reason. It did not matter what her husband felt or did not feel for her. But she knew one thing for certain. She wanted him back by her side where he belonged.

There was a long pause and Montgomery finally shook his head with uncertainty. "There will be rules."

"I wouldnae have it any other way," Liadain said hopefully.

"The first time ye donna listen—

She held up her hands in mock defense. "I will. I give ye my word."

"Then give me your word ye willnae poison my food."

She smiled sheepishly. "I give ye my word. Ye willnae regret this."

Shaking his head, he sighed. "I already do. Mount up, Lady MacGregor."

When Montgomery mumbled something under his breath about women, Liadain smiled. She knew at that moment he could be trusted—well, that and the fact that he did not kill her for tampering with his food.

Thirty

THEY ARRIVED AT HIS MAJESTY'S ESTATE ONLY TO FIND
their liege had taken his leave for a bit of sport. Declan
was disappointed his liege was not in attendance but also
relieved, knowing that the king would eventually return.
He was somewhat surprised that once he was delivered to
His Majesty's doorstep, Dunnehl did not linger to torture
him by gloating. Perhaps the English peacock had fled
back to Northumberland for the luxury of his own bed.

Declan sat in the bowels of the castle, waiting for
his liege to return. After riding with the haughty
Englishmen for so long, the silence of the dungeon
was a welcome relief. If another man made reference
to him being a Highland barbarian, Declan was ready
to let his true Highland colors show.

Damn English peacocks.

He settled back and tapped his foot impatiently.
It should not be too much longer now. While he sat
questioning Dunnehl's personal preferences, the heavy
wooden door to his prison flew open.

"What the hell are ye doing here?" Declan asked,
his voice unintentionally going up a notch.

Ciaran rolled his eyes. "Saving your arse once again." Ciaran and Aiden walked through the door, and it banged and locked behind them. "We donna have much time, Brother. Ye owe your wife a great deal," said Ciaran.

Declan's eyebrows shot up in surprise. "My *wife*?"

"Listen to us verra carefully."

⁘

Liadain was exhausted, miserable, and somewhat relieved that the end was in sight. After Montgomery sort of forgave her for tampering his oats, he actually turned into a formidable companion. He lit the fires every eve and even managed to catch a rabbit or two for the spit. She could only imagine what conditions her husband was forced to endure.

"Laird MacGregor is definitely ahead of us. He is more than likely already with His Majesty," said Montgomery reassuringly.

"Aye, well, I am nae going to relax until I am certain. How much farther is it?"

He grunted. "Ye mean from the last time ye asked me?"

Thundering hooves stopped them in their tracks as King James's banner rounded the bend from the opposite direction. Liadain and Montgomery were partially hidden along the path and conveniently out of the way when a group of men in hunting attire encircled the king and traveled into the estate. Trailing behind the party was a familiar face.

Liadain briefly hesitated, wanting to first contemplate her actions, but her emotions quickly won out. "Viscount Cranborne!" she shouted.

Robert turned his mount and approached. By his blank expression, she could not say whether or not he was surprised to see her.

"Lia…er, Lady MacGregor. What are you doing here?" He shifted in the saddle, his features clouding with uneasiness.

"Montgomery? Would ye please give us a moment?" Liadain asked. With a short nod of his head, her faithful companion pulled his mount a few yards away. "What are ye doing here, Robert?"

"I asked the same of you."

"I am here for my husband. He has been falsely accused of an attempt on King James's life. Mayhap ye have heard, but then again, I see ye have been hunting with the men. Ye are indeed a verra busy man, *Viscount* Cranborne."

He promptly ignored her taunting. "I have heard. Please accept my apologies. If there is anything Elizabeth or I can do for you…"

"Anything ye can do for me? Surely ye donna think MacGregor guilty of such a ridiculous accusation?" she asked, her voice rising unintentionally.

"Liadain, why don't we move inside? You have journeyed far."

"I donna care how far I have traveled. I am going to clear my husband's name. Surely ye understand and would do the same for your wife. I am curious if ye would help me," she said with a mask of innocence.

"If there was anything I could do—"

"If there was anything ye could do, ye would help me to clear MacGregor's name," she said abruptly.

"Of course."

"Then tell me, Viscount Cranborne. Do ye know of a way we could prove his innocence? Set my husband free?" Liadain didn't give him a chance to answer and then quickly added, "I must ask ye. Have ye any acquaintance with Lord Dunnehl, Catesby, Percy, or a man named Fawkes?"

His mount started to prance and Robert's expression confirmed the truth of what she already knew.

"Why do you ask?" A subtle warning laced his voice. "Listen to me. You do not recognize the dangers of asking such questions."

"Pray tell. I know *exactly* what I am doing. Ye see…I discovered that my brother, your dearest friend, kept notes of every meeting, every conversation, and every plot his devious mind devised. When I found the papers were in Archie's own hand, I had to come here personally to deliver them to King James. Och, Archie was quite thorough. In fact, he even had a map of Parliament House that indicated the path a man would take to kill His Majesty."

"Liadain…"

"But *Robert*, ye havenae even heard the best part," she said. "Imagine my surprise when I found a document that implicates ye as well."

Uncertainty crept into his expression and he replied in a low, tormented voice. "Before I journeyed to Spain, I met with those men. I knew Archie and Dunnehl were conspiring to remove King James from the throne. I will not deny my hand. But you have to believe me. That was before Spain—*before* I met Elizabeth. My wife and my son are my life, my reason for living. They mean everything to me. Please do not do this. I beg of you."

There was a heavy moment of silence.

"And what of me? Ye would let the man I love hang for a crime he didnae commit to save your bloody arse." When he did not respond, her blood boiled. "All these years I dreaded being Archie's half sister. My brother was a cruel man, but he was also verra cunning. When ye live under the same roof with someone for so long, ye donna tend to realize the great deal of knowledge that has already been passed down to ye." Her tone hardened. "Ye will listen to me verra carefully, Viscount Cranborne."

After Liadain finished her cursing tirade, rancor sharpened her voice. "Ye will speak with the king. Ye will do everything in your power to free my husband. And if ye donna, I will take the paper with your name on it and personally hand-deliver it to His Majesty… and your *wife*. Ye will lose it all, Robert. Your precious title, your wealth, your wife, your son, and I will make certain ye lose your life." Liadain spat out the words contemptuously.

Robert glowered at her and turned away.

∽

Declan stood flanked by his brothers. For a moment he had a memory of Ciaran and Aiden soothing over tempers when he was caught sampling the wares of a merchant's daughter. When he thought back, he remembered many of those times, more frequent than not. He always challenged, pushed the limit, and his brothers were always there to pull him out of his latest catastrophe. He could not help wondering whether there would ever be a time when his brothers realized

enough was enough—when they would let him
handle his own mistakes. He was thankful that Ciaran
and Aiden's revelation was not to be made on this
particular day.

King James had summoned them for a private
audience. As guards escorted them to His Majesty's
study, Declan could not slow his racing heart. He had
thought the truth alone would set him free. But what
if they could not convince the king of his innocence?

Aiden slapped Declan on the shoulder. "Everything
will work out. Be truthful and try nae to be—well, ye."

"Thank ye for the reassurance, Brother," Declan
said dryly.

"'Tis probably wise for ye both to remain silent
and let me do the speaking," said Ciaran in an
authoritative tone.

As they entered the study with two armed guards,
King James replaced a book on the shelf. "The
MacGregors. You have come here to bargain for your
brother's life?"

They all bowed their heads. "Your Majesty."

The king pulled out a chair and sat down at the
table. Leaning back, their liege rubbed his brow.
"Please, by all means be seated and enlighten me."

Declan took his seat between Ciaran and Aiden. He
could not help feeling like a scolded child. He bowed
his head and remained silent. To be truthful, he was
thankful Ciaran did the explaining because he did not
know where to even begin.

"My liege, I can say with certainty that my brother
did not shoot the arrow that struck ye. When my
brother took his leave from court, he traveled directly

to Glenorchy." When His Majesty looked doubtful, Ciaran added, "I have something to prove my
brother's innocence." Unfolding the papers, Ciaran
placed them on the top of the table.

King James sat forward and folded his hands. "Well,
go on. I am listening."

"The sister of the Earl of Argyll, my brother's
wife, discovered a hidden study in the walls of
Castle Campbell."

"How convenient," the king said dryly.

"The papers are written in the earl's own hand. At
first we found a detailed map of Parliament House."
Ciaran pushed the map in front of King James. "As ye
can see, markings are upon the roof and all lead here
to a spot marked 'X,'" Ciaran said, tapping the page.

Ciaran replaced the map with the next piece of
proof. "This next page has dates and times of meet-
ings with Argyll at which the removal of someone
of great power was discussed, including his demise at
Parliament House."

King James's expression darkened with an unreadable emotion. "And all this was found in Argyll's
hidden study? And how is it that this information
does not implicate your brother?" the king asked, his
accusing gaze riveted on Declan.

Ciaran cleared his throat. "The last document
uncovered has the names of the conspirators," he said
in a low, tormented voice. "Some of the men are
familiar to me and some arenae." He pushed the paper
forward and the king reached out to take it.

"There is more than one?"

There was a heavy silence as His Majesty read the

names of the men who plotted to seal his fate. Curses fell from their liege's mouth and his anger became a scalding fury. "Fawkes? The man has already been hanged. He was caught guarding thirty-six barrels of gunpowder for the purpose of blowing Parliament straight to hell. The man would only admit that he acted alone. And Dunnehl…he wanted so desperately to escort my guard to Castle Campbell. Thinking back, he was also the man who planted the idea in my head that MacGregor…So if Argyll and Dunnehl conspired against the realm, who the hell took a shot at me? MacGregor, you are the only one skilled enough to land that shot."

Declan shifted in his chair. "The only one that ye know of, Your Majesty. What of Graham? The tournament ended with the two of us," he said the words tentatively as if testing the idea.

"He left for Spain. My men verified this." King James regarded Declan quizzically for a moment. "If not you, then who took the shot?"

Declan needed to convince his liege of his virtue. It was never too late for the truth. "Your Majesty, ye awarded me Castle Campbell and a bonny wife. I donna hold anything against ye and have naught but respect."

The king's eyes narrowed. "If I remember correctly, you were not exactly thankful that I wed you to Argyll's sister. In fact, you were furious. You had the motive and the means to want to kill me, MacGregor."

"I understand how ye might think as much, Your Majesty, but to speak honestly, I have grown to care for my wife. In fact, I donna deserve her. She is too good for me and by far the best thing that has ever happened to me."

Ciaran glanced sideways in surprise.

Declan rubbed his brow. "If I may, Your Majesty, I have an idea."

❧

Liadain waited in the hall outside King James's study with Montgomery. She could not stop herself from pacing. Once the pacing grew old, she stood and shifted from foot to foot. Her husband's fate was being decided and she was not by his side. She needed to be in there. She could not bear the thought of what would have happened to MacGregor if her brother had not kept such detailed notes. She gave a silent prayer of thanks to Archie for being such a methodical tyrant.

The door opened and King James was flanked by two guards. She gave a low curtsy as he walked by without acknowledging her presence. She quickly stood and rushed to the study as four armed guards came out of nowhere from behind her, one of them pulling her firmly by the arm to the side. The men stormed in and escorted her bound husband out with Ciaran and Aiden in tow. A troubled expression crossed all of their features.

"MacGregor!"

"Healer, what are ye doing here?" Her husband's last word was muffled as she shook off the guard and threw herself against his broad chest. Her arms encircled him and then her hands moved all over him. She needed to make sure he was unhurt.

"I donna think now is the time," MacGregor said wryly.

"Husband, are ye injured? I have been plagued with worry." Her eyes were bordered with tears.

"I am fine."

She glanced down at his bindings and then at Ciaran. "Liadain, ye need to come with Aiden and me. Now," Ciaran ordered.

"I am nae leaving my husband," she said with firmness. Four brawny Highlanders stared back at her, along with four English guards. She lifted her chin and met their gaze straight on.

"Healer, look at me." MacGregor's voice was soft but alarming. "'Tis verra important that ye stay with Ciaran and Aiden. These men will take me to the dungeon. I have proof of my innocence, and on the morrow, I will take His Majesty's men to get it. Now stay with Ciaran and Aiden." He gestured to the guards that he was ready, and the men started to escort him away.

As she was about to speak of the papers, Ciaran reached out and grabbed her arm. "Liadain, ye will come with us."

She hesitated, blinking with bafflement and totally bewildered at their odd behavior. Did they show King James the papers? Why was her husband still bound and being taken to the dungeon? What evidence did her husband have? She was so confused. When she glanced back at MacGregor, her dream came back to haunt her. She would not let it end this way without him knowing…

"Husband, I love ye!"

Thirty-One

DECLAN STOPPED ABRUPTLY AS THE HEALER'S WORDS hit him like a stone catapulted into his chest. A firm nudge from the guard brought him back to reality. He could not glance back, for if he did, he would take his wee bonny wife right there where she stood. The lass loved him? After everything he had done to her, every horrible word he had ever spoken to her, his wife loved him. He could not understand it. And yet, it was truly delightful. His mouth curved into a smile.

Ciaran and Aiden would fill the healer in on their plan. Once King James had his trusted men spread the word regarding the papers, Dunnehl, Catesby, and Percy would be more inclined to make a mistake. That was the easy part. Now they just had to flush out the man who took the shot.

The guards threw Declan back into the dungeon and closed the door. This plan had better work. Settling back in the confines of his prison, he thought it was ironic how life takes turns. Declan MacGregor was known as a rogue across the Highlands for his expertise in bed sport, a title he would now willingly bestow on another. Out of all the lasses he bedded, not one of them ever uttered a single word of love. Granted, he had never believed in such a ridiculous idea, but for some reason when his raven wife spoke the words, they were something he clearly desired to hear. His heart swelled with a feeling he had thought long since dead.

His eyes burned dryly from sleeplessness and his back ached between his shoulder blades. There would be time for sleep once he was back in his own home, in his own bed, and with his own wife to share it with. Until then, he mused on the smoldering passion that he had thrilled her with.

Not much time had passed when the keys to Declan's prison jingled and the lock opened. Dunnehl ambled in and the door shut behind him.

"Are they treating you well, MacGregor?" the portly lord asked, studying the unaccommodating surroundings.

"Unlike ye pampered English, I could live anywhere. Where have ye been, Dunnehl? I thought ye would have been here to gloat." Declan paused. "Do ye think it safe for ye to be in here with me alone? After all, I am naught but a Highland barbarian—verra uncivilized."

"I'll take my chances. There have been rumors surfacing of papers drawn in Argyll's own hand that implicate and give the names of men who plotted against His Majesty. Is this true or perhaps another attempt to cry for freedom?"

Declan had a hard time trying to wipe the smug expression from his face. "Worried are ye?"

"Let me tell you what I think, dear boy. You will soon face the hangman's noose and I believe you're nothing more than a frightened dog. If you had any proof, you would have presented it. You do not play a good hand of cards and your time is running out." Dunnehl's eyes darkened and a wicked smile played on his lips. "Argyll's sister, on the other hand, looks ripe for the picking. I'm sure she will need consoling after the death of her Highland husband. I will be more than happy to provide her with the comfort she deserves." The cur turned on his heel and knocked on the door for the guard.

"Donna fret, Lord Dunnehl. Ye, Argyll, Catesby, Percy, and Fawkes can all sleep peacefully in your soft beds this eve—well, Argyll and Fawkes are already lying in theirs. They have been waiting verra patiently for ye. It willnae be long now before ye join them."

Dunnehl stiffened and did not turn around.

The plan was in motion.

❧

Ciaran, Aiden, Calum, Seumas, and Montgomery watched their backs. They could not risk being spotted. Each had carefully taken their leave from the estate and covertly gathered at the edge of the forest before the setting sun. Ciaran needed to make sure that everyone knew his role well. There was too much at stake and he would not chance his brother's life.

"Ye werenae followed?" Ciaran asked, his senses on alert.

"Nay," the men answered in unison.

"Liadain?"

"Stays with Viscount Cranborne's wife," said Montgomery. "She wasnae happy, but I have her word she willnae interfere. Besides, Cranborne gave his word he would watch over her as well."

"Good. Now listen verra carefully," Ciaran said to the men. "There will be at least two chances for a clear shot at Declan: when the guards break for the midday meal or when they stop to break camp this eve. Calum and Montgomery, ye two will keep watch on Dunnehl, Catesby, and Percy, while Aiden, Seumas, and I will tarry along and search the forest for the man. Do ye have any questions?"

The men shook their heads. "Nay."

Ciaran nodded. "Good. Lest I need remind ye, this is Declan. Eyes and ears open, alert at all times. Montgomery, I am counting on ye."

"I have your back," he said.

"Let us find this man and put an end to this. *Seun Dè umad!*" *Spell of God about you!* Ciaran said firmly.

"*Feun Dè tharad!*" *The hand of God over you!*

❧

After Lord Dunnehl met with MacGregor in the dungeon, Dunnehl sent word to Catesby and Percy. In the darkened hours of the night, the men met secretly in the stables. Dunnehl needed these men to see reason. There was a very good chance that they all would be exposed and everything they'd worked for thwarted. And he refused to be brought down by a bloody Highlander.

"Take him out," ordered Dunnehl. When Catesby and Percy exchanged a silent glance, their look infuriated him even more. "Did you not hear me? Bloody Argyll wrote down everything. If the king gets his hands on those papers, we are all dead. Kill him. We cannot risk it. I know he did not speak this to the king or we would already be in the hangman's noose. MacGregor's words mean nothing. He will need those documents as proof. Kill him before we are implicated. I should have known never to trust Argyll," he snarled.

Tapping his finger on his chin, Dunnehl narrowed his eyes. "There is something bothering me, though. MacGregor never mentioned Cranborne. If Argyll wrote down all our names, why did MacGregor not mention Viscount Cranborne? Hear this, if I am charged, I am taking everyone with me."

"What difference does it make if he did or did not name Cranborne now? He accused us all. If MacGregor hands over those papers to King James, we are all dead. I will take the bloody Highlander out before he even gets close to Castle Campbell, but I will have to ride out now to get ahead of him. You and Catesby ride ahead to Castle Campbell and find the damn papers before it's too late. I'll deal with MacGregor," said Percy, shaking his head.

Dunnehl glared at Percy. "Try not to make a jumble out of it like you did with the king, Percy. You missed the shot."

"I never miss twice."

❧

Declan had to admit that he'd had brighter ideas than this. As he sat bound upon his mount for appearances, he cautiously glanced around at his surroundings, knowing that at any moment someone could be lying in wait. What the hell had he been thinking?

Although the guards surrounded him, the archer had two chances: when they stopped for the noon meal and when they set up camp this eve. At least, that was according to Declan and Ciaran's calculations. Unfortunately, the conspirator was not on the same schedule.

When the guard rested for the midday meal, nothing out of the ordinary happened. Not that Declan desired to be a marked target, but he was sick and tired of being branded a traitor. He craved his life back and yearned for his bonny healer.

Ciaran and Aiden were somewhere near. Even though he could not see them, he could feel their presence. They were kin and would do anything for one another. Although, Declan had to admit that his sisters-by-marriage frightened him a little. If anything happened to his brothers, their wives would have his bollocks on a platter. He shifted at the thought.

The longer the men journeyed toward Castle Campbell, the more restless and irritable he became. The corner of Declan's mouth twisted in exasperation as he thought how much he resented simply being placed in this situation.

"How are you holding up?" asked a guard beside him. It was the same guard who had escorted him from Castle Campbell.

Declan's smile was without humor. "I want this resolved."

They had traveled several additional miles in silence when the guards halted abruptly. An overgrown tree splintered across the trail. When the tiny hairs on the back of Declan's neck rose, his attention reached full alert.

His eyes darted around nervously. Damn, he needed to concentrate. Where would he make the shot? *Think MacGregor, think.* God's teeth! He felt like a lamb waiting for the slaughter. He refused to be a sitting target. He was sliding from his mount when an arrow struck him in the arm and he fell to the ground.

Springing to his feet, he turned to the guard. "Cut my bindings!" His arm burned like hell, but it was more of a nuisance than anything. Had he not shifted, the arrow would have struck his heart.

The guard hastily pulled out a dirk, reached around Declan, and cut him free.

Declan spotted his bow and arrow and quickly grabbed it. "I need this," he said to the guard.

He thundered into the brush after the guards, scouring the landscape relentlessly. The foliage was too thick and he could not see a damn thing. Men yelled in the distance as they pulled out their swords and chopped away at the thicket. A man could easily mask his appearance anywhere in this terrain. Curses fell from his mouth and his nostrils flared with fury. He vowed to catch this man and personally send him to his maker.

They were losing precious light when Declan spotted his brothers with Montgomery and Seumas. He studied Ciaran and Aiden struggling to walk through the brush, their legs tangled by the thistles and nettles. No man could have made an escape so easily. Damn, the revelation hit him like a nail to the head.

The shot would have been from the air. No sooner did Declan open his mouth to warn the men when Ciaran shouted his name.

A branch snapped directly over his head. Without thought, Declan lifted his bow and shot the arrow at the center of the dark-clad figure looming above. The man grunted and fell out of the tree into a thicket near Declan's feet. Declan threw back his head, a cry of relief breaking from his lips.

Ciaran, Aiden, and Seumas cursed the nettles as they pulled the man out of the brush. Was that...*Percy*? As the realization sunk in, Declan could not believe it. That had been brilliant. Pretending not to be able to shoot a bow and arrow but actually mastering it. Percy had fooled everyone, including him. And to think, he had actually instructed the man on how to hit the mark.

Declan leaned against the tree. Damn, his arm hurt like hell.

"Ye got him," said Aiden with a brief nod. "Ye are hit." He reached for the arrow and broke it off in a single snap.

"An diobhail toirt leis thu." The devil take you.

Aiden smirked. "I have heard worse from ye, Brother. Pull out the other end or I will have to do it for ye."

"And why do I get the sense ye would thoroughly enjoy that?" Declan lifted his arm and let his brother pull out the other end of the arrow, grunting when it came through.

"And *that* was for Aisling. She will be angry I had to be away so long."

"Fair enough."

Ciaran spoke with the guard and then walked over to Declan with his laird-ish swagger. For the first time in his life, Declan realized leadership suited his older brother. "Your name should be cleared. The guards will take Percy's body to King James, and the men have already gathered Dunnehl and Catesby. They will all be secured."

Spotting the blood, Ciaran leaned over and examined Declan's wound. "'Tisnae too bad. Only a flesh wound. Ye need to get that cleaned and cared for so it doesnae fester."

Declan's mouth twitched with amusement. "Ye know? I happen to have a verra bonny wife who is a talented healer. I have a feeling she will take good care of me."

Montgomery growled and everyone looked at him. "Talented healer, my arse. Be sure nae to fire her ire or aye, she will take good care of ye all right." When the men cast him a puzzled gaze, he chuckled. "Ye know Lady MacGregor was verra determined to come here. When I told her she couldnae come after ye, she tampered my oats with Auld Wife's Huid and made me run."

There was a moment of silence, and then all of the men threw back their heads and roared with laughter—well, all except Montgomery.

❧

"God's teeth, healer! That burns!" whimpered MacGregor, gritting his teeth.

Liadain wrapped her husband's arm with a clean bandage. "Ye are a grown man. Ye uncovered a plot to bring down the entire realm and yet act as though ye are a wee lad that cannae handle a little scratch. 'Tis only a flesh wound, Husband."

"'Tis only a flesh wound? I took an arrow aimed for my heart."

When he placed his hand over his heart, she could not help but smile. She covered his hand with her own and tapped his fingers playfully. "But it missed."

MacGregor's eyes widened and he leaned back with a dramatic flourish. "But it missed? I could have been killed."

Liadain leaned over her husband and brushed a brief kiss to his lips. "Aye, but ye werenae." She gathered the soiled cloths and supplies, and placed them in the bowl on the table.

"I heard what ye did," he said playfully.

She sat down on the bed beside her husband. "What did I do?"

"'Tis a wonder Montgomery still wants to be the captain of my guard. He will now be careful of eating anything ye put in front of him."

"I was worried about ye. He was standing in my way. That was the end of it." She shrugged.

"God's teeth, lass, I hope ye donna become cross with me," he teased.

"Ye will know if I do."

There was a heavy pause and he looked her over wantonly. "Ye risked your life to come after me. I cannae say that I approve, but I am joyful ye are here and safe."

"I am your wife. I should be by your side. Always."

He lifted her chin with his finger, his grin irresistibly devastating. "I want to kiss my wife." His lips feather-touched her with a gentle persuasion and she quivered at the sweet tenderness of his kiss.

She kissed him, lingering, savoring every moment. It had been too long since she held her husband in her arms. His lips were so warm and sweet on hers. It was a kiss for her tired soul to melt into.

Gently, he eased her onto the bed, an eager affection coming from him. He pulled back and she noticed he was watching her intently. Something intense flared in his eyes and there was a tingling in the pit of her stomach.

"Say it again," MacGregor said barely above a whisper. His smoldering gaze never left hers.

"Pardon?"

"What ye said when the guards took me away. Say it again," he repeated softly.

Liadain was actually trembling now and her eyes were full of tears. She could feel her throat closing up. An inner torment began to gnaw at her. She had been truthful when she said the words, but she could not bear to look in her husband's eyes when he rejected her. Her spirits sank even lower and she did the only think she could think of.

Moving her body, she was attempting to wiggle out from underneath him when a firm grip halted her in her tracks. MacGregor pinned her back down on the bed. They were so close that she could feel his breath on her lips. She gazed at him as a hot tear trickled down her cheek.

He wiped her wet cheeks with his thumb. "Healer, why do ye weep?"

She dropped her lashes quickly to hide the hurt that was sure to come. She shook her head but did not speak, trying to hide her misery. She was silent and defeated.

"Liadain…"

At the sound of her name, her eyes flew open. She was about to speak when he placed his finger over her lips.

"I want ye to listen to me verra carefully. I love ye. I loved ye from the first time I placed my dagger to your bonny throat. Ye are kind, gentle, everything I am proud to call wife. I surely donna deserve ye. The gods have truly blessed me. I was a daft fool for treating ye with such disrespect. I promise ye that I will try to be the husband ye so deserve. Let us start by ye calling me by my Christian name. Give me another chance to win your heart, *a ghràidh." My love.*

"Declan, ye already have it. I love ye, Husband."

∾

Liadain was eager to depart, but the men wanted to remain until Dunnehl and Catesby met their demise. She could not say she understood the reasoning, but perhaps the men sought a bit of closure. For as much trouble as Lord Dunnehl had caused their entire clan, she guessed the MacGregors wanted to make sure the beastly man's death was final.

Ciaran, Aiden, and Declan had received an audience with the king that morn and all charges against Declan had been dismissed. His Majesty even expressed his gratitude to the MacGregors for catching Percy. As Liadain waited in the courtyard for the men to depart, she summoned Robert.

When he spotted her, he approached her hesitantly. "Lady MacGregor."

"Viscount Cranborne. I wanted to speak with ye

before we departed. I know I threatened ye that I would speak with King James about your dealings if ye didnae free my husband. As ye see, there was nay need due to Archie's papers."

Strong arms encircled her from behind. "Are ye ready, Liadain?" asked Declan, giving her a gentle kiss on the neck.

Turning, she raised her hand and brushed her husband's cheek. "Aye, could I have a moment?"

"Of course."

She pulled Robert a few steps away from her husband. Then she reached into her bosom and pulled out a paper. "I see the way ye have changed. Your love for your wife and son is so clear. For that reason *alone*, I didnae speak of your involvement to my husband." Her eyes narrowed. "Donna let me regret this decision. I strongly suggest ye donna let MacGregor see this as I cannae be responsible for his actions."

She hesitated and then handed Robert the paper. "I believe this belongs to ye. Cherish your love for Elizabeth and your son, Robert."

He took the proof of his wrongdoing and she turned on her heel.

She would've walked to the ends of the earth to free her husband. But she recognized love when she saw it. And Robert truly loved Elizabeth and his bairn. Perhaps love could change a person. At any rate, she couldn't tear Robert away from his family if she didn't have to. As she approached her husband, Robert called after her.

"Lady MacGregor!"

"Aye?"

"You are nothing like your brother." A smile lit Robert's features.

As she turned back, Declan nodded to Robert. "What was that about?"

"It was naught. I merely gave him some advice about Elizabeth."

"Cranborne is right about one thing," Declan said, pulling her close and kissing the top of her head.

"And what is that?"

"Ye arenae like the bloody Campbell. Ye will forever be a MacGregor, Liadain."

Read on for an early look at

To Wed a
Wicked Highlander

**Coming September 2013 from
Sourcebooks Casablanca**

Glengarry, Scotland 1606

My Dearest Alexander,

If you are reading this, I have joined your beloved mother. Do not be saddened, my son. First and foremost, you are a MacDonell. Never second guess yourself.

I hope my words, though not spoken, will bring you some peace. Now that you are laird, you may find the lairdship is not all you expected, but the entire clan is now in your hands. It is up to you to keep our clan safe and provide for them during the harsh Highland winters. I know you will be a kind and giving chief, as I raised you to be such a man. My wish for you, my son, would be that you become a better man than I was.

The first order you should attend to is seeking a wife. My only regret is that I did not live to see your son. You are the last of the MacDonell line. It is your responsibility to carry on the name of our kin. When all else fails, I know my beloved sister will torture you until you do.

Donald has been the captain of my guard for as long as I can remember. Treat him with the respect and dignity he so deserves. When his service is no longer needed, see to it his coffers are full. As we discussed, John will replace Donald as the captain of your guard.

I have never been disappointed in you, Alexander, and I have no doubt you will fulfill the duty that befalls you. And lastly, at all costs, keep the stone safe within the walls of the Rock of the Raven.

Laird Dòmhnall MacDonell of Glengarry

Alex sat in the chair behind his father's desk, now his own desk, shaking his head. "Father mentions to keep the stone safe within the walls of the Rock of the Raven. What stone?"

Donald's eyes narrowed. "I donna know."

"Why would he write me and then nae explain his words? This doesnae make sense."

"Your father sealed the letter and gave it to me over a year ago. Mayhap he meant to speak with ye and then became ill. But he ne'er mentioned anything to me about a stone. If ye donna know of what he writes then this stone is probably already safe. It almost sounds like some type of bauble."

"I will speak with Aunt Iseabail. Father may have spoken to her." Reaching into the drawer, Alex pulled out a pouch and placed it on the desk in front of

Donald. "I thank ye for the years of service and your continued loyalty to my father."

"It was my honor to serve him. I wish I could do the same for ye, but I am afraid these aging bones are weary. John will serve ye well. If ye ever want or need for anything, ye need only ask. Your father was a dear friend to me and ye as a son." Donald rose and picked up the pouch. "Ye will make a fine laird, Alex."

Alex watched Donald walk out the door and then once again, he glanced at the opened letter. He couldn't help but wonder if there was anything else his father had neglected to mention.

The remainder of the afternoon remained a blur. All he was mindful of was the fact that last eve he stood over his father's lifeless body and now he returned to stand over his father's grave. There was no turning back time. He must accept the inevitable fact that his sire was truly dead.

A flash of despair stabbed at him and the pain in his heart became a sick and fiery gnawing. His mother had long since passed and his father had practically raised him alone. It was always the two of them, and now there was one. The knowledge that he was now Laird Alexander MacDonell of Glengarry knotted and turned inside him, for he was a man who faced a harsh reality.

It was time to take his father's place.

୬ঔ౿

Lady Sybella MacKenzie huffed. "I donna know why 'tis so important I learn to do this. Why is it expected that women must learn to sew and stitch? 'Tis truly ridiculous and has nay value whatsoever. I feel as though I'm losing my mind."

"Nay wonder, Sybella, ye arenae concentrating. Look at your stitching. What a mess." A smile played her cousin-by-marriage's lips as Mary tucked her nut-brown hair behind her ear. She was petite and fragile-like, everything Angus would favor in a woman. "When ye wed, do ye want your husband to have tattered clothing? He would look like a fool."

Sybella giggled. "It doesnae matter if his clothes are tattered. Men always look like fools."

"Angus takes pride in his appearance," Mary added.

"And my cousin takes ye for granted. Why do ye want to sit here bored to tears when we could be out in the open air?"

Mary promptly ignored her, resuming her latest project, while Sybella glanced around the ladies solar. She shook her head at the womanly touches. Dainty pictures of the fairer sex wearing delicate gowns hung on the walls. There were flowers and all of the feminine furnishings someone would expect to be placed into a room where the ladies were presumed to congregate. How very original. Who made those rules? She would love to hang the bow she shot which landed her four rabbits in one single hunt. She wondered what the ladies would speak to that. The women of propriety would surely shudder, including Mary. At least it would be another conversation piece other than the same acceptable boorish subjects.

For as long as she could remember, Sybella craved to do manly things with her brother, never interested in stitching, bonny dresses, or womanly conversation. Why would she be when women spent most of their time gossiping about one another? Men on the other hand were brutally honest in their words and moved on. She much preferred the latter of the bunch. And although she was a lass, her brother never treated her differently. She loved that about Colin. He would often take her fishing and hunting and never minded her coming along.

Sybella sprang to her feet, dropping the embroidery to the floor. "'Tis a beautiful day and ye are clearly wasting it. I dare ye to stop what ye are doing and come out and enjoy the sun." When Mary hesitated, Sybella knew she was going to relent.

Placing her stitching on the table, Mary rose and smoothed her skirts. "Verra well. Ye will continue to plague me until I do. *Dè a chuireas mi ort?*" *What shall I wear?*

Sybella smirked and her tone bordered on mockery. *"Dreasa breagha."* A pretty dress. "Donna be ridiculous."

Mary did not try to mask the vague hint of disapproval upon her face. "Must ye always speak with such sarcasm?"

"When ye are being foolish, aye." Sybella headed toward the door and turned her head over her shoulder. "Grab your cloak and I will meet ye in the bailey."

"Ye know? One of these days ye are going to meet your match. I wish to be there when ye do."

"There has ne'er been such a man." To be honest, there was one, but she made it a point never to think of the brute. She wouldn't give him the satisfaction.

Sybella ambled through the bailey and waited for Mary.

"Cousin."

Sybella turned around and Angus nodded. "Your father wants to speak with ye in his study."

"Mary and I were just taking our leave to the village. Does he want to speak with me now?" she asked, disappointed.

Angus ran his hand through his brown locks. "Aye."

"All right. Please tell Mary I'm with Father."

She made her way to her father's study and when the sound of heated voices argued from within, she placed her ear to the door. She couldn't hear a single coherent word.

The voices silenced.

"Enter, Sybella," called her father from the other side of the door.

How he could have heard her was beyond her comprehension. She pushed open the door and her father was seated behind his large wooden desk with Colin. When neither man looked pleased, she realized this might not bode well for her.

"Come in, Daughter. I wish to speak with ye." Her father gestured for her to sit and his tone did not display the reason he had wanted to see her.

She couldn't help but study her sire's graying hair, broad shoulders, and handsome visage. The man had a commanding presence about him and didn't even need to speak. She knew her mother's death must be so hard for him to handle.

She glanced at Colin and her brother cast a

bleak, tight-lipped smile. His eyes were dark and unfathomable.

Her father leaned back in his chair and folded his hands over his stomach. "I donna expect ye to understand the ways of politics, Sybella, but ye know as much to realize marriages are often arranged to better our clan."

She heard herself swallow, not sure she liked where this conversation was headed.

"Since your mother has passed and ye nay longer care for her, not to mention with our conquest of Lewis, the MacLeod—"

She stirred uneasily in the chair. "Surely ye arenae going to offer my hand to the MacLeod, Father," blurted out Sybella with a trace of panic in her voice.

"I wouldnae think of it," said her father. "Howbeit there is another clan in which we wish to keep the peace."

Perhaps it was her own uneasiness, but her misgivings increased by the moment. She had an underlying feeling in the pit of her stomach that the next words which escaped her father's lips would forever seal her fate.

"The MacDonell of Glengarry has recently passed and we need to make an alliance. I am offering your hand to his son, the new laird of Glengarry. And I am fairly certain he will accept my offer."

Her mouth dropped. "Ye cannae offer my hand to that man." Fury almost choked her. "He is naught but an arrogant, brooding, conniving excuse for a man and I willnae have him—ever! He is our enemy! All of the treasures in the world wouldnae make me wed—"

Her father's voice hardened. "This isnae open for debate. My decision is final and there is nay more to discuss. Besides, ye have ne'er even met the man."

Sybella growled in frustration. She certainly wouldn't tell her father that as children she and Colin snuck onto the MacDonell's lands for a swim at the waterfall. And she most definitely wouldn't speak of the fact that Alexander MacDonell caught her and stole a kiss from her. God's teeth, she had never spoken of that day to anyone. The rogue still made her blood boil when she thought about him, his kilt riding low on his lean hips, that arrogant swagger. Not that she ever thought about him—well, maybe sometimes.

She fingered a blond curl behind her ear. "I know enough that our clans have been warring for years. Why would the MacDonell even want a MacKenzie for a wife lest nay one will take his bloody arse?" she asked.

Colin's voice broke miserably and then he cleared his throat. "We need to make an alliance with the MacDonell," he simply stated.

Her father rose and sat down on the edge of the desk. He gazed down at her and smiled. "Think about making your mother proud, Sybella. I need ye to gain your husband's trust and be a dutiful wife. For now, that is all I ask of ye."

"I donna understand, Father. The MacDonell has been our enemy for years. Why now?"

"Ye arenae to speak of this to anyone. Do ye understand?" She nodded as he continued. "For a verra long time our clan has been blessed with good fortune because we have been gifted with a seer.

There are less than a handful of men who know of this and I want to keep it that way."

"*A seer?*" She sat back, momentarily rebuffed.

Colin's voice was calming. "I have seen it with my own eyes, Ella. Our conquest on Lewis was the last he foretold."

"Who is this seer and why have I ne'er heard of him if he is a MacKenzie?" she asked doubtfully.

"For your own safety, 'tis better ye donna know. Dòmhnall MacDonell was quiet and circumspect in burning our church to ash when his real purpose was to steal our clan seeing stone."

"Seeing stone? Seer? What are ye talking about? Ye cannae tell me ye honestly believe in such tales." Sybella scrunched up her face in annoyance. When she started to become agitated by her father's words, he reached out and grasped her arms.

"Listen to me."

She was startled by the tone of his voice.

"Our seer cannae foretell without his seeing stone which disappeared while our church was engulfed in flames. We know Alexander MacDonell's father stole the stone and 'tis held somewhere within the walls of Glengarry. So there is another purpose for your vows. I need ye to find the stone and return it to your clan where it belongs."

Sybella pulled back. "I donna understand. Are ye and Colin in your cups?"

Her father's eyes darkened. "Cease your tongue and listen. Once ye find the stone, I will take care of the MacDonell. I would ne'er make my daughter suffer under the same roof as a bloody MacDonell," he spat.

She wasn't exactly sure what he meant by 'taking care of the MacDonell,' but right now, she was more concerned about speaking her vows to her father's enemy—her enemy.

She sat back and rubbed her hand over her brow. She needed time to absorb this. How could she speak her vows to the man who had haunted her dreams for years and then be expected to betray him? Worse yet, what if she was caught under her enemy's roof with no means of escape?

The truth was that Sybella would do anything to make her father proud. She had always wanted his acceptance, and just because she wasn't a man did not mean her sire shouldn't place his faith in her. She was a MacKenzie through and through. And after all, she had her father's blood, did she not? There was no sense pondering the inevitable. Her father had never asked her for anything, and now, he called upon her to help the clan. This just might be the perfect opportunity, a chance to prove her worth to her father.

"Ye can trust me, Father. I will recover the stone and make ye and the clan proud."

Acknowledgments

A very special "thank you" goes out to the following people:

To my agent, Jill Marsal, for your endless encouragement.

To my editor, Leah Hultenschmidt, for supporting my dreams.

To the unsung heroes at Sourcebooks: it truly takes a village.

To my girls, Mary Grace and Beth, my biggest fans, who could probably recite every manuscript I've written verbatim. Thank you for holding my hand through the blood, sweat, and tears. Mary Grace, you continue to be my rock.

To my husband, who escorts me to every Scottish and Renaissance festival under the sun to "research" and never complains—eye rolls, but never has complaints. I love you!

To my mother, who was so proud of her romance-writing daughter who finally found herself on this side of forty-ish. Although you are watching from above, Mom, I have comfort in the fact that you read my first two books. I will hold your praise close to my heart, your lessons not forgotten. And even though you begged me to write a most unpleasant fate for Lady Rosalia's mother, I hope you are pleased with these *Bad Boys*.

And as I will never forget your words, I pray you will always remember mine. I love you, Mom. Always.

About the Author

Victoria Roberts writes sexy, Scottish historical romances about kilted heroes and warriors from the past. An avid lover of all things Scotland, she simply writes what she loves to read. Prior to ever picking up a romance novel, she penned her first young-adult novella (never published) at sixteen years old. Who knew her leather-studded motorcycle hero would trade in his ride and emerge as a kilt-donning Highlander wielding a broadsword?

Victoria lives in western Pennsylvania with her husband of nineteen years and their two beautiful children—not to mention one spoiled dog. When she is not plotting her next Scottish romp, she enjoys reading, nature, and antiques. For more information about Victoria, visit her website at www.victoriarobertsauthor.com.

Temptation in a Kilt

Victoria Roberts

—— ❧ ——

She's on her way to safety

It's a sign of Lady Rosalia Armstrong's desperation that she's seeking refuge in a place as rugged and challenging as the Scottish Highlands. She doesn't care about hardship and discomfort, if only she can become master of her own life. Laird Ciaran MacGregor, however, is completely beyond her control…

He redefines dangerous…

Ciaran MacGregor knows it's perilous to get embroiled with a fiery Lowland lass, especially one as headstrong as Rosalia. Having made a rash promise to escort her all the way to Glengarry, now he's stuck with her, even though she challenges his legendary prowess at every opportunity. When temptation reaches its peak, he'll be ready to show her who he really is… on and off the battlefield.

—— ❧ ——

"Wonderful adventure with sensual and compelling romance." —Amanda Forester, acclaimed author of *True Highland Spirit*

For more Victoria Roberts, visit:

www.sourcebooks.com

To Wed a Wicked Highlander

Victoria Roberts

—⁂—

Torn between his duty and his soul mate, what will this Highland bad boy choose?

When a beautiful traitor is discovered under his own roof, Laird Alexander MacDonnell is faced with a decision he never thought possible. He's sworn to protect his clan, but following his duty will mean losing his heart forever to the woman who betrayed him—his wife.

Lady Sybella MacKenzie is forced to search for her clan's ancient seeing stone under the roof of her father's enemy. But when she finally finds the precious artifact, ensuring her family's survival will mean turning her back on the man who has captured her soul.

Praise for *Temptation in a Kilt*:

"An exciting Highland adventure with sensual and compelling romance." —Amanda Forester, acclaimed author of *True Highland Spirit*

"Filled with everything I love most about Highland romance…" —Melissa Mayhue, award-winning author of *Warrior's Redemption*

For more Victoria Roberts, visit:

www.sourcebooks.com

True Highland Spirit

Amanda Forester

—————— ❦ ——————

Seduction is a powerful weapon...

Morrigan McNab is a Highland lady, robbed of her birthright and with no choice but to fight alongside her brothers to protect their impoverished clan. When she encounters Sir Jacques Dragonet, she discovers her fiercest opponent...

Sir Jacques Dragonet is a Noble Knight of the Hospitaller Order, willing to give his life to defend Scotland from the English. He can't stop himself from admiring the beautiful Highland lass who wields her weapons as well as he can and endangers his heart even more than his life...

Now they're racing each other to find a priceless relic. No matter who wins this heated rivalry, both will lose unless they can find a way to share the spoils.

—————— ❦ ——————

"A masterful storyteller, Amanda Forester brings new excitement to Scottish medieval romance!" —Gerri Russell, award-winning author of *To Tempt a Knight*

For more Amanda Forester, visit:

www.sourcebooks.com

The Trouble with Highlanders

Mary Wine

With her clan on the wrong side of the struggle for the Scottish throne, heiress Daphne MacLeod, once the toast of the court, is out of options…

Norris Sutherland once helped Daphne, but she walked away from him without a backward glance. Now she's in deep trouble and needs him more than ever. But he may be lost forever…unless she can somehow convince him to forgive her.

Praise for Mary Wine's Highland romances:

"Mary Wine brings history to life with major sizzle factor." —Lucy Monroe, *USA Today* bestselling author of *For Duty's Sake*

Hot enough to warm even the coldest Scottish nights…With a captivating leading lady and terrific pacing." —*Publishers Weekly* Starred Review

"Not to be missed." —Lora Leigh, *New York Times* #1 bestselling author

"One gripping plot twist follows another…kilt-tossing, sheet-incinerating lovemaking." —*Publishers Weekly*

For more Mary Wine, visit:

www.sourcebooks.com

New York Times and *USA Today* bestselling author

The Bridegroom Wore Plaid

Grace Burrowes

❧

His family or his heart—one of them will be betrayed...

Ian MacGregor is wooing a woman who's wrong for him in every way. As the new Earl of Balfour, though, he must marry an English heiress to repair the family fortunes.

But in his intended's penniless chaperone, Augusta, Ian is finding everything he's ever wanted in a wife.

For more Grace Burrowes, visit:

www.sourcebooks.com